Ghost in
the Surf

Ghost in the Surf

A Kami White Para(normal)legal Mystery

E.L. Oakes

Kenmore, WA

Epicenter Press
6524 NE 81st St.
Suite 2
Kenmore WA

For more information:
www.Epicenterpress.com
www.Camelpress.com
www.Coffeetownpress.com

For more information go to: www.camelpress.com
www.eloakes.com

Cover design by Dawn Anderson

ISBN: 9781603816571 (Trade Paper)
ISBN: 9781603816588 (eBook)

Produced in the United States of America

CHAPTER 1

Santa Cruz: Late Wednesday Morning

SANTA CRUZ GREETED me with her typical mid-August cool foggy breeze and a thick overcast sky, almost as if she was welcoming me back. She was still, in many ways, the town I'd spent much of my childhood in; a little bit sleepy, a little bit wild, and one-hundred percent Coastal California. But the city had grown in fits and starts, and it seemed that along the way, I'd grown up with it.

Traffic flooded around me as I turned onto Ocean Avenue and hunted for the address I'd been given on the phone. New construction crowded alongside old buildings; ramshackle lots side-by-side with gleaming concrete buildings marked the growth the town had taken over the years. I found the correct address and hunted for free parking, a growing rarity in Santa Cruz, then climbed out of my weary old Kia and took a deep sea-damp breath before striding up and opening the door.

I'd never been in a morgue before, so there was that. Not that "that" was much of a comfort. It wasn't really what I'd pictured on the drive over the Santa Cruz mountains from my workplace in the East Bay. Outside, the ocean breeze was pushing the gloomy, clinging grey mist away up into the mountains, but inside the office the walls were painted a cheery light blue, and the fixtures were stainless steel and brushed chrome. Clean, but bright. With a smile that felt more like a grimace, I joked, "No organs?"

The woman who greeted me at the desk, and whom I took to be an assistant of some kind, looked at me strangely. "What?"

"I thought morgues had, like, organs in jars? Brains and hearts. Sciency stuff? That kind of thing?" What was I supposed to say? You called me about a corpse? A corpse that they had to be wrong about. They had to be wrong. Please let them be wrong.

"Ah… no." She flashed a disapproving glance. "Not here."

"I'm sorry. I'm Kami White. I was asked to make an… identification." Identification. I suddenly hated that word.

Her demeanor shifted immediately, and she stood and gestured for me to follow her. "This way, please."

She was middle-aged, of indeterminate Asian descent, with greying brown hair and dark eyes, slightly rotund, but she moved with the grace of a dancer. I didn't want to follow her through the doorway into that smaller, white-painted room, but somehow, I did. I squared my shoulders and stepped in, and then I was standing in front of the cold sterile table. I knew full well that under that clean white cloth was a body, but I didn't want it to be Charles. Maybe it was a dummy. Maybe this was all some sick joke. I looked around to see if our crowd of surfer buddies was hiding in the office, waiting to pop out at me. If this was an early birthday gag, it wasn't a funny one. The woman pulled back the sheet slightly and there it was; an empty shell that wore the face of my dear friend and employer.

The hope I'd clung to smashed into shards. Charles Hanford was dead. Dragged under by the unforgiving Pacific and tossed back to the beach as only an empty shell. Drowned.

Oh, there were pieces of him there. Above his closed eyes was his wave of silver hair, still sandy from the surf; the little scar above his brow from a youthful bar fight in Munich; his smooth-shaven square chin. But nothing else of his spirit remained.

My boss. My confidant. My Charles. Gone. A stillness came over me, and everything seemed to stop. I think I said something, muttered, "Yes, that's Charles. Yes. That's him." Or maybe just "Yes." And then I whirled and fled the room.

Just as a point of reference, fleeing works better when one is cognizant of any signs on the door, especially the ones that read "Pull to Open." My hands hit the unyielding brushed chrome handle with a sickening crack as I ploughed head-first into the unmovable barrier of two-inch thick safety glass.

The next time I opened my eyes I was staring up at the crisp white ceiling and the woman leaning over me, looking seriously into my face. "Don't move. I'll call an ambulance."

Brushing her hands away, I pulled my yoga-trained muscles together to sit up, a hot flush of embarrassment washing over me. "It's okay. I don't need an ambulance. Besides, aren't medical examiners doctors? Where's the doctor?"

She straightened suddenly, standing back from me. "I am the doctor." Then she shrugged faintly. "I'm a forensic examiner. I don't do live people."

"Great. I'm still alive." I gave a grin I hoped wasn't too embarrassed looking. At least, my body was alive. The rest of me felt numb, emotionally overwhelmed. I let her open the door this time and staggered out into the corridor.

"Are you sure you don't want an ambulance?"

"Yeah, I'm fine. Not dying, I promise." I felt blood return to my brain by way of my cheeks. What kind of idiot runs into a glass door? "Just clumsy. Sorry."

In the corridor, I slid down, squatting with my back against the oblivious blue wall, and tilted my head back, eyes on the ceiling with its stark white fluorescents that turned everything to ghastly shades of white and grey. My fingers hurt where I'd hit the door handle, and I flexed them cautiously, reassured I hadn't sprained anything. Bruised but not broken.

Charles was dead. And what was I supposed to do now?

"Kamera!" My full name, surprisingly correctly pronounced—"Kam-eey-rah," not "kam-ruh"— came from the end of the hall, and I whirled at the sound of a familiar voice. For a moment my heart surged, wanting it to be Charles. It wasn't. Of course it wasn't.

My cousin, Captain Patrick Tamsin, aka Trick, was in his on-duty Coast Guard blues, his six-foot four-inch frame taking up half the hallway. "Patrick," I uttered his name in disbelief.

We'd both inherited our looks from our Granny Jazzy, but the lean, flat-chested, square hipped look that makes me look totally boy-town no matter how much makeup I wear or how flirty a dress I put on gives my cousin the appearance of a Norse god, albeit a clean-shaven one. His blond hair always lays in attractive waves, while mine frizzes up in a blur of curls that I have to keep shorn short to prevent sheep-like woolliness. Granny Jazzy's wide, pale blue eyes give him a mystical insightful gaze. They make me look like Gollum. I struggle against high breezes and car exhaust, but Patrick is solid as a rock. And a rock was just what I needed in this storm.

He approached with long, swinging steps, a seaman's stride, and squatted down in front of me. "Hey, cuz."

I rocked forward onto my knees and into his arms, burying my face briefly against his powerful chest. Trick is two years older than me, and only my half-cousin by blood, but throughout our childhood, he'd always seemed more a brother to me than my own flesh-and-blood brother. His arms came around me in powerful hug, and I allowed him to support me for a moment before drawing back.

"What are you doing here?" And why, I realized, did he seem to have been expecting me?

"I was waiting for you," he said simply. "I was there. My boat got the call about a surfer in distress." He held me at arms-length and blinked. "You have a spot your forehead. Looks like a bump. A friggin' water balloon. What'd you do?"

"Their door attacked me." I felt my forehead gingerly with my fingers. There was a tender spot, but no swelling at all. "You're messing with me."

"Rather, she attacked our door." The medical examiner

joined us and handed me a clipboard with information to fill out. "I'll get you an ice pack. Are you sure you don't want an…"

I sighed, feeling stupid about running into the stupid door to begin with. "If you say ambulance, I'll sue your door for assault."

Patrick did that thing where he scrunches up his nose and digs his left thumb into the socket of his right eye. He usually does that when he thinks I'm overreacting.

"Really, I'm fine. Thank you," I muttered. I blinked again, trying to blot out the entire morning, turning back to Patrick. "I didn't want it to be him."

Patrick met my gaze for a second, his gaze sad and serious. "I'm sorry, Kam. And I'm even more sorry, but the police are waiting to talk to you. I held them off but they're in the main lobby."

"The police? Why the police?" It was a surfing accident, wasn't it? I grabbed Patrick's arm and forced his gaze back to mine.

"Unattended death, Kam. They have to take a report."

"Unattended? He was surfing, wasn't he?"

Before Patrick could answer me, the M.E. (The paperwork informed me that her name was Dr. April Chee.) returned with one of those single-use first-aid chemical ice packs, and explained that the morgue would release the body for burial after an autopsy. Autopsy. I knew what that entailed and I didn't want to think about it.

"From first glance, this looks cut and dried," Dr. Chee continued, "and if that remains the case, I should be able to release him right away. If my findings aren't congruent with an accident, then there will have to be an investigation."

I looked to Patrick, but his expression was closed. "Why would you think it wasn't an accident?"

"It's just routine, Miss White. I'm very sorry for your loss."

I signed everything from my safe-zone on the corridor floor and handed the clipboard back up when I was done. She handed me a small plastic bag with Charles' valuables in it. An entire life in one plastic bag. "Thank you. Please let me know if there's anything else I can do." Because I felt utterly helpless.

Patrick took my arm and pulled me up, ice pack and all. "You ready?"

I wasn't. I crumpled the ice pack over my bruised knuckles, squared my shoulders, and let him lead me across a long corridor and through a set of double doors into a lobby area where two uniformed police officers were waiting. They introduced themselves as Officers Bryant and Ortez.

I didn't want to deal with them, especially when the first words out of Ortez's mouth were, "You're the next of kin?"

"Not exactly." I sighed. "I'm his emergency contact. I have power of attorney for when he travels...Charles and his sister don't get along."

"Didn't." Officer Bryant corrected, and I felt myself stare at him in disbelief.

"So, you are his...?" It was obvious they were waiting for me to say girlfriend.

"Girl Friday," I tried to smile. "I'm the paralegal for Charles' law firm, Hanford Legal Services." I didn't mention that Charles and I were the entirety of Hanford Legal, unless you counted the cat. "I run the office."

"And you didn't go surfing today?"

I clenched my sore hand and took a deep breath. One thing growing up in Oakland had given me was a distaste for beat cops. I'd seen too many of my classmates harassed for no other reason than the color of their skin or the street they happened to be walking down. I reminded myself that these were tourist town police officers, not Oakland street cops, prayed for patience, and continued, annunciating slowly. "No, I was in San Amoro, running the office. Look, what's this about?"

"Just routine, ma'am."

"My grandmother is the ma'am, Officer Ortez." Patrick fired a warning glare in my direction, and I took a deliberate pause before continuing. "I'm sorry. I understand routine, but I really can't tell you anything. Charles left a note saying he was going surfing, along with a to-do list. I thought…" I choked. I tried to be angry at these cops asking stupid questions, but it hurt too much. I couldn't find the anger, just the overwhelming feeling of loss. Patrick's hand landed on my shoulder, steadying me. "I thought he'd be back by two. We have client meetings this afternoon… I really should get back. I need to notify people, close the office…"

"You can in just a moment." The cops exchanged glances. "Do you know why he would go in to surf alone?"

"He wouldn't. Are you telling me there was no one with him?" That cut through the haze my brain seemed to have wandered into. Patrick's words came back to me. Unattended death. How could that be? "He doesn't surf alone. He's big on safety."

Ortez and Bryant exchanges glances before Ortez asked, "Had he seemed normal lately? Acting like himself? Was he depressed?"

Depressed? It took a few beats, glancing between their intense, curious gazes, before I realized just what they were suggesting. "You think he killed himself? No, oh no. If Charles was going to commit suicide, he would have done it years ago, after his partner died. Not now. Charles loves life. The business is finally to the point where he can take off and surf in the middle of the week. He was happy, enjoying himself."

They were eying me with some skepticism so I shook my head and continued with as much calm as I could muster, "He wouldn't commit suicide." I could feel my patience running out by the syllable and I'm afraid it showed. "I don't believe for a second that he killed himself, and neither should you. He wasn't suicidal and he doesn't surf alone. If you think his drowning was anything other than an accident, please, find out what really happened."

The cops looked a little taken aback. "I'm sorry we had to suggest it, ma'…" Bryant's words faded quickly, and he gulped a little. "I mean, Miss White."

"If we're done here?" I hefted my shoulder bag, hoping they

would get the hint.

"For now, but we may need to contact you again when we get the coroner's report."

I handed them my card and Patrick steered me away from them and out the door. "C'mon. Let's get you some coffee."

HE TOOK ME TO THE surfer-centric Fin's Coffee on Ocean Street. I don't remember ordering, but soon I was seated at one of their round wooden tables and there was a hot cup of caramel latte in my hands. I sipped slowly, feeling the warm sweetness soothe my tight throat while I tried to put my thoughts in order, my eyes focusing on the vintage Long Board Invitational posters that decorated the walls.

"What happened, Patrick? What happened to him?"

My cousin looked at me with sad eyes, his strong hand cradling his paper cup of straight black coffee as though it were something fragile, a baby bird in need of rescue. "The call came in around eight this morning, just 'surfer in distress.' Well, ninety percent of the time these things are just kids horsing around, but we always check them out. When we got there, there was a board floating out beyond the break-water, so we launched the rescue dinghy. We found the body in the surf. Kam," he didn't look at me as he admitted, "I knew who it was the second I saw his watch."

Charles' prize Suunto Elementum diver's watch. I slipped it out of the bag from the coroner's office and held it in my palm, admiring the shining metal, the sturdy glowing numbers. My thumb brushed over the smooth sapphire crystal lens. Unbreakable. Made for life. "He loved this stupid watch."

"I know." Patrick glanced away from me, letting me have my private grief. "I wanted to call you, you know, when I realized it was Charles, but there are procedures to be followed."

"Did he drown? I mean, he did, right?"

"That's the coroner's preliminary finding, Kam. But you heard her. A full report will take a little while," Trick sucked in a deep breath and leaned both elbows on the table. I recognized that look. I'd seen it the day he had to tell Granny Jazzy he'd decided to join the Coast Guard instead of going on to law school. I'd seen it the day his mother went to prison the last time. There was something he felt he needed to say, but didn't want me to hear.

And he knew darn well that I wasn't going to fall for his prevarication. "Whatever it is, just say it."

"It's a civilian matter now, so I shouldn't say anything," he prevaricated.

"I'm a civilian, so you'd better say something." Okay, so threats against a member of a branch of the US military probably won't win me any elections, but since he was the son of my mother's brother, I figured I could get away with it. "Or else."

"Or else?" A half-smile tugged at the corner of his mouth, but respecting the circumstances, didn't break any further. "Okay. But this stays between us, right here, right now." When I nodded, he sighed again and said bluntly, "It didn't look like a surfing accident to me. I'm not saying it wasn't a surfing accident, just that it didn't look typical. I'm not saying you should go off half-cocked."

"Half-cocked? What's that supposed to mean? I don't half-cock. I'm not a half-cocker!"

People glanced our way, and I'm sure they thought I meant something I didn't. Patrick had the good grace to look chagrined. "You're right. You just pump both barrels and fire in the same breath. Remember when Kenny came home with his bike all messed up and said he had an accident?"

My brother had tried to claim he'd been run off the road by a car. I'd inspected his bicycle, then hunted down the bullies who dared mess with my baby brother. "I was right, though, wasn't I?"

"You went after those kids before Granny could even talk to their parents!"

"Kenny was never going to admit to being bullied, so I did

what I had to do."

"You made a wild assumption and went after kids three years younger than us." Patrick shook his head. "You can't do that this time, Kam. Surfing accidents happen. You know it. I know it. Even to guys like Charles. Maybe he had an aneurism or something. We just don't know."

I hated to admit it, but he was right. I wanted action, I wanted to fight. I wanted to expend all of this something that I was feeling into something that meant something. But you can't fight the ocean. You can only go along with it. "And no one saw it happen? No one was on the beach when you got there?"

"Kamera…" And this time his voice was official Coast-Guard-Cutter-Captain serious. "Don't do this. My bet is that the coroner will find evidence of a heart attack or stroke. Something like that. Until there's some kind of evidence otherwise, this was just an accident."

Just a surfing accident. Nothing more than that. But even my summer-time sibling, one of the few people in the world I trusted, couldn't convince my heart that it was true.

"He wouldn't have gone into the water until the others got there. He wouldn't have surfed alone." I said it with confidence that I didn't feel. "And he was a strong swimmer. We know that beach. We've been out there almost every weekend this summer. Charles isn't reckless, he's not foolish. He knows what waves he can handle and which to leave off. He's always warning me about it. Judge the water. Watch the water. Know what I'm getting into…" Patrick just listened as I ranted out all the reasons that Charles wouldn't drown… Or had he? "Shark?"

"No bites. No blood." My cousin leaned back casually in his chair, one leg cocked, arm resting on the back of the seat. He was garnering looks from every female patron in the house. Some ladies just like a man in uniform, I guess. A man in uniform who looks like a Norse god, especially. Patrick was oblivious to the appraising glances.

"Jellyfish?"

"Maybe. Was he allergic?"

"Not that I know of." I shook my head, thinking. "And we haven't seen any sea nettles close to shore all summer long. Why now?"

"Strange currents, cooling water, food pattern shifts... Even just one injured jelly being washed into shore could sting. But usually the stings are minor. Not a problem for a man Charles' size." Trick shrugged. "He was really sandy when we pulled him out. Like I said, no blood, but with all the sand I wouldn't have seen any bruises or stings. If there are, the coroner will find them. There are a lot of factors, Kam. Until you have the coroner's report you can't rule out heart attack, leg cramp, or even just a bad undertow. Could be he just caught a bad wave."

Caught a bad wave. We all did that from time to time, didn't we? A bad wave that curled too soon, slapped you under the water and pinned you against the sand and gravel in its wash, held you down until you thought your lungs would burst. I sipped my latte, but barely tasted it. Patrick and I grew up spending summers together in the safe haven that Granny Jazzy and Grandpa Dan's beach-house provided us; him from his drug addicted mother and out-to-sea father, and me from the uncertainty that was my mother in Oakland and my father somewhere in the India Himalaya. And I was watching him now and recognized a familiar doubt in his eyes. Doubt that echoed my suspicions. "But you don't think so?"

"I told you. I have doubts. But I'm not saying anything more. I'll put everything in my formal report, though, so it will be on record."

"C'mon. You can't just say that and not tell me what you think."

"I told you, it's a..."

"Civilian matter. Fine. Does your crew still hang out at the River Dog after shift?" I made like I was standing up to leave.

"What?"

"If you won't tell me, I bet one of your crew will. May cost me a fortune in beer, but if I can't get my own cousin to come clean with me..." Not that I'd actually follow through on the threat. I couldn't afford that much beer.

"God, you are so stubborn. Sit down." Patrick glanced around us, but no one seemed to be listening. He lowered his voice and leaned in. "Fine. Here's what's bothering me. The body was in the surf, but his board was floating out beyond the break. The tether wasn't broken, the Velcro was open. It's like... he left his board and tried to swim in." His gaze met mine. "I've surfed with you guys enough times to know he's experienced. He's surfed all over the world. Charlie would know that safety is on that board, not in the breakwater. Even if he came off the board and was injured, the surf should have carried both the board and the body in the same direction. That's why I mentioned aneurism before. Maybe he was disoriented or confused."

"He'd left his board?" Or had it taken from him, maybe. But that begged the other question. "And he was alone? Why would he go in alone? Unless there was someone with him, someone who left. Maybe someone tried to rob him?"

"He was wearing his watch, and his phone was still in his armband when we found him," Patrick reminded me. "So, he wasn't jacked for his gear."

I stared into my coffee, watching the creamy surface swirl as my mind raced. Nothing made any sense.

"Kam? Why did he have you listed as next of kin? I mean..." And there was a curious suspicion behind Patrick's gaze. "I thought you just worked for him. You weren't... I mean, if you were having an affair..."

My broken heart stopped aching long enough for a laugh to escape. "Patrick, Charles was gay. His partner, Arthur, died around the same time Jack and I split up. We are...were... friends. That's all. I think he saw me as the daughter he couldn't have...and I..."

"Saw him as a father?" Patrick was probably the only person in the universe who knew how much my father's decision to stay in India and divorce my mother had torn me up. A father you only see for two weeks out of the year isn't a father at all. "Sorry, Kami, I was just curious. Why you, and not a family member?"

"Oh god." I groaned as I realized I would have to deal with Juliet. "He only has a sister left living, and they don't get along. She doesn't like anyone," I muttered. Charles' sister was a piece of work and I didn't want to think about dealing with her. I changed the subject. "When Arthur died, we agreed that I was likely to be the best person to be his fiduciary, since I usually knew better where he was and what he was doing, especially when he was traveling. Patrick? Do you know who called in the body in the surf?"

"I don't know. I just get the radio dispatches. I can check the logs for you, if you want." He stood and straightened his uniform. "I'll take you back to your car and then I've got to get back to the boat. A lot of last-hurrah summer tourists out there looking for trouble. Are you staying on this side of the hill? Want me to call Granny Jazzy and have her make up a room?"

I shook my head. I needed quiet and space to think. The last thing I needed was my hyperactive grandmother fussing all over me. "I have to go back to the office. I need to call people, cancel appointments. Take care of business..." What was I supposed to tell our clients?

Trick patted the curls on top of my head, like he had since we were kids. "Call me if you need anything."

I shook my head.

"I want to see the beach." One last time. Because I was never going to surf there again.

IN THE STATE PARK PARKING lot above the beach, Charles' black SUV was still sitting in his preferred parking spot. His annual park pass was on the dash, which was probably why the park service hadn't gotten around to towing it away yet. I rolled my Kia up alongside it, kicked off my black flat-heeled pumps, shoved them into my rugged canvas messenger bag, and rolled up my pants-legs. My law-office wear, standard black slacks and white blouse, wasn't exactly beach appropriate. The morning fog had burned off so the Santa Cruz sun was bright and clean overhead, and the sea-salt breeze was cool. I hadn't brought sunscreen or even a hat—ten minutes in that sun and I was going to burn to a crisp—but I wasn't sure I cared. Everything felt strange and unexpected; the sensations of sand beneath my feet without my water shoes, the ocean-breeze against my body without my wet-suit; even the glaring sparkle of sunlight on the water seemed foreign. I jogged down the steps, the worn wood comforting beneath my bare feet. There were more tourists than I expected for the middle of the week but down the beach, where the surf rolled in soft waves as the tide waned, I could see the usual gang hanging out waiting for the tide to turn. They saw me and waved.

Jude Booder was squatting on his board, dry practicing his pop-up. He looked like a grasshopper. "Kam, yo, sis," he greeted as I approached. He'd been my brother's best friend in high school, but I had no idea where their relationship stood these days. I'd stopped speaking to Jude Booder years ago, but he never seemed to have noticed that fact. "You hear about Charlie?"

I nodded a brief "yes," and then turned my back on him. Back when I left Jack standing at the altar waiting for me to walk down the aisle, Jude told everyone that I'd done it because I was secretly in love with him. I swore that I'd never speak a word to him again and I meant it. A nod didn't qualify as a word in my book.

Andelle headed me off and gave me a quick hug. The visiting New Zealander was wet-suited and her curly dark hair was yanked back in a messy pony-tail, but she wasn't wet and there was no sign she'd been in to surf. By contrast, Manny, an aging beach rider who showed his years in deep sun-wrinkles and silver-streaked sun-bleached hair, was damp and sandy, and his breath was quickened as if he'd just come in from the waves and run up the beach. Rick was wet as well, and out beyond the break I could see Shane and Tory turn their boards to ride back in. Doc, who was an actual doctor in real-life, waved half-heartedly with one hand. He was sitting on a towel in the sand with his favorite hybrid board at his side and a bottle of sports-drink in his hand.

Nicky Gratz, my on-and-off best friend, was lying stretched on a towel, her eyes covered with thick prescription sunglasses, and the rest of her covered with sunscreen and very little else. She rolled on her side and tilted her sunglasses to blink up at me with her hyperopic gaze. Ask Nicky to identify a blob in the water beyond the break and she could tell you what it was right down to the exact species of porpoise, but ask her to identify a person two feet away and she'd tell you it was a fence post. The glasses helped. A little bit.

"Sucks, Kam."

There's a thing that happens when you spend days in the surf with like-minded people. A kind of verbal shorthand springs up, one laced with curse words, surf slang, and breath-saving silences. When you've been best friends since third-grade surf camp, complete sentences were pretty much optional. I acknowledged Nicky's assessment of the situation with a grateful nod. "They found him in the surf?"

"CG pulled him out there." Andelle gestured, her dark eyes glancing at the spot and glancing away again.

"It was 'Trick's cutter." That was Jude Booder. He'd edged up between me and Nicky, striking a surf-board model pose that was probably for my benefit. I ignored him.

"I was with him early this morning. We surfed a couple waves," Doc spoke up, shielding his green eyes from the sun as he glanced up at me. "But I left to drop the kids at practice. I wanted to get back before the waves died down, but ended up running by the office. By the time I got back…"

"Were any of you here when it happened? When he actually…" My mouth refused to finish the sentence.

There were slow head shakes all the way around. Nicky sat up. "Sorry. Only got here an hour ago, K."

Manny shook his head. "Got here late today."

Manny the Man missed the good surf? That was about as rare as him actually paying for lunch. I turned back to Doc. "When you got back they were pulling him out?"

"Already had him out. I told them I was a doctor and offered to help, but Trick said it was too late. They wouldn't let me through." Doc's head lowered. He was in his forties, bald but for a ring of reddish hair around the back of his head, and broad hazel green eyes. He was freckled and tanned nut-brown from his active lifestyle, but today he looked grey and washed out. Just how I felt. He reached behind him and handed me Charles' surf-gear duffle. "I packed everything up, but wasn't sure what to do with it."

"Thanks." I shouldered the bag, trying not to look at it. "So, none of you were here when he went in the water?" Of all the things that didn't make sense, that was the big one. "Was anyone else here?"

Andelle thought for a minute. "Not when I got here, not the surfer crowd, anyway. A couple fit-bitters and a dog walker or two…" She hesitated but shook her head, her curls cascading around her face. "All I really saw was the Coast Guard and the beach patrol…"

"Me, too." Rick admitted.

That's all I would have noticed, too. Couldn't blame anyone for watching the show.

Nicky pushed to her feet, her long tan body stretching out of the sand like an Egyptian goddess birthing from the desert, and dusted the sand from her towel. We're exact opposites, Nicky and me, but I count her among my few and dear friends. She's tall and well-figured, her Native American blood blending with her Western European heritage in exotic wild-child fabulousness. There wasn't anything Nicky couldn't do if she put her mind to it, with the result that she put her mind to a great many things. Currently, she was a part-time mechanic, part-time surf-shop employee, part-time student, and part-time coastal wildlife rescue volunteer. There wasn't a lot that Nicky did full-time. "I'm packing in. There's good waves, but I'm not feeling it. You staying, Rick?"

Speaking of doing things full time, I wondered if they were dating again. I raised an eyebrow to Nicky, but she ignored me and Rick nodded. "Yah. I gotta work off this tension."

Nicky gave him such a casual wave that I had to guess that they were off-again in their... well, whatever it was the two of them had. Welcome to Coastal California. I mean that in the best way. Relationships, especially casual ones, always seemed to come easily for my best friend in a way that they just didn't for me. Nicky glanced around the group. "Give us a ride, Andelle?"

Nicky rarely seemed to have a running car among the half-dozen wrenching projects parked in her father's junkyard lot, including her constant favorite machine, affectionately called the FrankenStang. At that moment, Nicky's lack of transportation provided the perfect solution to one of my problems. "Hey, Nicky? Do me a huge favor and take my Kia, please? Charles' car is still in the lot here and I'd like to take it back to the office before it gets impounded. I'll catch up with you later?"

"Yah, okay. But don't wait to call." Nicky took my keys with a faint smile and gave me a sandy and powerful one-armed hug that might have dislocated my shoulder if she hadn't released it almost right away. "Anything you need, I'm right here."

Tears snapped to my eyes but I let the sun burn them away. "Thanks, Nick."

"I'm outer, too. Don't feel much like going in now," Andelle agreed, casting one last glance to the sandy grey surf. "You'll let us know when the funeral is, yeah?"

"Yeah. You know I will." I stood for a row of hugs from the gang. When I skipped Jude, he moved to the other side of Doc, apparently angling for a second try, so I was grateful when Manny stopped in front of me, his body effectively blocking

Jude Booder from approaching.

"Jude'll watch my gear. I'll walk ya back up to your car." And I got the impression that he wasn't just being chivalrous.

I waved good-bye to Doc and ignored Jude Booder. Manny jog-walked beside me as I made my way back up the beach. He's insanely fit for a man of his age and habits, a 70s leftover that had never really grown up. At least Granny Jazzy had done adulthood before slipping back into her artist-hippy ways. I didn't think Manny had ever done anything aside from spending his days hopping up and down the coast in his camper van, selling his custom-made surf waxes (and, I suspected, less legal things) out of the back while looking for waves. I doubted if he'd ever had a steady job. He did make a good wax, though. He knows all the water conditions and watches to learn your surf patterns before making up exactly the right stuff to meet your needs. Spendy, but worth it.

He waited until we were out of earshot of the others and then said, "You think Charlie really just swam out there and drowned hisself?"

I appraised Manny with a guarded glance, but I didn't know what I was looking for. He just looked like washed-up old Manny in floral Bermuda shorts and a red T-shirt that had sun-faded to pink. "Where were you this morning, Man? Usually you're the first one here."

Manny ran a hand through his shaggy sun-bleached, more grey than blond, hair and gave an embarrassed half-laugh. "I ran into some old friends last night, an' one was named Jose Cuervo. Forgot to take my heart meds, I guess, so mornin' came a lot later than usual. Guess I'm lucky it came at all. I got here just as the rescue cutter came across the bay, so I booked it down the beach."

He paused and glanced back down the beach. "There was a van in the lot when I parked, a green van. An' someone was standin' at the top of the stairs with binocs, just watchin'. I got halfway down the steps, but when I glanced back at the landing, they was gone."

"Did you go back up?"

"Nah. I saw the cutter put out the launch and knew somethin' bad was up. I wasn't gonna worry about some whale-watcher."

"It's not whale season."

"Tourists don't know that. They think we got sunny shores and whales all year long." He shrugged. "But here's the thing buggin' me..." We were climbing the stairs now and paused at the landing so Manny could point out where he saw the stranger. "When I come back up here to get my gear, the van was gone. Wit'out a permit, costs five bucks to park in the lot—that's why I park over on the side street—why pay five bucks and not go down to the beach?"

"Maybe it was a jogger who'd already done his run?"

"An' that's another thing." Manny pointed to the spot at the top again. "That coulda been a guy or a gal. They had a hoodie on, pulled low. Figured it was just the morning chill, but, well... Wish't I got a better look at them, but I din't really think about it 'til I come back up and realized the van was gone. Thought it was weird. It's probably nothin' but something about it just ain't sitting right."

"Nothing about this feels right." I admitted in agreement. I fished out my office keyring with the spare to Charles' SUV on it, jabbed the unlock button on the fob, and was satisfied with the clear beep of the car alarm shutting off. No one had messed with the SUV, at least. I opened the back hatch and dropped his duffle in. I wondered where his board was, but guessed that it was probably still on Patrick's boat. "But the coroner says it was drowning, plain-old garden variety. Just because there was a van in the parking lot, you think something happened to Charles?" I shook my head. "He drowned, bro. Caught a bad wave. That's all."

Manny chucked me on the shoulder lightly. "You keep tellin' yourself that."

I intended to. It was just a bad wave.

CHAPTER 2

———

San Amoro: Wednesday Afternoon

CHARLES' SUV WAS stronger and more stable than my little Kia, the padded steering wheel cushiony-smooth under my fingers as I navigated the winding dangers of Highway 17. 17 crosses the Santa Cruz Mountains through Patchen Pass between Santa Cruz and the San Francisco Bay Area. During peak times the journey can take two hours, but on a slow afternoon it takes less than forty minutes. No matter what the traffic is like it's a dangerous road, narrow, hemmed in by sheer cliffs and tall trees, with boulders that can break loose and crash into the road in heavy rains. It's a scary drive on a good day, but somehow the soft seats and easy handling of the car eased my mind. Charles' radio was on a jazz station and I left it, even though I'm not all that fond of jazz. It didn't feel right to change his settings.

Once out of the mountains, Interstate 880 zips along the bottom of San Francisco Bay through San Jose, and then angles northward toward Oakland. Concrete squares filled with tech companies, car lots, and industrial complexes line the major freeway in a straight shot up through Fremont and Hayward. At rush hour, it's hellish, and rush hour can happen all day every day. Near Fremont, I bailed off the freeway and took surface streets the rest of the way to San Amoro and 542 Marin Ave, the office building that housed Hanford Legal.

I loved 542 Marin Ave. From the first moment I saw it, I knew I wanted to work there. It's a beautiful little office building, grey stucco, turreted like a little castle on the front corners, with arching front windows downstairs, and small square windows upstairs. If you squinted just right, in the late afternoon lighting the stucco looked like stone. Sometimes, I imagined that it had a battlement on the roof. Parking Charles' SUV in the lot behind the office, I slouched around to the front door. Hanford Legal was in Suite 1A (Charles loved to switch the numbers around so it read like the steak sauce. It resulted in me having to chase a lot of couriers, promising them they had the right address.) 1B, next door, held Mallory Kent's insurance brokerage. Mallory was in, but his back was to the window. I knew that I had to tell him what happened, but I didn't have the energy just then. I unlocked Hanford Legal and started to flip the Closed sign around to Open out of habit. I managed to catch myself in time. There was no Hanford Legal anymore.

I found myself frozen in place, staring around the office at the walls laden with collectible artifacts and artworks. So many beautiful things that Charles had collected. What would happen to them all now? And what was I supposed to do? I was the Girl Friday of a legal office that didn't have a lawyer. I was, for all intents and purposes, unemployed, but I couldn't just walk away and leave our clients hanging, or ignore the work half-finished on my desk.

Hoover, Charles' hairless Sphynx cat, ran to greet me, bounding to the top of my antique walnut desk, an energetic lanky mass of big-eared felt. How do you tell a cat that his human isn't coming home? I picked him up and snuggled him until he struggled to get down. He ran to Charles' office door and then back to me. Maybe cats already know these things?

Or maybe ghosts knew how to talk to cats?

A faint frisson of cold washed down my spine as I

remembered our office's other occupant. I turned to the 14th Century French suit of armor and whispered our resident ghost's name with reverence. "Evrett?"

Evrett's armor was exactly as I'd left it, his left gauntlet loose at his side, his right resting on the hilt of his sword, his sabatons comfortably spaced in their bracings, his visored sallet helmet closed and still. I observed the knight's empty shell and waited, but there was no sign of the Crusader. Not surprising. That wasn't how our office haunt operated. I whispered into the silent office. "Charles is gone... Evrett, can you see him? Can you hear him?"

Could he carry a message to Charles? Another shiver slid down my spine. Or, maybe, was Charles here?

"Evrett?"

Silence greeted me. Gawd! I was an idiot talking to a ghost who, in all the time he'd been in our office, had never once answered me. As far as I knew, Evrett's presence was limited to knocking things over and shifting his armor around when no one was watching. Expecting an answer from him was insane. Well, maybe I was losing my mind. So what else was new?

A sudden knock on the door drew my attention, and I glanced at the clock on the wall. Crud. The divorce filing! I'd completely forgotten all about it. Vanessa Toreski stood on the front step, her two-inch yellow heels a perfect match to the yellow leather short coat that she wore over a sleek blue silk dress. Her currently blond, enough to hide the grey, hair was swept back from her cheeks in a carefully air-dried and hair-sprayed style, and her grey eyes were keen in her Botox-perfect face. Vanny was pushing fifty, looked like a well-strained thirty-eight, and everything about her, from her gleaming Jaguar to the Hawaiian Island sized diamond on her finger, screamed that she didn't really belong in downtown San Amoro. Not for the first time, I wondered why Vanny came all the way down here to see Charles for her legal work. She probably could have done the paperwork herself, seeing as she was currently divorcing husband number eight, but if she wanted to slum it in San Amoro and pay me big bucks to do it, who was I to complain?

I dashed over to the door without checking my appearance or bothering to brush the tear-tracks off my face. Taking a deep breath, I slipped the dead bolt with a tentative hand, and opened the door. "Vanessa. I'm so so..."

She bowled past me without so much as a hello. "I am so sorry, Kami! I was at the South Street Gallery, and I completely lost track of time. I know I should have called, but what can you do? I hope you have my paperwork ready? Not that I'm in any rush, but Robert is just so tiresome these days. He used to be fun, you know, now he just wants to sail on the Bay and watch the television. Those ridiculous crime shows, you know the ones, where they always solve it with science? I need to divorce him before he takes it in his head to get rid of me." She raised a peaked and perfectly plucked eyebrow, eying me up and down. "Your eyes are all puffy. Are you feeling alright? Allergies getting you down?"

"No. Oh no. Look, Vanny, I'm very sorry that ..."

"Oh no. They aren't ready for me, are they?" Her tastefully made-up face fell into a frown and I thought swiftly. I didn't want to lose the one client I could handle on my own, and I didn't know yet what I could legally say about what happened to Charles and what it meant to the business. I wasn't ready to tell anyone what had happened to Charles. The whole world would have to know soon, but right now I needed it to be my secret grief.

I scrabbled in my bag for the files. "I was going to call you, but then I thought, you were coming by anyway, and we could do this in person." I was winging it, flipping through the paperwork and consulting my notes. "Um. I wanted to ask... about... Why don't you have a seat?" That bought me a few seconds and I snatched the first thing that I thought could be problem if she didn't want the divorce contested. "The yacht.

The yacht was an anniversary gift to you and Robert from Robert's business partner."

Vanny had perched herself carefully on the edge of one of the reception chairs. "Yes. 'The Miracle I.' What about it?"

"Well, it was a gift to you both. The pre-marital agreement you and Robert signed before your wedding doesn't consign gifts. You have the yacht listed under your assets, but under California's joint property la…" My voice trailed off as Vanny leaned forward in her chair, her perfectly pouted lips spoiling the lineless illusion that her makeup provided.

"I want the yacht. He can have the vacation house we bought together."

I consulted the paperwork. "The one in Mexico or the one in Denver?"

"Mexico. And Denver. I don't care." She waved a slickly manicured finger in the air. "I'm sure you can sort it all out. I'm not trying to be complicated, Kami. I'm just ready for the next thing in my life."

The next man, she meant. Poor Mister Number Nine, whoever he turned out to be. "Okay. I'll edit these up and get them ready to go. Early next week at the latest, all right?" I fanned my notes, pretending like I had this all under control. I was a licensed document preparer, but I hadn't done this big of a filing without Charles looking over my shoulder. He'd always been there to help. If Robert decided to contest the terms, I'd need to corner Reginald Burroughs for help. And that train of thought brought me back to Charles' death. I needed to call Reginald anyway.

Vanny didn't look thrilled about next week for the timeline, but she smiled graciously as she stood up. "Please keep me posted, Kami, and if you or Charlie have any questions, or anything else comes up, please let me know right away."

I decided that "right away" didn't mean "right now"and referred only to her paperwork, and not to Charles' death. "Thank you, Vanny, I'll do that. I'll get this wrapped up and give you a call."

She paused one last time, taking in my rumpled office-wear with sudden clarity. Her eyes narrowed, and I tensed, but she glanced out the window and then back at me to ask, "Is the high-wader fashion coming back in? I just loved that look. Showed off my ankles. The rolled pants thing is a nice new twist on it."

"I read about it in Vogue, thought I'd try it." I mumbled, feeling my cheeks blaze. "It's quite comfortable."

"Well, you have the ankles for it, but those shoes need updating, dear," Vanny suggested cheerily before she finally left, sliding an oversized pair of designer sunglasses over her pert smooth nose as she drove away from the office.

I sat down at my desk and unrolled my pants-legs, releasing a shower of sand that Hoover found fascinating enough roll in, scattering it all over the rug. With a sigh, I headed back to the File Room closet where the vacuum cleaner was kept. I was well aware at this point that I was stalling, but sand is sand and antique oriental carpets are well above my paygrade, especially when I was uncertain when I'd ever be paid again.

Suite 1A hosted three rooms; the reception area where I worked, Charles' office, and then the File Room, which is at the end of the hallway, past the door to Charles office. Just beyond the File Room, there was a bathroom with a sink and a shower that's just big enough for a really skinny midget, or maybe a lean Sphynx cat. At the back of the file room was a locked door that opened into the back corridor of the building and out into the alleyway. From the back corridor, a narrow set of stairs went to the upstairs offices. 2A was the daytime den of Morri Morrimont, our resident cruciverbalist, and across the hall was 2B, empty ever since the chiropractor renting it was sued for practicing without a license. He gave me a free spinal adjustment once, and I guess I'm lucky he didn't pop something the wrong way.

In Charles' office, I stood still and looked around at the dark wood cabinets, the comfortable furniture, the artifacts he loved to collect on his travels. Hoover jumped up on the desk and gazed at me with curious eyes. I rubbed his chin as I came around the desk, and knelt to open the cabinet that concealed the wall safe. My fingers punched in the code and I opened it but ended up sitting cross-legged in front of the opened door, staring at the contents. Hoover crawled onto my lap to poke his head in, but determined there were no treats inside and wandered off, leaving me to pull out the cash-box, which contained the petty-cash for the office, the cameras and audio recorder for taking evidence, the stack of confidential invoices for the month, and then, under that, the black binder labeled, "Charles H. Personal." My hand hesitated, unwilling to pick it up. Unwilling to touch it. Maybe I should have called Reginald Burroughs first. After all, I was just an employee. I just worked here. Was this my place? Should I call Juliet?

Juliet. The very name made my gut clench. No, Charles had named me fiduciary. I was responsible, not Juliet. Finally, I snapped my hand out, grabbed the binder by the edge, and jerked it out of the safe. It was somehow lighter than I'd expected. Not heavy at all. I shoved the rest of the contents back into the safe and slammed it shut, feeling the lock engage.

Binder safe under my arm, I went back to the File Room, where the coffeepot, microwave, and mini-fridge lived. I dragged the vacuum out of the closet, and then scanned the contents of the mini-fridge. There was one yogurt that wasn't yet expired, and there were plenty of plastic spoons. I hauled yogurt and vacuum out to the reception area, much to the dismay of Hoover, who believes the vacuum cleaner is the Anti-Christ out to suck up his little kitty soul. He disappeared while I cleaned up the sand, but mysteriously reappeared the moment I sank into my comfortable mesh-backed office chair and opened my yogurt.

I really didn't have any more excuses, so I bucked up, and rang the first person on Charles' contact list; the estimable Reginald Burroughs, Attorney at Law.

"Oslo and Burroughs, please ho…"

"Ray! It's Kami. Don't put me on hold! I have to talk to

Reginald and it's urgent." Rayanne is a competent receptionist, but she loves to push that dang hold button. The day that the Grim Reaper comes for her, she's going to put him on hold.

"Is this…?"

"It's Kami White from Hanford Legal, and I have to talk to Reggie, please."

"I'll see if he's…"

"Please just transfer me, Ray. It's kind of an emergency. Whatever he's working on, he'll want to talk to me. It's important." Why was I in such a hurry to deliver bad news? Because this was going to be one of the hardest things I'd ever done and I wanted it over with. "Don't put me on…"

BEEP

Hold music, classical something or rather with violins, sang through the line.

Forget it. This shouldn't happen over the phone anyway. I shoved my phone in my pocket, gave Hoover a hug and the remainders of my yogurt, collected my shoulder-bag, and checked my appearance in the reflection from a glass-covered, framed Native American Chilkat weaving. My pants legs were a little rumpled, but I'd gotten most of the sand off and looked mostly presentable. I'm not going to make most fashionable paralegal of the year anytime soon, but San Amoro is in the San Francisco East Bay, between Fremont and Oakland, and the pace is more laid-back and casual than the high-powered attorney-scene of Silicon Valley or the urban chic San Francisco legal set.

It took less than eight minutes to drive across town to the Bayfront three-story complex that houses Oslo & Burroughs in a top-floor office suite. From the elevator exit, a panorama window gives a stunning view out across the Bay. On a clear day, you can see southward down to the long, flat expanse of the Dumbarton Bridge, a thin grey line against the dark blue-black waters of the Bay, and north all the way to the engineering monstrosity of the Bay Bridge and the distant towers of Oakland. Today I didn't pause to admire the view, but walked straight through to Rayanne's desk in the tastefully decorated offices of Oslo and Burroughs. She looked at me, blinked, and then looked at her phone. Sure enough, a hold light was blinking. I pulled my phone from my jacket pocket and held it out to her.

"Ten minutes?" It was a good thing I was too grief-worn to growl. "I'm still on hold and I drove all the way over here? Did you even tell him I called?"

"I…" Rayanne must have realized she was on the verge of an unexpected strangling because she punched a button on the phone. "Mr. Burroughs? Kami White is here to see you."

"Kami? Send her through." I heard Reginald Burroughs' angelic Welsh accent roll richly, even through the tinny intercom speaker.

He was waiting in his office doorway, leaning insouciantly against the frame. His black suit was immaculate; his dark hair fell in a classic wave over his forehead. What Nicky was to me, so Reginald Burroughs was to Charles, only with a couple of decades more time together tacked on. Reggie was nothing like his stuffy name implies. He's an Oxford man with a law degree from Stanford, sure, but he was also world traveler with an easy-going demeanor, as at home in a Monte Carlo casino as in a yak herder's yurt. He might be in his late thirties or he might be over fifty; it was impossible to tell. What is certain was that he's dead handsome, with amazing-looking black hair shot through with silver and a killer easy-going smile. He's also, much to my everlasting disappointment, and like so many of Charles' oldest friends, raveningly gay. Reginald was a little like a Special Edition Rainbow Version George Clooney.

I took a deep breath as he greeted me cheerfully, "Kami? What brings you by? I told Charlie I'd send the briefs over by courier tomorrow."

They'd met as boisterous students at Oxford and had been best friends ever since. Their adventures were far more epic than mine and Nicky's, but they'd also had half a lifetime more of them. They'd been two young queer men in a world that didn't understand them nor approve of them. No wonder they'd both wound up in the Bay Area. Charles and Reggie were brothers that surpassed DNA. And now I had to tell him the unthinkable. I clenched my trembling fingers into small fists. "Reggie?"

Something in my voice, in my eyes, must have clued him because he stepped back and gestured me into his office. "Sit down, kiddo. What's wrong?"

As gently as I could, as calmly as I could, I explained that Charles was dead. I felt tears welling again, but somehow managed to keep my voice steady. When I'd finished, the silence stretched into forever, but I couldn't find another word to fill it.

It was awhile before Reggie recovered enough to say, "Has anyone told Juliet?"

"No, you're the first person I called. I reached into my shoulder bag and pulled out the binder. "This was in the safe. I know you handle his legal affairs and…"

"Peter does. I'll give him the paperwork." He sighed his business partner's name, and the sound went straight to my soul. "We'll make him call Juliet. He's good with difficult clients. Is there anything you need?"

"I'm not even sure what I'm supposed to be doing. Legally, I'm not even sure where I stand. I mean, he named me his responsible party, but what about the business? Should I close out the office? I guess I need to contact our clients. And are we supposed to plan a memorial? Or is that up to Juliet? We have a few days because they can't release the death certificate until after the autopsy."

"Autopsy?" Reggie's voice dropped off as he absorbed that. "Why an autopsy? Kami? What happened?"

Oh. Right. "It looks like a surfing accident," I admitted. "They found him in the water this morning. But it qualifies as accidental and unattended, so… autopsy."

"Surfing…" Even without his tone, I knew Reggie didn't like surfing. He wasn't fond of water as anything other than as a softener for his single malt Scotch. "He loved surfing."

"I know. I wish I'd gone..." My commiseration was interrupted by my cell phone ringing, or rather singing. "Hot hot hot flatbread, hot hot hot flatbread, at SuperPita today!" I yanked it out of my handbag and checked the caller ID. Mom. I told it to ignore the call, but the moment with Reggie had been broken. He was staring at me with wide eyes.

"What the hell? Why is the SuperPita jingle your ring tone?"

There was really only one reason to ever have the SuperPita jingle as your ring tone. "The phone was free and the data plan is super-cheap. I just have to put up with a few ads." Because when you were trying to put yourself through law school while working in an office, free and cheap always sounded good. "It's not that bad."

"SuperPita?"

"And Nino's Pizza. The one that really drives me nuts is Reggae Carpet Cleaning. Clean your carpets, fahst, mahn." I groaned. "The map application is terrible. It always wants to direct you to the nearest of their advertisers and it uses them as landmarks, like 'continue one mile past SuperPita, turn left at Pizza Palace. If you need fuel, Gas Plus is on your right.'"

Reggie was watching me disbelievingly. "You know new phones don't really cost all that much, right?"

"Reggie," I reminded as gently as I could, "I don't even have a job anymore. Not even sure what I'm going to do next."

He nodded, his voice incredibly soft. "We'll get through this. Everything at the office will need to go on hold until we can start probate, and that can't start until the death certificate is released. If you need legal sign-off on anything you're working on that can't wait, swing by. Peter and I will help."

"We have two open civil court dates. I'll contact the clients and file change of counsel to Oslo & Burroughs? If that works?"

He nodded, "You take point as paralegal, and we'll do whatever is necessary."

I stood up. "I'll call you tomorrow, okay?"

Reggie walked me to the door, then gave me the strongest hardest hug ever and for a breath's space, grief was a shared weight.

As he let me go, he muttered, "Kami, whatever you need, I'm here."

With Patrick and Nicky and Reggie all there for whatever I needed, how was it that I felt so all alone? "You, too, Reggie." I held up my cell-phone. "I'm just a SuperPita jingle away."

Neither of us could really smile at the joke, but we both tried.

I DROVE BACK TO THE office, pulled out a legal pad and started to make a list. People to call. Appointments to cancel. Papers to file. Paralegals generally work under lawyers and our legal responsibilities are limited, but I was certified as a document preparer, so at least that much of the work I could finish. Everything else, I was going to need Reggie's help with. The only thing I knew for sure right now was that the office felt cold and empty. Across the street, the warm, inviting lights of Reese's Café beckoned.

I was just about to make a break for those comforting golden lights when I heard footsteps on the back stair. Morri was coming down. And he didn't know. Oh god, I was going to have to tell him. I looked around for somewhere to hide.

He knocked at the back door before using his emergency key to come in through the file room. "Poppet?"

It only took one glance at his wizened face to know that he knew. A war correspondent journalist in his previous life, Morri Morrimont spent the afternoons of his retirement in the office over mine writing word-puzzles. He tended to be jaunty, with a mischievous grin and sparkling eyes, and his wiry frame was a coil of energy just waiting to spring into action. Normally, he was a ray of sunshine in my life. That moment, he was another grey shadow, haunted by memories of too many friends lost. "Morri, I…" I choked off my words and sighed.

"You already know, don't you?"

"Came over the radio a bit ago." No clever pun or witty remark. No wordplay at all. He just held out his arms and we hugged. I have a perfectly good grandfather, and I love my Grandpa Dan, but if we're allowed to choose our family then I choose Morri as my honorary grandfather. It doesn't hurt that his wife runs a cookie shop and makes the most amazing snickerdoodles ever.

That was when I realized someone was standing behind him. A vaguely familiar man, but I couldn't place him. Was he a client of the business? Medium height and build, he had dark hair and dark eyes, and was younger than I would have expected, but with a solemnity that marked him as one of faith.

"I don't know if you remember Father Joseph Talbon," Morri asked more than stated. "He was a friend of Charles."

"Father Talbon." I blinked, held out my hand for shaking. "Of course. You were part of the ghost research group that tracked down our knight for us."

"Just call me Joe." He shook my hand lightly and smiled. "Yes. I helped out with your crusader. And I enjoyed many a chess night with Charles at Morri's."

Thursday Chess Club Night. Of course. Joe is a good name, so I was instantly inclined to like him, but I also felt a hint disrespectful at calling a priest by his given name instead of his title. I decided to compromise.

"What did they say on the news?" I asked Morri as I turned on the electric teakettle and fixed us each a cup of my mom's special herbal mint-chamomile tea. Her label on the tin promised "soothing calm," something I thought we all needed. I gestured Father Joe to Charles' comfortable office chair while Morri and I appropriated the leather sofa.

Morri settled back, gazing around the familiar room with weary eyes that lingered briefly on Charles' carved marble chess set in the corner. I made a mental note to ensure that he got it. "They reported that a surfer drowned this morning, but they didn't release the name until just a bit ago. I looked out and saw Charles' car pull in and I thought, well, that they must have got it all wrong…" He glanced at me with a hint of his old mischief. "We're journalists, not gods, you know. We make mistakes from time to time. Then I saw you get out and, poppet, I knew the minute I saw you it was true. I conjectured that you could use some moral support and called in reinforcements. You look like the world has ended."

I leaned on his bony shoulder, exhausted. "It feels like it has ended. What am I supposed to do now?"

"What did they tell you at the hospital?"

"I had to go to the coroner's office. They said that there has to be an autopsy. That they'll release the body for burial after that. That they'll release the death certificate after the autopsy. I already took all the paperwork to Oslo & Burroughs."

Father Joe smiled sympathetically. "I'll help with the arrangements if you'd like. I believe Charles mentioned having a plot beside Arthur's already prepared. I'll check on that for you."

I should have guessed he would have. Charles wasn't one to leave things last minute. Not like me. When I die, hopefully they'll think of something useful to do with me. I hear that you can be turned into soil for a tree now. Or donate me to science, maybe. "I don't know how much of that is up to me, but I bet Reggie will do everything he can to make sure we have input."

"And you've talked to Reginald Burroughs?" Morri continued softly. "What did he say?"

"That he had to talk to Peter Oslo about the …" The word "will" stuck in my throat. "The paperwork. Peter was handling Charles' affairs, not Reggie." I sighed. "I can't think what else I'm supposed to be doing."

"Then I think there's really only one thing to do for right now."

I drew back and looked at Morri, and he smiled, warmth glowing in his eyes. "Go home. Go home and take a bath. Have some wine. Have some soup. Get some sleep. Don't worry about anything until you've taken care of yourself."

I started to agree, but Hoover butted my hand, looking for chin rubs. "What about Hoover? I can't take him to my place. No pets allowed. And he can't stay here all alone. I guess I can take him to Mom's. She's cat-sat for him before."

But that would also mean telling Mom what was going on, and I wasn't up for that. Not just yet.

Morri scooped up Hoover and picked up his harness and his little hand-knit sweater, this one in blue with white stripes. (My mother provides Hoover with an unlimited supply of sweaters. She adores Hoover, possibly more than she adores me and my brother. At least, she's never knitted me a striped sweater.) Morri dressed and harnessed the cat with deft hands. "I'll take him home with me tonight. Mrs. Morri won't mind at all. I still have some food left from when Charles went on vacation, and we'll make up the spare litterbox."

"What about Helliqat? Won't she mind?" Mrs. Morri had found Helliqat abandoned in a dumpster behind Happy Cookie. The little black and white kitten was a complete terror to everyone else, but utterly devoted to, and protective of, Mrs. Morri.

"She'll just have to be good with it." Morri buckled Hoover into his harness. "We'll go next door and break the news to Mallory Kent and then we'll be off home. You lock up and do the same."

Father Joe handed me his card. "If you need to talk, any time, day or night."

I didn't need to talk. I was exhausted from talking. I hugged Morri one more time, unable to find the words to express my gratitude.

I LOCKED UP THE SHOP, but I didn't want to go home. I crossed the street to Reese's Café and ordered a bagel with cream cheese and a double chocolate brownie. Usually at this time of day, from the second floor, you could look across and see Morri head-down at his desk or standing in front of his whiteboard sketching out puzzles. Or you could see me typing away at the computer downstairs. This afternoon, all the lights were off upstairs and in Hanford Legal. As I watched, Mallory Kent switched off his neon OPEN sign, and turned off his lights, too. The whole building was grieving.

The sight broke my heart even further, so I went back downstairs, selected a table away from the windows, opened my briefcase and extracted Vanny's preliminary divorce filing. I didn't read it. I was starting to feel sorry for Husband Number Eight, the soon-to-be-poor Mr. Toreski. Charles had helped Vanny develop an airtight pre-nup, so aside from the changes Vanny requested, it was all pretty straightforward as long as Robert Toreski didn't object and contest the terms. I needed to formulate a divorce decree as tight as that prenuptial agreement.

Instead, I ate my brownie without tasting it, picked at my bagel, and thought about Charles, how generous he'd been. How kind. How supportive. He'd been in the next table over, just a few feet away, on the afternoon that I delivered his usual lunch, a tuna sandwich and a fruit cup.

… I'd taken the time to pick out the grapes and replace them with strawberries.

"Remind me to leave you a good tip, Kami."

"You better." I'd smiled, but I was tired from staying up late studying and then opening the café that morning. "I need all the tips I can get if I'm going to afford textbooks."

Charles blinked, glanced at his sandwich and then back at me. "I didn't think of that. I always had plenty of money for books and supplies."

I knew he was a well-off lawyer, and I knew he'd gone to Oxford—Oxford, which to me was some far away exotic land of higher education that I could only dream about—and that he came from money. I was tired, I was irritable, and I didn't need someone rubbing their wealth in my face right then, not when I was working full-time and taking night classes and didn't know if I would be able to afford food next week or if I'd drop dead from exhaustion before my next shift. "Yeah, well, some of us didn't come from rich families. Some of us came from single parent families where we were just grateful to have food on the table and clothes on our backs. And some of us have to work our hind-ends off to follow the dreams that you just had handed to you on a silver platter."

As soon as the words fell out of my mouth, I knew there'd be no tip for me. Nope. He'd probably order Reese to fire me on the spot! And I'd totally deserve it.

But Charles just looked at me, with those kind hazel-brown eyes that seemed to see through and beyond, and said, "Would you like a job?"

"I…uh…what?"

"You're studying to be a paralegal, right? You want to become a lawyer some day?"

I did. I absolutely did. "Yes. I don't want to make tuna sandwiches forever, but…"

"Legal secretary duties to start, Monday through Friday, nine to four, time off for exams and studying, and I'll help you make full paralegal, and with law-school after that. I can pay you twice what Reese is."

"And what do you get out of it?" I was instantly suspicious.

"I get a legal secretary, which I desperately need, as well as someone who isn't afraid to speak her mind and tell me what she really thinks of me, which I also need." Charles winked and swiped a hand through his greying hair, grinned as he added, "And who can make a hell of a tuna sandwich."

… Something splashed into my latte and I belatedly realized that it was a tear. And once they started, they didn't seem to stop. Fortunately, I practically lived at Reese's in my off-time. I studied there, ate most of my meals there. Sometimes, when they were very busy, I'd take a turn bussing tables or pulling espresso. Reese never took me off the payroll, and a couple dollars here and there never goes amiss, even if I did mostly use them as credit toward coffee. Point is, I was family at Reese's. So, when I decided to have a quiet breakdown in the corner, no one even flinched. One of the taxi-cab driver regulars dropped a stack of napkins in front of me and patted my shoulder on his way out.

Five years. And where had they gone? I was a full paralegal now, and I was taking law classes at night and online, working toward my law degree. I'd learned more about working law with Charles than I ever could have just working at a coffee shop. I'd also learned a lot about running a small business, from finance and paperwork to maintaining a company website. Hanford Legal had nearly doubled in clientele, and we'd lately been talking about taking on an actual receptionist so that I could focus on my paralegal duties.

And now Charles was gone, and Hanford Legal was gone with him.

I finally followed Morri's advice and collected my old thrift-store bicycle from the rack in front of the office. It didn't pay to have a nice bike in San Amoro. Anything that looked good would be stolen out from under you in ten seconds or less. I'd had Old Thrifty for almost ten years. Maybe it had been blue once upon a time, but was now a faded eggshell with a few rust spots showing through. No one ever stole Old Thrifty, no matter how hard I tried to let them. I slowly peddled through the summers-end gloaming back my little efficiency apartment, where I lay awake on my found-free-on-the-corner love seat and stared at the ceiling until dawn.

CHAPTER 3

———

Santa Cruz: Friday Morning

"THE CAUSE OF DEATH really was accidental drowning? No extenuating circumstances?" I was looking right at the death certificate, but I didn't believe it. I didn't want to believe it. "May I see the full autopsy report?"

The coroner office receptionist, a woman my age with a brown bob, wearing a brown sweater and a tired demeanor, stared at me as if I'd sprouted horns. Maybe I had. It had been a rough week, after all. "Well, we don't normally release that to individuals. Unless there's going to be an inquiry, I mean."

"I understand it's unusual." I placed both hands on the counter and leaned in. It would probably have been more effective if I could loom over her, but I tried to make up for my lack of height with a stare-down. "But I would like a copy."

The receptionist shook her head tentatively. "Miss…White? Is it? I know we all want to see a reason in an accidental death like this, and it's natural to seek meaning in what happened, but sometimes, things are just accidents. There's no rhyme or reason. Autopsy reports can be traumatic for loved ones. Maybe it's better to…"

"Maybe it's better if you give me a copy of the full autopsy report." I held out my hand, and hoped it wasn't shaking.

"Please."

"Miss…"

"I said 'please.'" I tried to summon up some De Niro and Pacino. Or, at least, what De Niro would be like if he was a cross between a young Meg Ryan and an angry toothpick. Don't make me not say 'please.' "As his legal representative, I'm formally requesting all documents pertaining to the death of Charles Hanford. I can get it to you in writing if you'd like."

Technically, Peter Oslo was his legal representative, but he hadn't had time to come, and Reggie hadn't wanted to come with me. I was acting as a paralegal in the authority of Oslo & Burroughs and as personal fiduciary to the deceased. She turned away without another word and started photocopying documents out of the file.

"And how many copies of the death certificate will you need?"

Ten was the number that Reggie had given me when I told him where I was heading and asked if he would come with me, which he'd emotionally declined. "Twelve, thank you very much."

Minutes later, I was in Fin's Coffee ordering an iced caramel latte—not as good as Reese's—and waiting for Patrick. I had the official autopsy report in my hand, but one glance at it reminded me that I was a legal professional, not a medical professional. I picked out the words I understood, checked the chart that showed where abnormalities were found, and read the section about seawater in both the lungs and the stomach. He'd swallowed water trying to stay afloat. I turned the report over, sucking at the foam on top of my latte as I registered that bit. He'd swallowed water, which meant he'd suffered, struggled. He'd fought for life.

Patrick swung in the door, his usual sea-swayed stride taking him to the counter where he ordered a large coffee, black, and an oatmeal cookie. My cousin was as predictable as the tides. I raised a hand and he joined me.

"He didn't kill himself." I tapped the downturned report.

"And it wasn't an accident."

Patrick eyed me up and down. "When was the last time you slept?"

"Last night." For about two hours. The sofa in Charles' office was comfortable enough, but Hoover wasn't used to sharing.

"You're going to make yourself crazy. You have to let this go. Hold the memorial, grieve, do whatever you have to do, but let it go."

"Like you with Kelli-Ann?" Bringing up his divorce was mean, and I knew it. Maybe I still had De Niro in my brain. "That's rich advice coming from you."

"Death isn't the same as a break-up." Patrick let my jab glance off him and picked up the paperwork from the file, glancing it over. "Death is final. You can't fix things after they're dead. What makes you so sure it wasn't suicide?"

"If you want to die, you go under water to breathe it in. You don't fight to stay above water and swallow it in the process."

"You're grasping, cuz. There's a million reasons that he could have swallowed water." Patrick went back to the report, looking again. He muttered words under his breath; hematoma, abrasion, etcetera, and I was reminded that he was a certified EMT/First Responder. Maybe he had more sense of what it all meant than I did. Suddenly he stood up. "We need to talk to the coroner."

"I thought I was grasping?"

Patrick shot me a raised eyebrow and added a curled lip. "And I thought you wanted to understand why Charles died?"

As we walked down the street to Patrick's Jeep, our coffee cups in hand, Patrick took the outside curb-edge of the sidewalk. My cousin, the chivalrous. "Afraid I'll fall into traffic?"

"Afraid if you piss me off, I'll push you." He chuckled a little. "You never change, do you? Still always see the worst in things."

That startled me a little. "You think I'm a pessimist?"

"You tell me. Why did you leave Jack?"

"Because I hate him," I answered coolly, but a hot blush hit my cheeks. I pretended it was sunburn, even though the Santa Cruz morning fog had yet to burn off. It was a mean move on Patrick's part, and it didn't matter how right he was, I wasn't about to admit that I was too scared to hold on to something precious for fear of how it might go bad later. I wasn't about to admit that Jack was one of the best things that had ever happened to me. Like Charles. The good things always leave. It was safer to run. Though, on reflection, running to another state in a wedding dress via a Greyhound bus was probably not the right way to leave. "I left Jack because he was impossible."

"Uh huh." That was all Patrick said about that. I figured it served me right for bringing up Kelli-Ann, so didn't try to retaliate.

WE ARRIVED BACK AT THE coroner's office and the woman at the counter tried to hide when she saw me, but Patrick strode up and asked loudly to see the coroner who had performed the autopsy. The receptionist stepped up when she realized it was Patrick and not me that she'd be dealing with. Patrick gave me another raised eye-brow glance and mouthed, "What did you do?" at me.

I flexed my shoulders in a "dunno, wasn't me" shrug and pretended to be very interested in the privacy notice that was posted on the wall. My brain didn't seem to be word-enabled at the moment, and I just barely skimmed it, finding two misspellings and a misplaced comma. Patrick signaled, and I followed him back to a small office. On the walls were shelves of medical manuals and journals, and on the top shelves were some plastic anatomical models. I decided it was creepy. Dr. Chee joined us. She winced when she saw it was me. "Hello, how can I help you?"

Patrick held out the copy of the autopsy report. "You were the one who completed the autopsy on Charlie? Charles Hanford?"

"Ah. Yes. Mr. Hanford was in incredibly good shape for his age." Dr. Chee smiled with a hint of envy. "Surfing must have agreed with him."

"Surfing killed him. I'd hardly call that agreement." I didn't mean to snap. I swear I didn't. Once you start carrying De Niro, it's hard to put him back down.

Dr. Chee blinked, and her expression shifted to one of hurt. Oops. Guess there was a reason she worked with dead people. Before I could apologize, Patrick nudged my shoulder and said in his most polite tone, "Shut up, Kami," before turning back to the doctor. "I wanted to ask a few questions about this report?"

"Ah. Yes. Okay, whatever I can answer, but everything is in my report."

"What does this mean? I didn't recognize the abbreviation." Patrick pointed to the report.

"Nonspecific skin lesions. There was a lesion on his left hand and a couple on his feet."

"His feet?" I glanced at Patrick. Charles hadn't shared my obsession with surf booties, preferring to feel sand (and seagull poop, and all the other icky ocean stuff) between his toes. "Jellyfish stings, maybe?" We were back to the jellyfish theory?

"It could be." Dr. Chee's dark eyes flicked to me and then away again. Great. I'd scared the doc again. Pretty soon the entire Santa Cruz coroner's department was going to be hiding from me. If I died in Santa Cruz, they'd probably just mark my death as a heart attack without looking too closely. "They were small, though. More like insect bites?"

How do you get insect bites on the bottom of your feet?

"Or like an allergic reaction, maybe? Some kind of hive?" Patrick was ahead of me. We'd always been competitive, even as children. He could run faster, jump higher, surf better, but I could swim further, run further, and was way better at Scrabble. Having him beat me at quiz-the-doc was annoying.

"I don't think Charles was allergic to anything." He'd traveled all over the world. We'd eaten hundreds of meals together, surfed the same waters, and bicycled the same insect-buzzing trails at Chabot Lake Regional Park. "He never mentioned it. Even mosquitos didn't seem to bother him." But they bit the heck out of me.

The coroner shrugged. "Ah. Well, the body hasn't been moved to the mortuary yet. I can take a closer look and send samples for further testing, but since those lesions don't affect cause of death, I'm not sure it justifies the expense. And it could take weeks to get the panel back from the lab."

"Do it. And if the expense is a problem, you can bill it to the estate through Oslo & Burroughs Legal Firm." I handed her Reggie's card. "Just one more question. How often do you find water in the stomach of drowning victims?"

"It happens." Dr. Chee pulled down a model from the wall, and I realized that the lungs inside the plastic rib-cage were soft and squeezable. "As a drowning person struggles for air, they bob in the water. The pressure," she squeezed the base of the lungs and the model exhaled, "presses air out and sucks water in. The body's natural reaction is to try to swallow the water, to channel it to the stomach instead of the lungs."

"If they're struggling not to drown." I confirmed, glancing at Patrick. He met my eye and looked back to the model. "If they want to die, if they're suicidal, just how much do they struggle for air? The cops suggested he was trying to commit suicide, and that's ludicrous."

"My ruling is accidental death due to drowning, not suicide, and that's what the legal entities should focus on. I'm sorry. I'm just a physician. I can tell you what the body does and how it works, but the why is something else entirely." Dr. Chee tapped the model on top of its bald, featureless head. "I can tell what happened, but only the deceased themselves can tell you why."

So, that was no help. The only deceased I knew didn't tell me anything at all. "Patrick, was there anything else on the report?"

My cousin shook his head. "I think this is enough for now. May I call you if I have more questions, Doc?"

"Ah, yes. I'm happy to help anyway I can." She shook her head. "I know when a healthy person dies like this, it can be hard to understand. I wish I had answers for you."

I shook my head. "Thank you, Doctor Chee. I appreciate you taking the time to talk to us. You're right that it's hard to understand. Impossible, really. Too many things don't add up."

She frowned, studying me for a moment. "I'll take some samples from those lesions and run them through the lab. Maybe I missed something." But her expression said that she wasn't the sort to miss things.

"That's all I ask, thanks."

We left the coroner's office, the receptionist woman refusing to meet my eye as we walked past her desk. On the sidewalk, I reached for Patrick's arm and gave it a squeeze. "Thanks, cuz. You were awesome in there."

"I'm awesome everywhere." Yup. That's my cousin. "Can I keep this report for a couple of days? I'm on duty tomorrow, but I'd like some time to look it over again, see if there's something we missed."

"Yeah, of course..."

"Kami!" Andelle appeared on the sidewalk, her long legs bare below short-cropped denim cutoffs that reached the top of her thighs and wrapped her curves tighter than a shell on a turtle. She wore a pink baby-girl T-shirt that read Surfin Princess. Jude Booder was walking behind her, and his eyes weren't on her T-shirt.

"Andelle." I gave her a hug, met Jude Booder's eye and looked away again— a cat hello; silent but effective.

"And who is this?" She eyed Patrick up and down, and he returned the favor.

"Patrick Tamsin, my cousin."

Andelle registered surprise and then her expression turned even more interested. "Cousin. Nice. I've heard a lot 'bout you. The gang says you've a wicked backside reverse." She held out her hand to Patrick, "I'm Andelle Lakely, but all my friends call me Delle."

No, we didn't. Only the guys trying to get into her size two denim-cutoffs called her that. The rest of us called her Andie. But Patrick fell for it hook, line, sinker… Hell, he took the whole darn rod. He moved in closer than necessary and took her hand, not in a business-like shake, but more of a gentle squeeze. "Kia ora, Delle. And my friends all call me Trick."

That was true, at least. Trick was a stupid nickname that he'd given it to himself when he was twelve and I was eleven. We were trying to master a frontside snap. He was the first of our small herd of cousins to do it, and afterward demanded that we all call him Trick. I called him something that rhymed with it. Granny Jazzy overheard me and I was beached for the rest of the day and had to wash the dishes for a week. Granny Jazzy can hear a bad word uttered from five-hundred feet away. I'd swear to that, but she might hear me.

"Yeah?" Andelle was staring into Patrick's eyes.

"You ever surf Wainui Beach? I hear its sweet as!"

Sweet-as? Why had Patrick suddenly gone one-hundred percent Zealand surf-bum trying to impress her? Wasn't it enough that he was hot, charming, and captained a Coast Guard cutter?

Andelle blinked and smiled charmingly. "Yeah. It's good."

This was getting nauseating. Time to move it along. "What brings you two down here?"

"Tide's out until five or so. Thought we'd head over to the surf-shop and see what's new." Jude Booder spoke up suddenly. He was glaring at the spot where Patrick's hand had only just released Andelle's. "Delle and me are looking for new boards."

Ah, Jude Booder. Always one to live in his own world.

"Bro, how can you afford a new board?" Patrick said what I was half-thinking. "I can't even afford a new board."

Jude shrugged, his unkempt hair falling over his plug-pierced ears, which just added to his grasshopperish appearance. "All the vacation birds turn sell back their gear before they head back home. Some of 'em don't even use the stuff. Sometimes ya can find something good real cheap."

Even a used board of average quality wasn't exactly cheap. I eyed Jude again, but there was nothing about him that said he was lying. "Well, you guys have fun."

"When's Charlie's funeral?" Andelle asked suddenly. "I'd like to come."

"And we should hold a Paddle Out." Jude Booder surprised me with words that I actually thought were lovely to hear. The Paddle Out, revered custom among surfers since the early Hawaii surf days, was a memorial, a sacred good-bye specific to surfers and their peers. It was a good idea, even if it was coming from Jude.

"The coroner's office just released his body." The words felt stiff as I spoke them, like tiny arrows. "I'll let you know as soon as the arrangements are made. It's my understanding that he left instructions with his lawyer, but I haven't seen them. As to a Paddle Out…"

"I'll start setting it up." Patrick spoke up. "That's a good thought, Jude. I'll talk to Doc and then let y'all know when and where."

Andelle gave me another coconut sunscreen scented hug, and they walked off down the street, but she glanced back over her shoulder at Patrick and winked. Whatever Jude Booder thought he had going with her, he certainly didn't. Patrick winked back and I smacked his shoulder the second she looked away. "Dude, seriously. Eyes front and center."

"What do you know about 'Delle?" He rubbed his arm and gave me a little push in return. Because that's what family is for.

"Andelle? Not much. She's got a wicked gorgeous roundhouse, cleanest I've seen. Better than Manny, even."

"Manny's is pretty clean." Patrick agreed.

"Anyway, she's probably headed back to New Zealand as soon as the weather shifts, chasing the waves." I didn't want Patrick to get his hopes up about her, but he gave me a serious look.

"Do me a favor. Run a back-ground check."

"What? On Andelle?" I shifted and glanced back at

Andelle's departing back as it disappeared into the tourist crowd outside the surf shop. "Why do you want a check? You can't date someone without full disclosure or something?"

"Because wherever she's from, it's not New Zealand. I've surfed every beach in New Zealand." Patrick's pale blue eyes fixed on me just as the sun broke through the fog. "Wainui is crap. Over-crowded, baby beginner waves…Any Zealander who surfs will tell you that."

It took me a second to register the implication of that. "Wait. You set her up? Maybe she was just being polite?"

"Kia ora, bro. Now, I've got to get back." He waved the file at me. "I'll take another look at this and see if there's anything else that catches my eye. You gonna be okay?"

I nodded. "I'm heading back to San Amoro. I need to talk to Reginald about funeral arrangements and everything. And start closing out the office. I guess I need to start job-hunting, too."

Because without a lawyer, a law office was kind of pointless. Without Charles, I was suddenly stunningly unemployed.

"Okay. Call if you need anything."

"You've done so much already, cuz, but I'll call you if I think of anything."

He walked away, and I stood still and filled my lungs with damp ocean air. I still had time before meeting up with Nicky to get my Kia back, which was just fine with me. It would be building to a hot and humid afternoon in San Amoro, and I really wasn't looking forward to the harrowing drive over 17 back to the Bay Area. Since I had an hour to kill, I decided to track down Doc. My new smartphone helped me out, pointing me to a small medical complex with dentists, doctors, and psychologists all sharing neatly laid out wood-sided block buildings. The Internet told me Doc was Dr. Jerry Jameson and that he was a neurological specialist. Neurology? Wasn't that brain stuff? Why did I think he had something to do with feet?

The diagrams on his office wall clarified that for me. The feet, apparently, are full of nerve endings. And apparently when

they hurt it feels like needles. Or fire. The posters made me feel
pretty uncomfortable, really. I stepped up to the counter and
the young man behind the desk looked at me and then at the
reception computer with a slightly furrowed frown. He looked
far too young to be a receptionist. I really hoped he wasn't a
doctor.

"Do you have an appointment?"

"No, I don't. This is actually a personal visit. Is it possible
Dr. Jameson has a moment to talk to me?"

"I don't know." The young man rolled his chair to the back
door of the reception area and hollered, "Dad! Lady out here
says she knows you!"

He rolled back to me and for the first time I saw the family
resemblance in the shock of reddish hair, the vivid freckles,
and the slightly buck-toothed smile. "Oh, you're Doc's kid?
The older one, I'm guessing?"

"Yeah. He's makin' me work for him part-time to pay off
the…" The kid ducked his head and mumbled something that
sounded like "broken window" under his breath. "How do you
know Dad? You're not one of his women, are you?"

His women? I choked, snorting back a laugh. "No. No, I'm
definitely not one of his women. We surf together sometimes."

Used to. Used to surf together. I had no intention of getting
back in the water anytime soon.

"Oh." The kid registered this for a second. "Is this about
Uncle Charlie?"

Uncle? Another Hawaii tradition dragged into the
California surfing culture. Any good friend who looked out
for your kids like their own became an uncle or auntie. And
if the kid knew Uncle Charlie, then he was family. That's just
how it worked. I smiled warmly. "Yeah, it is. I'm Kami. Maybe
he mentioned me?"

"Yeah! You're the peach!"

"I'm the…what?"

"Uncle Charlie always said he wouldn't be able to come
surfing on Wednesdays with us if you weren't being a peach

and running the office. I always pictured you as more pink."

I felt pretty pink right then, actually. Somehow, I managed to hold out my hand. "Nice to meet you."

"I'm Rodney." He shook my hand quite seriously just as Doc came out from the back. I hardly recognized him in his professional garb; a white lab-coat and spectacles in lieu of wetsuit and goggles.

"Kam! What brings you by? We were just about to close up for the day. I was finishing some paperwork." Doc skipped the hand-shaking formalities and gave me a solid hug. "How are you doing? I was about to take Rodney for burgers. Want to come?"

How much caffeine had Doc had? I tackled his questions one by one. "I came by to talk about arrangements for a Paddle Out. Patrick is putting it together. I'm holding up, barely. And I'd love to join you for burgers. You'll have to drive, because Nicky still has my car. Did I miss any questions?"

Doc chuckled. "I think that's everything."

"Doc?" I paused next to a diagram that showed small arrows pointing to specific points on the bottom of the feet. "What does this mean?"

"Those are just reflexology points. The feet are like a roadmap to the rest of the body, full of blood vessels, sweat glands and nerve endings. Some people believe that stimulating specific spots on the foot can help stimulate and heal other body parts."

"Like acupuncture?"

"Exactly." Doc shrugged, stripping off his lab coat and hanging it on the hook behind the reception area door. "I figure, it can't hurt and, if nothing else, it can help my patients feel more in control of their conditions. By the time they come to me, they've often already seen a number of specialists, and sometimes there aren't any real answers. We just keep trying treatments until something works."

"Hmm." I looked at the diagram a moment longer, remembering the "nonspecific lesions" on Charles' feet.

Patrick had the report with the coroner's diagram in it, but if memory served, they didn't seem to line up with the diagram on the wall. I'd have to take a second look to be sure. Doc was smiling at me, his expression open and warm. Was I grasping for clues where there weren't any? "Where do you want to go for burgers?"

We ended up at the Hawaiian Grill. It wasn't quite an institution, but it tried hard to promote the Santa Cruz feel with surfboards on the walls, accented by tropical décor. We ordered lunch and found a table near the back. Rodney ordered the same thing as his father. In fact, he seemed a lot like his father, only quieter. He was seventeen and a high school senior. "I've already been accepted to Berkeley," he told me unapologetically. "But I really want to go farther away. Out of state."

"And I told you, start filing for scholarships." Doc reminded. I had the feeling this was a discussion they'd had a number of times.

"If you'd pay me for working in the office…"

"Which I will as soon as you pay off the new windshield."

I had a feeling I didn't want to know that story. "Doc, can I ask you about the morning Charles died? I mean, I don't want to bring up stuff in front of Rodney if you'd rather…"

"Rodney's mature enough to handle things," Doc said confidently.

I glanced to Rodney and could well believe it. The teen dipped a fry in ranch sauce and saluted me. "Okay. It's just… Manny said he saw a van in the parking lot? Do you remember seeing anyone in a van coming or going when you left or came back?"

Doc closed his eyes and breathed in slowly, his voice taking on a meditative cadence as he remembered. "I climbed the sea-stair. I'd left my gear with Charles so I wasn't weighed down. I pulled on a sweatshirt over my wetsuit and tossed a towel down on the seat of the car." He opened his eyes and shook his head. "I don't see a van. There's Charles' black SUV, and there's an older model sedan. No green van. No, wait… as I was leaving, passing the park kiosk, there's a green van outside the gate. Looked like it was waiting for something. Or maybe had taken the wrong turn and wanted the campground instead of the day-use area?"

"Did you notice the license plate?"

Doc blinked and looked at me across the table. "Sorry, no, the angle was all wrong. It had side-windows but they were blacked out."

"Well, that's not creepy or suspicious sounding at all." Rodney interjected with the kind of blatant sarcasm that only a teen-ager can muster. "So, do you think someone killed Uncle Charlie?"

I shook my head. "I don't know what to think, Rodney." I glanced back to Doc. I'd barely picked at my teriyaki burger. It smelled amazing but every tiny bite stuck in my throat like glue-soaked cardboard. "I looked at the autopsy report today and there was water in his stomach, which doesn't say suicide to me. You're a doctor, so you'd know more about that than me, I think. And Charles wouldn't have gone into the water alone. If he'd drowned accidentally, someone should have seen something. I can't help thinking that something went wrong somewhere."

Doc nodded, closing his eyes again. "I didn't look back when I left. We came out of the surf, I settled my gear, and he was getting his water bottle out of his duffle." His expression stilled and fell into sadness. "You never think that's the last time you'll see someone. Why didn't I look back? Why didn't I wave good-bye?"

After a moment, he continued quietly, "I wasn't paying particular attention, but I don't remember anyone else on the beach. No, there were two women jogging with a dog, but they were already well past us."

"Don't trust beach-runners with dogs. They never scoop

their poo," Rodney stated facetiously, then he frowned. "I don't like thinking that someone killed Uncle Charlie."

"None of us do, Rod." Doc reassured, before opening his eyes and looking back at me. "But I guess that's the question, isn't it? Who would want to kill Charlie? I mean, it just doesn't make any sense."

"It makes more sense than thinking that he paddled out beyond the surf, left his board, and then tried to swim back in and drowned. If the coroner had found, oh, an aneurism or a heart attack or something, anything, I wouldn't even be thinking it." I tried to say it gently, but the question had been weighing too heavily on my mind the past two days. "When you got back to the beach, who all was there?"

Doc seemed surprised by the question. "Well, everyone. Jude, Andelle, Mark and Manny. Nicky, Rick and Shane hadn't gone down to the beach yet, but were watching from the lot… Tory, of course. All the usual weekday crowd. The beach patrol was there, and Patrick's rescue crew. Too many people."

The weekday surfers, those who didn't have full-time jobs or had adjustable schedules, lived for the water and kept the surf-report open on their smartphones in case they could make it to the beach for an hour. I glared at my supposed smartphone, which had thus far refused to display the actual surf-report to me, but directed me to every surf shop that had bothered to pay the advertising group to be included in their directory. "And you were gone how long?"

"Close to an hour and a half… I shouldn't have gone by the office on my day off. The phone always seems to ring and I always end up answering it. I used to joke to Charles that I needed one of you in nurse practitioner form."

"Okay." I sighed. "Well, if you think of anything else, please let me know."

"Nino's Pizza, Hot, Tasty, Fresh" my cell phone sang out. I excused myself and headed outside to answer it. It took me three tries to unlock the screen, and I was afraid it would go to voice-mail before I managed it. Finally, I got it and squealed a quick, "Don't hang up! I'm here!"

"Kam? It's Reggie."

"Hey. What's up?"

"I have a fax here from the Santa Cruz coroner. Were you the one who ordered them to run extra tests and charge them to the estate?"

"You know darn well it was me." I smiled tightly, but knew he couldn't see me. "Something isn't sitting right, Reggie."

There was a long silence. "Well, okay. But if those tests come back with no results, then you drop it, okay? There's no sense putting all of us through more grief."

"There's sense in it if it tells us what really happened out there."

"Just be careful you don't find out more than you want to know."

What was that supposed to mean? "I'm just looking for the truth, Reg. It's what Charles would do if he were here. I'll drop off the death certificates for Peter when I get back over the hill. Talk to you then." I hung up on Reggie with his warning still echoing in my ears, and headed back to the coffee shop, where Nicky met me with my Kia. After a few days of my old bicycle and that morning's jagged commuter bus-ride over to Santa Cruz, there was something comforting about the worn fabric seats and the vinyl steering wheel, all adjusted and broken in to fit just me. It was the only thing that seemed to fit in my life right now. Except that Nicky had pushed my seat back to accommodate her long legs and it took me ten minutes of sliding back and forth to get it back where it had been.

I DROPPED NICKY OFF AT her dad's junkyard car lot and headed back over Hwy 17 to the office. I'd timed traffic badly, the talk with Doc putting me behind schedule, and it took nearly two hours to get back to San Amoro. I dropped the death certificates off at Oslo & Burroughs, where Peter Oslo was waiting for me.

"Thank you for taking care of this, Kami. I know it couldn't have been easy."

I just nodded. Peter Oslo is one of those sturdy older gentlemen who can soothe nervous widows and panicked puppies with a single word. I didn't know him well at all, but on the occasions where I'd worked with him, I'd enjoyed the experience.

"I'll try to get probate filed by the end of day, but it's getting late," he continued. "I assume you know that Charles specified that you and Reginald were to handle his final affairs?"

"We'd discussed it once." I admitted, "Not as much as we should have. I mean... I didn't think..."

"Of course you didn't." Soothing soft Peter Oslo. Thank god for men like him. "Sudden deaths are the most difficult. Reginald is named executor of the will, and he'll be in touch with you shortly. I'll trust you and Reginald will take care of the funeral arrangements to Charles' specifications. As I said, I will start probate today, but I don't anticipate problems. Charles was very specific about his bequests and requirements."

"I assume the business is frozen until probate resolves? Then we can start dissolution?"

"You assume correctly." Peter smiled faintly. "Reginald mentioned that he'd already discussed transferring clients to us. If you need anything else, please let me know."

"To be honest, I have no idea what I need, Peter." I thanked him and slipped back into corridor, pausing to take in the stunning view across the bay. I'd always dreamed of an office like this of my own one day, top floor with a bay view, maybe a corner office, and the name White Legal Services on the door. Now, I was looking at dissolution of the business I'd helped build, unemployed, my law degree unfinished; that office of my own seemed further away than ever. I turned my back on the panorama and stepped into the elevator, letting it carry me down.

BUSINESS DONE, I HEADED BACK to 542 Marin Ave where a

sleepy and lonely Sphynx cat was stretched out full-length on my desk, awaiting the attention it had been denied all day. I scratched his ears and asked, "So what do you think happened?"

He purred and lolled his head against my hand. "Death by purring? That doesn't seem likely. Any more ideas?" When Hoover failed to answer me, I shifted my attention back to work. I had about a million clients to contact. I started with a form-letter for the oldest clientele, the ones who didn't pay retainers and hadn't had cases with us in more than five years, offering to transfer their records to the legal firms of their choice. The newest clients and those with current retainers and upcoming court-dates would be contacted by phone, in person. Normally, I like my job, but today it sucked.

And more so, it sucked because I wasn't getting paid for it. I had two week's pay coming, I hoped, but until Peter Oslo had a chance to sort out the legal end, I had no idea if the money was there or not. The six hundred dollars in my checking account wouldn't even pay my rent. I'd been too busy and too grieved to think about my financial status, but now it was starting to weigh on me.

I settled in the file room and started pulling out old client files. I'd kept meaning to update the company mailing list, but I'd just never gotten around to it. Now, I wanted to kick myself. I should have just checked names and put addresses into the computer software so I could print labels, but I kept finding my mind wandering, reading through Charles' old cases.

I was reading through an intriguing property suit when a particularly thick file sitting on top of a cabinet suddenly slid off. I immediately looked around for Hoover, but he was in his litter-box, enthusiastically digging his way to China. I'd either bumped the file with my elbow unintentionally, or—I glanced down the corridor to Evrett's armor—was it just my imagination or had his gauntlet shifted a bit? "Evrett? Things are bad enough without you making a mess!"

The knight was silent as always, but I imagined he was reproaching me for blaming my klutziness on him. I opened the file to find it was Vanny Toreski's collection of previous divorce proceedings. Seven divorces in total; all initiated by Vanny, and all with her coming out on top, both financially and socially. The husbands were all bad news, according to the filings. Abandonment, neglect, drinking problems, cheating. Inability to earn a living? That one made me laugh. Every one of them had earned plenty of money before Vanny came along!

My musings were interrupted as the front door swept open, afternoon breeze rushing in along with an overwhelming wave of expensive flowery perfume. Behind the scent soared Charles' sister, Juliet Hanford, diving in out of the blue like an RAF Hawker Hurricane wearing a floral print dress. Hoover's toenails clambered on the hardwood floor as he galloped down the corridor and out of sight. Juliet launched into diatribe before I could even speak.

"He wants to be buried here! In San Amoro! I demanded to take him home to England, to the family plot, but those lawyers!" she spat out, laying down fire across my terrain. I was defenseless. "They refused! They said that his final requests were written and sealed and would be honored. Lawyers. Awful creatures. Why did Charles have to become a lawyer? Not respectable at all." Her beady eyes snapped from me to the artwork on the walls. "They said he left you in charge of his memorial. You, instead of me. I'm his sister, for God's sake! What do you know about my brother? You're just a secretary. And that's another matter. You'll close out the accounts and that's it. I want you gone. If I knew a single thing about all of this, I'd do it myself." Her liver-spotted hand fluttered at the shelves of legal books, her wrinkled nose making it clear what she thought of the knowledge they contained. "I guess you'll have to do. Here's what I want for the memorial. Flowers will be in Oxford blue and white. Order them from Prisilla's Floral. No carnations. I hate carnations. They know what I want. It must be a proper Protestant service. None of this ridiculous butterfly-releasing, or balloon-floating everyone is doing these days. The music must be Bach, and hymns, of course. I like

'How Great Thou Art' and 'Thy Will be Done,' provided you can find someone to sing it correctly. If not, a string quartet will have to do."

"Yes, ma'am." I muttered, completely blitz bombed. I was glad Hoover had scrabbled for refuge, no doubt hiding in the file room closet. I scribbled down her funeral demands on my notepad.

"I can't believe they made us wait for an autopsy. Of all things. Ridiculous. Don't they know everyone just wants to put this behind them?"

I didn't look up and pretended to still be jotting down her funeral notes. "I guess there are legal formalities to be observed in an unattended death."

Juliet sniffed so furiously that I wondered if her little bulb of a nose would explode. "Get this place cleaned up. It's a mess."

"Yes, ma'am." I didn't see anything that looked like a mess other than the files all over my desk.

"Honestly, my brother was wasted in this dump. Good riddance to it all, I say." The front window shimmied in its frame as she slammed the door on her way out.

Released from attention, I slumped down, head on my arms. In the past, Charles had always been a buffer between Juliet and myself. Now I was just another target along her strafing run.

I gathered up the paperwork on my list, holding Vanny's file a moment longer. Had I really somehow knocked it over, or was it Evrett? Was our resident ghost telling me that I needed to buck up and get back to work and finish Vanny's paperwork before the office shut down for good? I wasn't up for outright laughing but I chuckled and set the file aside. It might make entertaining bedtime reading later. I could consider it background work for Vanny's current filing.

CHAPTER 4

San Amoro: Sunday Afternoon

"WE'RE HERE TO say farewell to a good man, my dear friend Charles Hanford." Reginald Burroughs' Welsh accent drifted to me across the neat rows of aluminum folding chairs and I wanted to pretend that he wasn't including me in these words. I wanted to pretend that I wasn't a part of these proceedings. That I didn't have to acknowledge that what he said meant that Charles was gone.

Per Juliet's request, there were flowers in Oxford blue. There were no balloons or butterflies. But there was also no string quartet, and there were no singers of grim Protestant hymns. Charles' favorite jazz playlist was running softly in the background, and while Father Joe's service was appropriately somber, it could hardly be considered traditional. When Reggie and I talked to Father Joe about the arrangements, he asked if I wanted to say something, to speak a eulogy, but as much as I love oratory, this one was beyond me. Reggie had stepped up to the plate. Not only was he a brilliant orator, he was also the only person I trusted to know what Charles would have wanted from this moment, from the final impact he would have on all of us.

I gave a surreptitious glance around the graveside

gathering. A sea of black and grey, with the obvious smattering of Oxford blue, mostly appropriately somber (and annoyingly expensive) met my eyes. If someone had been responsible for Charles' drowning, it could be any one of them. How many of these people were friends, and how many were merely clients? And how many of those clients were disgruntled? Speaking of disgruntled, Juliet Hanford was front and center, her all-black garb identifying her as chief mourner, but seriously? She looked like she was actually smiling!

Juliet bumped to the top of my suspect list. Who else looked out of place?

At the edge of the gathering, most obviously out of place, some of the surfer crowd stood together in clean, if not new, jeans and T-shirts, their tattoos showing and earrings glittering against the early autumnal gloom. Doc and his son were with them. Even Jude Booder was there. Most notable among the missing were Manny and Nicky. Nicky, I knew, thought funerals were for dead people, and that living people shouldn't attend. Manny had probably had another date with some Cuervo. They would be at the Paddle Out, I was certain, but I didn't want to be part of that, any more than I wanted to be part of this. I wasn't ready to forgive that water from taking Charles away. The irony of the funeral crowd appearing as an ocean didn't escape me, either. They were drowning him all over again.

"Charlie and I traveled the world together," Reginald was saying. "And when you see a man like that, doing the crazy things we did…" A few of the gathering chuckled, obviously having been there for some of those road-less-traveled moments. "Well, let's just say some of our not-so-fine moments were about as low as a human could go."

Another round of laughter. I'd heard the stories, even seen some of their antics first-hand. But to me, that man wasn't Charles. I didn't know the reckless youth that had graduated Oxford and traveled the world with his friends before settling in San Francisco to get a law degree and take the Bar Exam. I didn't know the man who dashed off on worldwide adventure vacations twice a year. That wasn't my Charles.

"I was going to tell you about some of those mad adventures, but what I found when I sat down to reminisce is that those ridiculous moments weren't what I remembered. It was the little things I remembered, little acts of kindness; giving his coat to a beggar boy in Vietnam, buying spices from old woman in Mumbai." Another half-smile tripped across Reginald's handsome face. "And he made me swear never to tell you why you all got spice boxes for Christmas that year."

I don't really cook, but I loved to open that box and smell its mingled scents. I liked to imagine I could hear that distant marketplace and taste the foreign and wondrous recipes those spices would make if I only knew how. Now, would those imaginings be replaced by memories of this moment? Would I ever open that box and not think of the man who gave it to me? Reggie was talking again and I straightened my shoulders, shrugging in my best suit-jacket that probably cost less than ten percent of most of the clothes at the gathering, and turned my attention back to the crowd. I was grateful to see that Morri and Mrs. Morrimont were there, seated in the third row back. Mallory Kent and Reese were both there, too. The Marin Street business owner's association was mourning one of their own.

"When we met back at Oxford, I was just the scholarship case from the Welsh mining country. Everyone said I wouldn't last a single semester. But I did, and I did it because Charlie believed in me. He never cared where you came from. All he cared about was where you were going. No matter what country we were in, from England to Ecuador—no matter what circumstances we were facing—Charles never saw class, color, sex, or race. He saw all of humanity as a family."

If Reggie blinked a little too hard and too fast, and swallowed a bit too long before continuing, who could have blamed him? My own eyes stayed surprisingly dry, but my throat ached with a sudden need to swallow the lump that rose in it. That. That man. That was my Charles.

"Once Charlie named you 'friend,' he never gave up on you, never stopped loving you."

And now Reggie really was looking at me. Straight at me. I looked away, back to the elegant but simple black coffin. But he still left me.

"Charlie was my best friend, and if there's one thing he taught me, it is that love is boundless and friendship is limitless." A tear broke free from Reggie's eye and I turned my head away.

I slipped out of my seat and moved off until the words faded to a soft hum, like a cocktail party two balconies over. I'd never exactly been touchy-feely with my, well, feelings, and my eyes simply refused to cry despite being surrounded by those openly sharing their grief. Tearless and tired, I just stood there staring at the coffin, feeling empty and terribly lonely. I wanted to be somewhere else. Anywhere else. Even while I was looking at that box that held Charles Hanford's body, my brain was off remembering some show I watched once about making chocolate. It showed these huge vats swirling around, all full of gooey melted brown stuff. That's what I was. Mixed up and dark and alone.

I closed my traitorous eyes that refused to weep.

"KAMI!"

With my eyes closed, I had no warning when Juliet Hanford suddenly stormed me out of nowhere, like a battle-ax in a black dress. She was wearing a funny black muffin-shaped hat with an ebony feather in the top. I thought they only dressed like that in old British drama shows, which was where Ms. Juliet Hanford would be right at home. She belonged to another time and place; a formidable English bulldog of a woman. I think she believed that heritage provided privilege, and she had inherited all of it.

"I'll be by tomorrow to sort out the office, Kami. You be there, ten o'clock, sharp. I don't want to waste my time."

I glanced back to the casket and the line of mourners I'd been trying to block out. Charles wasn't even in the ground yet and she wanted his stuff? I mustered a small, "But Juliet, we have to wait for probate to clear. You can't just come in and start taking things …"

"That's Miizz Hanford to you. And I certainly can. You don't dictate to me…"

"No. I can't." My conviction was fading by the minute. I wanted to be alone with my grief, not fighting the wicked witch. "But the law can. I'm not disbursing anything until the will has cleared probate."

"Who do you think you are?" Juliet's buggy eyes popped even further out of her puggy face. "You miserable little…"

"Cheeky snot," I said, unable to tear my now wide-open and stinging eyes from Charles' coffin to look his sister in the eye.

"Excuse me?"

I didn't have to look to know that her eyes had narrowed murderously at me. I kept my tone as convivial as one should at a funeral. "Cheeky snot. That's how you wanted to finish that, isn't it?"

"Listen, you two-dollar night-school twit," Juliet hissed, low enough that the other mourners wouldn't hear. "Charles is dead. Whatever thing the two of you had is over. You've no right to talk to me…"

"No." I sighed, glancing at her flat, overly-peach-pancaked face with a grimace. "I suppose I don't. So, I'll cease immediately."

Making good on the promise, I turned and strode away from her, up through the eucalyptus trees and identical flat headstones. The weather had no right to be this warm today, did it? Shouldn't it be raining? Misty? Fogging a bit? Something that said I was hurting, and the world needed to know it? Didn't the weather know that Charles Hanford was gone and I was alone?

I meandered through the cemetery until mourners started to wander away from the graveside gathering. I didn't want to answer any more questions, especially not from clients who wanted to know the state of their legal affairs, or, even more awkwardly, wanted to know exactly how Charles died. I'd said the word "drowned" so many times in the past few days that it had lost all meaning. He could have fallen a vat of chocolate or inhaled a cup of Earl Grey tea, for as much as the word defined an event. They had so many questions to ask me, but today wasn't theirs. It was mine. And I had questions of my own.

I dragged Charles' watch from my jacket pocket and checked the time. The Suunto Elementum watch was heavy; a big digital monster with a gazillion buttons and no instructions anywhere that I could find. The alarm had been going off every day at three o'clock since the coroner's office had returned it to me. I didn't know what was supposed to happen at three so I just pushed buttons until it stopped beeping. And it just kept on ticking, keeping time, not knowing the person who cared about it most was gone. Now, it read 2:45. The official graveside ceremony was supposed to end at 2:30, but people were lingering. I had fifteen minutes before the beeper started, so for fun, I buckled the silver monstrosity around my thin wrist. It looked like it would fit better around my ankle. I contemplated trying it, but the last thing I needed was funeral-goers asking if I was under house arrest.

Doc and Rick headed me off as I sneaked toward the gate and my bicycle.

"Kami? We'll see you at the Paddle-Out, yah?" Rick's gold earring glittered in the harsh afternoon sunlight.

"I don't think so." I half-smiled, but it felt like even that small effort would tear my face apart.

"You should at least be there." Doc reached out and shook my hand gently, his voice soft. He might be totally wicked and tough while wave riding, but off the board, he had a great bedside manner.

"Yeah, we'll see, okay? Thanks, guys." I hesitated, considering my next move. This might not be the time or place, but both of them were Santa Cruz regulars. There wasn't much that went on in the surf-world that they didn't know about. "Rick, I hate to ask this now, but has anyone new been surfing with the crowd lately? Someone maybe you haven't seen before?"

Rick glanced over the mourners, but shook his head. "Andie's newest, but she's been here all summer. Guess she's going back to Zealand soon, though. Why?"

Doc tilted his head and twisted his finger at the side of his head, a "she's nuts" gesture. "Kami thinks someone may have actually drowned Charlie." He gave me an apologetic smile. "I'm sorry, but look around you. Everyone loved him, Kam."

Rick tossed back his wave of dark hair and laughed. "Charlie? Why would anyone have something against him? He was a good dude."

"A good dude," Doc echoed.

"But now you mention it," Rick frowned a little. "Andie was spending kind of a lot of time with him. Like asking him to show her longboard moves and stuff. Can't see her drowning him, though. Can't see anyone doing that. We've all had a bad wipe-out. Can happen to anyone."

"Yeah. I hope I'm wrong." I gave them both hugs and watched them head back toward the parking lot. Andelle had been spending time with Charles? Like that wasn't weird?

I trudged back down the hill to retrieve my old thrift-store bicycle from the wrought iron gate of the cemetery, casting one last glance at the remaining mourners. None of them were looking my way, so I thought I'd managed a clean escape when I heard Reggie call warmly.

"Kami! Wait up."

I suppose I could have kept going, but I owed him for taking on the eulogy and helping me with the arrangements, so I braked and waited for him to close the distance.

"Reggie." I returned his hug awkwardly with one arm while managing to balance my bike upright. "Good show back there. Thanks for doing that. I know it couldn't have been easy, but you were awesome."

I wasn't sure that the word "awesome" should be applied to a funereal speech, but it was the truth. Reggie could bring up a funeral crowd just as easily as he could bring down a courtroom.

"You holding up, Kam?" he asked when he drew away, and I nearly dropped my bike, startled tears springing to my eyes.

Oh sure. Now they wanted to start the waterworks. Traitors. "I was until you asked," I muttered, embarrassed, rubbing a hand over my face. Of all the people to break down in front of! "How are you?"

Reggie shrugged with a dip of his head, his perfectly cut suit moving with his shoulder muscles. He didn't need to say more. He was as heartbroken as I was. "A few of us are getting together at Magillies on Main, just a few drinks and some memory-time. You're welcome to come with us. You were as much a part of Charlie's life as we were."

I considered for a half second but shook my head. I couldn't be around the legal eagle crowd today, any more than I could be around the surfer crowd. "I think I just need to be alone, but thanks. Really. I've just got some stuff to take care of."

Reggie watched me for a moment, his gaze serious. He opened his mouth as though about to argue my lame excuse, but instead, he shrugged again, a sad smile touching his lips. "Sure, kiddo. If you need help with anything, you've got my number."

"I may need help with Juliet..." I cast a wary glance back up the slope. "She seems determined to violate probate and I'm not sure that I'll be able to stop her."

Reggie's expression turned serious, something dark flickering behind his eyes. "Leave Juliet to me and Peter. We'll sort her. You just take care of yourself. You've got too much on your plate to have to worry about her."

"Thanks," was pretty much all I could think to say.

"Are you sure you won't come with us to Magillies? You'd be welcome."

I wasn't sure of that. The secretary hanging with the big dogs of the legal set? It just didn't seem, well, right, somehow. I declined as politely as I could.

"I'll see you tomorrow, then. Just stay away from Juliet and leave her to me."

I rode away before he could say anything else. It felt too much like charity. Like now that Charles was gone, his friends felt they had to look out for me. Well, they didn't. I could look out for myself.

I started to ride back to my tiny apartment, rubber bike tires swooshing comfortingly on the rough pavement of what passed for a bike-lane in San Amoro. But within a few blocks of home, I found myself crisscrossing back through downtown to 542 Marin Avenue.

I pulled Old Thrifty up to the white painted bike stand, not bothering to chain my rusty steed, and dug out my keys. Opening the door to 1A was like coming home to find that someone's stolen all your things. Oh, everything was still right where I'd left it the day before, but despite the clutter of shelved souvenirs and artifacts, medieval collection pieces and wall hangings, and the bookshelves overflowing with legal texts, it felt empty.

It felt left.

Like I did.

MY TIRED EYES, STRAINED WITH the effort to produce tears, attempted to avoid anything that reminded me of Charles, and finally focused on my desktop. Everything was right where I left it, except for the file that I'd left on my desk, Vanny's serial divorce file. That was spread all over the floor under my desk, pages scattered everywhere. "Hoover!"

The cat, sleek and tan, slinked out of the back room and pounced onto my desk, his oversized ears perked up hopefully. I scooped the hairless Sphynx cat up into my arms and snuggled him. He felt like a warm squishy felted lump. "Did you do this?"

Hoover admitted nothing, tilting his head up to sniff my nose, and I sighed. "You miss Charles, too, huh, baby?"

Hoover's deep purr resounded in my ear. He'd always had that purr, even as a tiny kitten. That's how he got his name, or at least, the one Charles always called him by. His registered breeder name is Ramses Arabian Night. Remembering Hoover's International Cat Association registry only served to remind me that was one more paper I had to track down and hide before that miserable Juliet could get it. If she thought he was worth a dime, she'd want him. Juliet. Just thinking about her name made my face hot. I hugged Hoover a bit tighter, but he squirmed in protest, reminding me that he was a warm squishy felt lump with serious claws. I let him go, setting him down to let him twine himself between my legs.

"She won't get you, Hoover. Or you, Evrett." I reached over and tapped the helm of the other occupant of the suite. The pressure of my hand caused the bellows visored sallet of the French suit of armor to shift, dropping the visor over the empty face-gap in the helm. Empty, or so I told myself, but truthfully, Evrett isn't always as silent as one of his antiquity ought to be. "I won't let her anywhere near you guys."

That last was said with far less confidence. How was I going to keep Juliet from them? Damn Charles for dying like this. Juliet Hanford was his last living relative and even without her money and power, she would have been a force to be reckoned with. As it stood, even all Napoleon's armies wouldn't have had a chance against her. What chance did a night-school twit like me have? I glanced at Evrett's sword with thoughts that were unworthy of a law-abiding citizen. I was going to need more clout than a sword and armor could offer.

As Juliet so graciously slammed me with at the funeral, I received my paralegal degree at night school while working in Reese's Café. Unlike the Hanfords, who boasted august relations with titles like "earl" and "duchess," my heritage is a mixed-nut bag full of third and fourth generation Americans with titles like "hillbilly" and "hippy." The closest thing to an earl in my family is Great Uncle Earl, famed for dying when a tornado dropped a chicken shed on his head. Family legend says that Guinness sent someone to measure the chicken shed to see if it qualified Uncle Earl for the record for death by largest weather driven object, but it had been smashed to bits and there wasn't enough left to measure. There was never any mention of what had happened to the chickens.

Juliet, on the other hand, had kings and queens in her lineage. Charles' family tree read like a Who's Who of British Important People. My family couldn't even manage an obscure Guinness record. Even with Oslo & Burroughs on my side, it was likely that once the will was settled and the probate cleared, I'd never see Hoover or Evrett again.

I WASN'T READY TO GO home, but I didn't feel like working, either. I went to grab a yogurt, and spent a moment staring at the map over the fridge. It was a beautiful hand-illustrated map of Europe with lines drawn in different colors, outlining different journeys that Charles and Reggie, and later Charles and Arthur, had taken. I knew Charles would want Reggie to have it. I didn't think it was worth anything monetary-wise; its only value was sentimental, and there was no way I was going to let Juliet have it. I pried it off the wall and stuck it in the back corridor, face to the wall, behind a few paint cans. As long as I was in the back corridor, I slipped out the back door to the back lot and pulled the car-cover over Charles' SUV, hiding it from curious (and greedy) eyes. Reassured of its safety, I went into Charles' office, and curled up on the comfortable old leather sofa. Tomorrow, I would go through my finances, see where I stood, and figure out what to do next. But that was tomorrow. Tonight, I just wanted to stop thinking. About everything.

I shared the last spoonful of yogurt with Hoover and curled

up under the old blue afghan, ready to sleep even though it was barely after sunset. My cell phone interrupted me with a double beep, alerting me to new text message.

"Chnese Fud, beer. Opn door."

It was from Nicky. I stood up and peeked out the high window in Charles' office to see her Mustang parked by the curb. I knew it was Nicky's Mustang, because, well, when most people think Mustang, they think gleaming red classic 1969 'stangs with chrome bumpers, or modern recent Mustangs, sleek of form in metallic silver-blue. Nicky's Mustang was, technically, a 1972, but half the parts were '71 or '73 that she had managed to wrangle into working. The engine rumbled like a bear caught in a pit-trap, and there was more Bondo and primer on it than paint. We called it the FrankenStang out of pure love. "It's a work in progress." Nicky always says. It's been a work in progress for about eight years, and even though she usually manages to keep it running, it doesn't really seem to progress into anything other than an uglier, patchier version of itself.

I wanted to text back "Go Away", but instead asked, "Kung Pao Beef?"

"Duh. Lemme in or I eat yur 4tun cookie."

I unlocked the door and let Nicky in.

She stood for a second on the threshold and I realized she'd never seen the office before. Her dark eyes scanned over the antiques in their cases, the art on the walls, the suit of armor. "Holy cow. You work here?"

"Just for a couple more days, I guess." I looked around one more time myself. "If Charles' sister has anything to say about it…I expect she'll sell the building. I'll probably have to finish cleaning everything out, making sure all of our clients get their files and stuff. Then… well… Glad you brought Chinese. This might be my last meal for a while."

"You'll find another job. You have like, street cred, in your profession. You have connections." Nicky started unloading the bag of food on my desk and pulled up one of the client chairs. "The armor is really cool."

"Yeah, that's Evrett."

Hoover leaped up and started sniffing hopefully at the little white takeout boxes. I scooped him up, took him back to the file room and gave him some extra kibble for a treat, telling him more for Nicky's benefit than his own, "Cats don't eat Chinese food, especially when I have to clean their litter boxes."

"What are you going to do with Hoover? You can't keep him at your apartment, can you? You can't let Charles' sister have him!"

"Seeing as I can't afford rent," I moaned, "I guess we'll both move to Mom's until I can find more work. Mom loves Hoover. She won't mind…"

Nicky was looking at me a little bit oddly.

"What?"

"You, umm… haven't talked to your mom, have you?"

"Not for a few weeks, why?"

"I just delivered a bunch of custom racks Dad welded up for her. Your old bedroom is now an herb-drying space. Dehydrators, racks, shelves…" Nicky kind of gulped a little. "Sorry. Thought you knew."

"Mom turned my bedroom into an herbarium?" I heaped my plate with Kung Pao Beef, General Tso's Chicken, and a sizable helping of veggie fried rice. Salty fatty goodness. "Today just keeps getting better."

We ate in silence for a few moments, and both froze when we heard a noise in the back of the file room. Then I realized it was Morri's key in the back-door lock.

"Morri?"

"It's me, poppet." He was still in his funeral suit, a dark brown polyester thing that he'd probably owned since 1970, when he was bulkier and stronger. It looked a bit scarecrowish on him now. "Saw a scary vehicle in front, and thought I'd best be sure you weren't being robbed."

Nicky laughed, and I introduced the two of them and explained about the FrankenStang, which Nicky took ribbing about surprisingly well.

"Yeah, I keep meaning to get around to priming and painting it."

"It's a wonder of the transportation age," Morri's usual wordy glee seemed to have returned. "A commendably cringeworthy conveyance!"

Nicky glanced at me in confusion, and I grinned as I explained, "That's a good thing in Morri-speak." To Morri, I continued, "Thank you for coming to the funeral today. It meant a lot to me to see you there."

He nodded thoughtfully. "Of course. Just hope some of my friends survive to attend my final kick-off."

"Oh, we'll be there. And we'll throw one hell of a party." I promised.

"I've time to bide before I bucket myself off to Hades." Morri smiled faintly, then glanced around the office. "Guess we'll all be rented out of here when Juliet gets her hands on it."

I hadn't thought about that. I was going to lose my job and the office, but Morri and Mallory's businesses were also going to be out on their ears. "No doubt she'll sell it to some developer who'll tear out the turrets and paint it beige." The thought made me want to start crying again. I crunched a fortune cookie in my fingers.

"What does it say?" Nicky prodded, quite literally with her chopstick, when I didn't unfold the paper and read my fortune right away.

I took a deep breath. "Believe in good fortune and it will always find you."

We all glanced around at our funeral feast, and the office I was soon to be evicted from and I couldn't help but laugh.

A soft clank came from the corner, and Nicky's eyes widened over her chopsticks.

"So, the old knight stirs." Morri stepped over to Evrett and leaned close. "If only we could hear your whispers, old man. What stories you could tell."

Nicky's dark eyes were accusing as she stared at me. "Wait…

you mean… it's real? The ghost? Your office is really haunted? I totally thought you were putting me on!"

"Chevalier Evrett," Morri said with a faintly disapproving frown, though his eyes twinkled, "is most certainly quite incorporeally corporeal."

"But how… where?"

I smiled and settled back in my chair as Nicky jumped up and studied the armor up close. "Don't touch him. The oils on your skin can cause tarnishing. Charles found him on one of his jaunts to France. He e-mailed and told me to arrange shipment of 'something nice for the office.'" I laughed remembering. It felt good to laugh at a memory of Charles, like he wasn't really quite gone. "I thought it would be one of those beautiful hand-crafted Provencal roll-top desks, maybe. All full of old cubbies that smelled like lavender. Instead, I got a crate full of old metal."

Morri, too, smiled at the memory. "Charles told me that the shop owner refused to sell it to him at first, warned him that it was haunted, had, in point of fact, driven its previous owner mad. Charles decided then and there he couldn't live without it."

"I didn't believe it when he told me," I said. "But a few months later, I made a crack about the Crusades, and suddenly my tea knocked over all over the brief I was working on. We don't joke about the Crusades here. Someone took his responsibilities very seriously."

"Takes. Still does." Morri corrected. "Fortunately, the provenance was peerless. It wasn't difficult to research the lineage and discover the name of our young knight."

If nearly six-hundred years could be considered young? Well, he'd been young when he died, relatively. In his twenties, not even my age, and already a battle-hardened knight. I relaxed and let Morri tell the story.

"He survived the battle of Nikopol only to be killed on the way home when his caravan was ambushed. His fellow knights buried him along the road and returned his armor to his family. When the family estate was lost due to tax debt, Evrett became just another asset to the estate and was sold off. Changed hands more than a few times before ending up in that shop. Between you and me," Morri winked mischievously, "I hope he drives Juliet mad."

"He won't." And I felt my spine stiffen. "She's not getting him. I don't care if I have to hide him the trunk of my car, she's not getting her hands on a single piece."

"Good for you!" Morri agreed, but Nicky was looking thoughtful.

"You know, we could do an investigation. See if Evrett has secrets he wants to tell us."

"Oh, we tried that, me and a few friends." Morri shrugged, eyeing Evrett with a cagey glance. "But our knight only seems to be interested in knocking things about from time to time, or making messes."

"He found my letter opener once." I pointed to my silver letter opener, a graduation gift from Charles when I finished my paralegal studies. "I thought a customer had stolen it. I couldn't find it anywhere. Suddenly, there it was in the middle of the office floor."

"He was probably afraid you'd use his sword instead." Nicky laughed a little.

"It's not his." Morri pointed. "You see the crest here? That's a different lineage entirely. The sword was added to the suit later. My guess is that his original sword was either buried with him on the crusade trail or is in the attic of some descended family member who probably doesn't even know his name."

"Even so, I'm pretty sure he doesn't want me using it to open letters." Not to mention that if I tried I'd probably open myself up.

"I'd still like to do an investigation! Like a proper ghost hunt! With cameras and recorders and stuff. Like Ghost Hunt on TV. I'd love to prove all this!" Nicky looked as excited as a ferret in a bucket full of plastic balls, and even though I glanced at Evrett to see what he thought— apparently, he thought we were beneath his notice— I knew I'd give in.

"Morri? You did it the last time. What do we need?"

"As Nicky has surmised, you will need cameras and voice recorders. A motion activated sensor would be convenient."

"Cameras and a voice recorder I have. Motion activated sensor, no."

"You'll want to turn off the lights. Electricity can interfere with the activity." Morri was looking around the room with a critical gaze. "I would recommend doing your primary research in this space as this is where Chevalier Evrett has been most active. Set up the movie camera so that the lens-view will not pick up glare from the glass cases. Take pictures when and where you sense motion. Evrett," Morri warned, glancing at the knight, "is not the most forthcoming subject. My recommendation is to keep your questions to simple yes and no answers, and ask him to knock or clank…"

"Once for yes, two for no." Nicky grinned. "I watch Ghost Hunt all the time."

"Ghost Hunt," Morri frowned faintly, but kept his tone encouraging, "is an entertainment spectacle. What you will be doing is quite real, interacting with a human spirit on another plane of existence. For the living to interact with the supernatural can be alarming, disturbing, and even have severe consequences. Take good care not to antagonize Evrett. I'm off home for the night, but you have Father Joe's number and he is available any time of the day or night if you run into something untoward."

Untoward? I never liked that word. And I didn't feel particularly good about this entire thing, but I dutifully opened the safe and pulled out the cameras and my new digital recorder. "I got this for taking depositions. It's not really high-end or anything."

"It doesn't need to be." Morri assured me. "In my day, we used tape recorders. Cassette tapes, you know." He held his fingers up in the size of a cassette tape. "Your little gadget can record for hours and you never have to pause to flip the tape over."

"I know. Us kids have no idea how good we have it." I paused, and collected the chess set. "He'd want you to have this, Morri."

Morri ran his hand lovingly over the wooden box. "We were an even match. You never knew how the game would go."

"He beat me every time." I admitted before I hugged Morri and saw him out, making sure he made it to his car and he waved as he pulled out. When I got back, Nicky had started hooking up the digital movie camera to my laptop.

"Not all night, now," I warned her, "I'm completely wiped."

Nicky looked disappointed, but agreed. "Probably for the best. I have to be at the ocean animal rescue early. It's my turn to feed the otters."

"Doesn't everyone?" I teased. I'd never fed an otter in my life, let alone a rescue otter. I turned on the digital recorder and made sure there were no other files on it while Nicky put clean memory cards in the digital cameras. "So, now what?"

She propped the video camera on the shelf and adjusted it around until the glass cases weren't in reflection range; no easy feat since half the walls were covered with displays. "Move those daggers. They pick up the light."

I glanced to the rack of antique sgian dubh, Scottish boot daggers, resting on a shelf between sets of law books. "Where to?"

"Somewhere Charles' sister won't see them?" Nicky winked at me, but to me, holding back Evrett was one thing; he was a human being, after all, albeit a disembodied one, but taking the daggers would really be stealing. I took the rack down and carried it into the office, stashing it in a cabinet.

"Anything else?"

"Nope. Shut off the lights."

I started at the bathroom and walked through turning off all the switches, including power strips. Nicky drew down the thick shades over the front windows, blocking out the street lights, and a sepulcher-like stillness came over the office.

Yellow glow seeped around the shades, etching the office in charcoal and sepia shadows. My voice couldn't seem to muster more than a whisper. "So, now what?"

"Now, we wait a bit," Nicky whispered back. "Just watch and listen, see if there's any activity."

Her words were followed immediately by a faint scratching.

"What?" Nicky startled, and I couldn't see her eyes in the shadows, but I'd bet a silver dollar that's how wide they were. "What is that?"

"Hoover in his litter box." I snickered.

She chuckled as she settled back onto the edge of my desk. "Oh."

"Should we ask questions?"

"I think usually we're supposed to wait until he shows up, but since we don't have all night, why not? I mean, he's usually here, right?"

Truth be told, I had no idea. Did he just hang around all day, silent and bored? Did ghosts sleep? "Evrett? Are you here?"

"If you're here, give us a sign." Nicky tapped the table. "Can you knock, or make your armor clank?"

Silence answered us.

"You can also talk to this machine. It's a recorder that can hear you, even when we can't." Nicky held up the recorder. "All you have to do is talk to it."

"If he's been around the office, he's seen me use the recorder," I reminded her, but she just shrugged at me.

"Never hurts to explain these things. I mean, what if he thinks chain-maille is the height of new technology?" Nicky waved me back into silence. "Evrett? Are you here?"

Silence. Nothing stirred.

"This is silly. He's never talked to me before. Why would he?"

"Evrett, can you knock? Like this?" Nicky reached out and rapped her knuckles on the desk twice.

I started giggling. "Who's there?"

"Kam! Take this seriously. You heard what Morri said

about respecting Evrett."

"I do respect Evrett. You on the other hand…" I shook my head, trying to stifle my irreverent snickers. But the truth was that I was exhausted and heart-weary and something had to snap somewhere. When Nicky called Evrett and knocked again, I had to bite my lips together and squeeze my eyes shut to keep from giggling again.

"Ask him something. Something personal," Nicky encouraged. "He knows you. He probably wants to help you."

"Evrett? Have you seen Charles?" I don't know why I asked that. I didn't want the answer. If Charles was stuck somewhere, wouldn't it be where he died? Out on the beach or forever in the surf? Was that how it worked? Evrett moved around, but Morri said he was attached to his armor- where it went, so he went. Did Charles go with his surfboard? I thought that was a better option than floating out on the ocean for eternity.

"You can knock once for no, twice for yes," Nicky reminded Evrett.

We both sat holding our breath, but there was no answering knock or clank.

Nicky spoke up again. "Evrett, was Charles' death an accident?"

"Now, how the heck would he know that?" I started giggling again. "Evrett was here at the office, not out on the beach. Can you imagine what all that saltwater would do to his armor?"

Nicky sighed. "You're right. Stupid question. Evrett, do you want to move on from here?"

I found myself holding my breath. I'd just lost Charles. I didn't want to lose Evrett, too, even if he really didn't want to stay. Ting. There came a single metallic plink, the sound of his gauntlets shifting. I felt Nicky spring upright. The office was cooling with the late summer evening, I thought, just the metal contracting with the temperature change, but Nicky wasn't deterred.

"You want to stay?"

Ting. Ting.

"Then you will." I promised unhesitatingly, despite my own disbelief. My heart was pounding faster. We were talking to Evrett!

"Evrett, is there something you've been trying to tell me?"

Two faint tinks of the gauntlets.

Nicky spoke up. "Does it have to do with Charlie's death?"

Two faint tinks.

"Was he murdered?" I blurted out.

Nicky smacked my arm, but Evrett's visor slammed down with a resounding clank. Was that a yes? Or a no? "Evrett? Did that mean yes?"

No faint sounds, no movement, no nothing. No matter how we pleaded or begged, or what questions we asked over the next half hour, Evrett was silent. "I think I made him angry, Nick. Sorry."

"I don't know. Why would that make him angry? I mean, you've been trying to figure out what really happened to Charles this whole time."

"Maybe he doesn't know any more than we do." I sighed. "Look, I really need to sleep, and you've got to get to those baby otters in the morning."

Nicky transferred the camera footage to a flash drive. "I'll go over this tomorrow and let you know if I find anything." She picked up Hoover and hugged him, letting him rub his nose all over her face. Animals just like Nicky. Then she hugged me so hard I thought she'd crack a rib. "I'll call you tomorrow. You get some sleep. Good night, Evrett! Thanks for the chat. You three stay out of trouble."

I was about to steal a pedigreed cat and an antique suit of armor from Juliet. I'd say staying out of trouble was the least of our worries. "Thanks for everything. I'm going to work a bit longer and then get some sleep."

Watching from the window, I heard the FrankenStang roar to life and pull out down the street. Alone in the office. I stretched out on the sofa in Charles' office and stared at the ceiling. The fortune cookie words kept coming back to me.

Believe in good fortune and it will always find you. I was trying to believe. I wanted to believe. Was wanting to believe enough for it to come true?

CHAPTER 5

San Amoro: Monday Morning

I JERKED AWAKE AT 7 am, a steeped sense of panic rising in my gut. Without bothering to shower or change, I leaped up and grabbed Hoover, stuffing him into his harness. I collected his food, water, and litterbox and dragged him upstairs to Office 2A, which was still empty, painter's cloths on the floor, ladder scaffolding against the wall. "Sorry, baby. You're going to have to stay up here today. Be a good boy, okay? Morri and I will check on you, all right?"

I unclipped the leash from the harness, and after taking a look around to make sure there was nothing hazardous he could get into, let him go. He instantly discovered the scaffolding and was happily hopping his way to the top when I left him.

Moving Evrett wasn't so easy. I started to drag him into the back stairwell, but who knew? 14th Century suits of armor are heavy! Let me paint a quick picture for you. I'm five feet, two inches tall, not counting the two inches that my hair stands straight up. If Pixar Films rendered me as an inanimate object, I'd be a Q-tip with yellow-blonde frizzy-curly hair where my cotton-ball should be. I struggle against strong breezes and car exhaust. In comparison, Evrett is solid 14th century smith-hammered battle steel with rivets the size of my eyeballs and hand-bent chain-maille thicker than a yellow legal pad. He might be only four feet, nine inches tall, but he's compact and built for war. The stairwell wasn't an option. But the little bathroom was!

Somehow, I wrestled him inside the small shower stall, managing to keep him mostly on his stand but banged my elbow and broke the soap dish in the process. I kicked the broken soap dish behind the toilet, threw a damp towel over Evrett, "Sorry, Sir!", and flung the dingy shower curtain closed.

I took a half-moment to glance in the mirror. A pathetically pale stick-figure in a wrinkled black suit with dark-rimmed, reddened eyes looked back. So I wouldn't be charming Juliet with my good looks this today. Maybe I'd manage to scare her away with my looks alone? I dunked my head in the sink, soaking it with water so cold it made my head hurt, trying to make my unruly mess of curls lay down. Reaching back blindly for the towel, I too late remembered it was on the suit of armor. Stupid. I shook my head over the sink like a dog, tossed my hair back from my eyes, and wiped my hands on my suit-pants.

I glanced at the antique German clock. 8:38. Enough time for breakfast. I glanced across at Reese's but decided I needed cheap coffee with cream and sugar. Lots of it. I gathered my laptop and the business information that I thought Juliet would want to know, slipped out the back door, and crossed through the alleyway to Main Street, where Magillies serves plain fry-up breakfasts until noon, and the coffee was cheap and plentiful.

At 10:00, replete with pancakes, eggs, and five cups of perfectly awful diner coffee, I headed back to the office, my brain ticking down like a NASA countoff, "T-minus thirty minutes to Juliet. T-Minus twenty-nine minutes to Juliet…" I checked Charles' SUV one more time, and went around to the front of the building.

And discovered a moving truck. I froze on the sidewalk,

the early morning East Bay fog clogging in my throat as I watched a gaggle of thickset guys wearing lifting belts and hauling hand-trucks rush in and out, loading the truck with the contents of the office.

I jumped in front of them. "What? What are you doing? Get out of here!"

They stared at me, then looked over my head. I turned to the doorway to find Juliet. "Gentlemen, please finish your work." She pointed imperiously back into the office. The movers obediently marched back inside. To my unpracticed eye, it looked like they'd already loaded half the office into the truck! I pulled out my phone and dialed Oslo & Burroughs with a shaking hand. "Juliet! You can't do this!"

"I think you'll find that I already have."

I glared at Juliet, blocking the door with crossed arms. "No, you can't! Nothing moves until probate clears. That's the law. You can inventory, but you can't just come in here like this. There are confidential client files and sensitive legal briefs. Items that belong to the law firm. You can't just bring strangers in here and start taking things!"

Juliet stood glaring at me, and I stood glaring at Juliet.

"Fine. Gentlemen? Take everything but the sensitive files and briefs. I trust Miss White here can show what not to touch." Juliet actually put her hand on my shoulder and shoved me aside, an unfortunately easy feat for a woman twice (three times) my bulk.

Rayanne answered, but when I asked for Peter or Reginald, she told me they were in a meeting and couldn't be disturbed. "Please disturb them! Charles' sister is here with a moving van!"

"They asked not to be disturbed." The line went dead as Rayanne hung up on me. Meanwhile, the movers were dragging out the antique German clock and the oak book cases.

"What part of nothing moves until probate clears did you not understand?" I jumped back in front of Juliet. "I will call the cops if I have to!"

"The cops? And what are they going to do? I'm his sister. He is dead. You can't keep me from what's mine." Juliet sidestepped with more grace than I would have thought possible, and barged down the hallway.

"Juliet!" I started to dash after her, and that's when I glimpsed, under the chair at the desk formerly known as mine, a glimmer of polished silver. Oh no. Evrett's head! I came to a skidding halt at the edge of the rug. "He was your brother. Don't you think you should... well, respect his wishes? I mean, until we know what's happening with the business..." I sounded like an idiot and Juliet paused to stare at me, her bug eyes disturbingly round and her pug nose tilted. So much for scaring her away. "I mean, don't you want to ... see what..."

Juliet stared inscrutably at me for a long moment and then waved a hand. "No need to get all emotional on my behalf, Miss White. Fetch us some tea and order some lunch for the moving crew, if you will."

"You want tea, there's a shop across the street. Get out or I'm calling the cops."

"You wouldn't dare. Take your belongings and get off my property." With that, she marched into Charles' office. The moment her back was turned, I hooked Evrett's visor on my toe and launched him toward the recycle-basket. Fortunately, I hadn't emptied it in two days and it was full of shredded paper, padding any clanking. I apologized silently and fervently to the former crusader. Looking up again, I realized the two mover guys who hadn't followed Juliet were looking at me, obviously waiting for directions.

"If you like lawsuits, then go right ahead." I stared at the empty wall where only that morning, the Chilkat weaving had hung, trying to keep memories at bay. My voice somehow managed not to break. "But expect accessory to theft added to your resumes."

It was no use. They barely spoke English. And I didn't care what Juliet said. This wasn't her property yet. I wasn't going to budge.

I grabbed the office phone and dialed Reginald Burroughs personal cell phone number. It went straight to voice mail. "Juliet is here. She's cleaning the place out! I need help. Now."

What was my next recourse? The movers were dragging furniture out of the file room. I called the San Amoro police department, spent entirely too much time trying to explain why I was calling, and was finally promised that they would send a car as soon as one was available. I should have reported skateboarders on the sidewalk or jaywalkers, and they might have come sooner. And then I grabbed my camera and started documenting everything, literally taking things off the hand trucks as the movers wheeled back and forth. No matter how many times I said, "Get out! Leave that!" I was overridden by Juliet.

By the time the police arrived the offices were nearly emptied, nothing left but bare wooden floors and shelves, blank walls and dark-stained framing. Juliet had taken my directions literally. The files remained, heaped in alphabetical piles where the movers had taken them out of the filing cabinets, but the sturdy wooden cabinets were gone. My work computer was sitting on the floor where my desk had been, but they'd taken my solid walnut reception desk, my ergonomic office chair; even my brass pen-holder. I'd had to snatch my silver letter opener out of a moving-man's hand. Everything that wasn't my personal property or confidential to Hanford Legal was gone. Every scrap of art, nearly all the furnishings; anything Juliet's opportunistic eyes had spotted had been gobbled away by her greed. Only the company safe, Charles' laptop, the old leather sofa, and the files, as well as the few things I'd hidden, remained. In the file room, the mini-fridge and microwave had been earthquake-bolted to the wall and they'd been unable to take them. If Hoover's litterbox had been there, they would have taken that, too.

"Who has the next office?" Juliet demanded as she walked out of the back room.

I shrugged, too despondent to care. She could read the

window for herself, couldn't she? "Mallory Kent. Why?"

"I think he might be dying." Her wrinkled pug-nose wrinkled even further. "Terrible wailing coming from in there. Perhaps you should call the police."

"I would do," I mumbled, belatedly realizing what the "wailing" was. Hoover was furious at being abandoned upstairs. "But you've taken the phones."

"Oh, don't be such a whiner." Juliet started to head for the back. "I'm just going to use the ladies before I see myself out."

That propelled me into action. My feet stumbled over each other as I launched myself in front of her. "Oh! No. You can't!"

"Terribly petty of you, after the consideration I've shown." Juliet bristled, glaring down at me, but I was done being flustered. Mostly.

"You can't. Because it's backed up. That's what I was trying to do before you got here… get it unclogged. It's stuck. Huge mess. Poo everywhere. Gotta call a plumber. I mean, right after I call the police to check on Kent. You know, if you're really concerned, maybe you should check on him?" I grabbed Juliet's arm and guided her toward the door, praying she didn't just mow me over with her bulk. "Why don't you just pop next door and knock and see if he's all right, and I'll finish getting the toilet fixed, and …"

Somehow, I managed to reach the door-jam and angle her out. Like a kitten wrestling an elephant. "Have a nice day, Juliet. I'll call you if anything else of importance turns up."

She started to turn to push back in, but at that very moment, the blessed officers of San Amoro's overworked underpaid police force rolled up, lights flashing, and Juliet climbed into her car and pulled out from the curb with a speed I hadn't seen outside of Nicky's FrankenStang.

"Thanks," I muttered to the cops as they exited their car, "But you're a little late. She already cleaned out everything." They politely took my report, which I tried to make as detailed as possible to get it all on record, but it was clear that since it wasn't a violent crime or a blatant violation of public safety law, they weren't very interested. They gave me a case number, and I swiftly slid the door shut and flipped the lock over, waving one last time through the small pane of glass. I dashed up the back stair and unlocked the empty office.

The poor neglected Hoover had apparently given up hope of rescue and with it, his yowling. He was coiled up in a ball, sound asleep on a stack of folded painter's cloth, with his wrinkly nose between his front paws, and his back legs curled to the side; an adorable felted lump of softly snoring feline. Something in my chest jerked a bit, and I had to resist the urge to snatch him up in my arms and snuggle him.

"Close call, buddy. Close call." I scooped him up and took him back downstairs. Then, hands on my hips, I looked around the office formerly known as Charles'. Everything that hadn't been built in, bolted down, or that was confidential to the business was gone. Juliet had even taken the potted Ficus tree in the corner. Of the furniture, only the old brown sofa remained. Apparently, it hadn't met Juliet's standards. In the closed cabinet, I found the rack of sgian dubh I'd moved the night before. I was glad that Juliet hadn't gotten her hands on them, not yet, anyway, but I was also glad they hadn't been out on display: I'd never stabbed someone before but Juliet was enough to inspire homicidal thoughts.

The oak desk and matching file cabinets were gone, and the open shelves were emptied of all but the most common of legal texts. The safe was cemented in, and I'd warned Juliet there was confidential business information in it. With shaking hands, I entered the combination to the safe and opened it, smiling to see it was exactly as I'd left it when I'd put the ghost hunting gear away the night before. At least I had some petty cash. The cameras, digital recorders, and the back-up hard-drives were all there, too. I picked up the digital recorder we'd used the night before and kept it with me.

IN THE FILE-ROOM, THERE WERE files everywhere, heaped

waist-high on the floor. I'd done my best to keep everything in order, but I knew I was facing hurricane-worthy chaos. Not knowing where to begin, I retrieved Evrett's helm from the recycling bin. I tried it on for size, something I'd never dared to do before, and felt a surge of cold at my back. Instantly, I pulled it off and held it in front of my face, looking directly into its slits with contrition. "All right, I'm sorry. I can't see anything through it anyway."

I took my time retrieving the rest of him from the bathroom. He seemed even heavier now, and I grunted as I lifted him over the shower-lip. I was just glad he wasn't wet. Oiling armor wasn't on my schedule for the day.

After wrestling Evrett back into the front office, I sat on the floor, my head hung. I held up the voice recorder, and backed up the recording from the night before, comforted by the sounds of my own giggles interspersed with Nicky's chastising voice. I had a friend like Nicky. How bad could things be?

"Do you know who killed Charles?"

"How would he know that?"

My own giggles again, setting off a set of faint chuckles in the here and now. And then another voice. Faint. Under my laughter. Almost whispered. Nearly unintelligible.

I played it again. And then again. Turned up the volume on the tiny recorder until Nicky's voice was a boom and my laughter was a roar.

Seev lajuant. Was that was what I was hearing? A male voice, clearly, sheev laj haunt? Shiv the haunt? Was Evrett asking about stabbing him with the sgian dubh I'd moved? I didn't think so. No one had been shivved. I stared at the knight, my chin resting on my knees. What did he mean?

French. Evrett was French. He spoke French, old French He wasn't saying shiv. He was saying suevre. I didn't know much French, most of what I knew came strictly from its Latin roots.

I grabbed my laptop and, sitting cross-legged on the floor, pulled up a French dictionary online. It took a few combinations before I came up with words that sounded and looked right. 'Suevre l'argent.'

Follow the money. Follow the money? What was that supposed to mean? Whose money? "I don't have any money, Evrett. What are you talking about?"

The knight remained silent. Maybe he literally meant follow the money, as in get back to work and finish the one paying job that I had access to. "Sorry, sir. I just don't get it. But thanks for trying." The one time he actually spoke up and I had no idea what he was talking about. I straightened up and headed to the office next door.

MOST WEEKDAYS, MALLORY KENT'S ROUND form can be spotted around the giant hanging potted fern in his window, rifling around in his desk or talking on the phone, his thinning hair framing a round face made ruddier by the purple ties he favors. Today was no exception and I found myself opening Kent's office with a timid knock.

"I'm fine!" Mallory yelled without lifting his head. The radio was on and he reached as though to turn it up higher.

"I know. It's me." I muttered, feeling a little sick as I ducked through the door. "I don't suppose you have a spare office telephone? Juliet took mine."

"I think I've got something for you." Mallory pushed to his feet, opened a cabinet at the back of his office and rummaged through a stack of boxes. "I was listening through the wall. It's hard to believe that woman was born from the same blood as Charles."

"She wasn't. She hatched. From an egg. Like any snake."

Mallory had the good manners to laugh. "Did she leave anything? That moving van was packed to the roof." He came out with a small box and handed it to me. "I bought a new office phone a few months back. This one works fine, but I wanted a wireless headset. This'll do for you, I think."

"Aw, thanks! I'll get it back to you as soon as I finish getting things sorted." I hesitated at the door. "I hid the things that mattered most. And she can't touch the client files, so I guess that's something."

"What are you going to do now?" Mallory asked sympathetically, his eyes moon-wide.

"I don't know. I have to think of our clients right now. They need me. They trust me. I need to find out where I stand legally as far as the business is concerned, and then... I don't know what. Find a firm to work for, I guess. Maybe one of the firms Charles did work with is hiring."

Mallory nodded. "I'll keep my ear to the ground. If I hear of anyone hiring, I'll let you know. Hey, you ever thought of going into business for yourself?"

"What? Me?" I laughed, a tiny laugh that I didn't feel. "I don't have a clue how to run a business."

The insurance salesman grinned, his chubby cheeks puffing merrily. "You've been running Hanford Legal for years now. I'd say you're darn good at it."

"Thanks. And for the phone, too." I backed out the door with a wave. "I'll return it as soon as stuff's settled.

"No rush." He waved me off with a chubby hand as he settled back into his chair.

I ESCAPED BACK INTO MY office, made a pot of coffee with the last of Charles' custom roasted Columbian bean, then settled on the floor with my last blank legal pad, my pen and a stack of phone numbers. With a long sigh, I dialed the first number on the list and started working my way down.

"Hello, this is Kami White, from Hanford Legal? How are you today? I'm calling to tell you there's been an accident, and we can no longer manage your case file. If you'd like, I'll be happy to courier your files to the lawyer of your choice, or you can pick them up."

After four or five calls, it felt like rote. I was on autopilot, just writing names and making notes.

I was less than a quarter of the way through my list when

a knock on the door disturbed me. I wasn't calling the simple cases for which I could finish the paperwork on my own, and I hadn't yet called the cases that were going to require the most attention. I both dreaded and begged for the interruption and I got up and unlocked the door without looking to see who was on the other side of the glass.

"Kam?" A wave of dark hair, dashed with grey just at the temples, appeared.

Reggie. I wasn't sure if I was relieved or dismayed to see him.

"Come in." If I'd felt messy compared to Juliet, I was positively scruffy next to Mr. Well-Dressed.

He stepped in and came to a sudden halt, his handsomely cut jaw jutting wide as he waved a legal folder stamped with his firm's seal at the empty room. "What the hell happened in here?"

"Didn't you get my message? Juliet. What else?" The name sounded disgust laden to my own ears, but Reggie smiled slightly before I continued. "She showed up with a van full of movers and took everything that I couldn't prove belonged to the business. She even took my penholder. With my pens. I called the cops but they were too late to stop her."

"Well, we'll have to see about that." His gaze fell on Evrett. "I see you managed to save a few things?"

"Confidential client stuff. The knight. The cat. And all the files and computers, everything in the safe... I had to call the cops but they didn't get here in time. Some things I knew he'd want people to have, like the chess set for Morri, your map, but..." I'd been able to put off that sick feeling in my gut while I was working, but now, looking around the empty room, it was back. "She was like a tornado. Just swept in with movers and a van and...well...I didn't know what to do."

"I wish I'd gotten your message." Reginald peered around himself as Hoover arrived to twine in and around Reggie's legs. Hoover associated Reggie with Saturday barbecues and hence made him a priority among his human friends. That cat would sell us all up the river in exchange for a bacon-wrapped prawn.

"Look, Kam, I didn't want to say anything yesterday..."

"Then don't say it today, either. I'm commending most of our clientele to your firm anyway. I'll have things cleared out of here in a few days and you won't have to bother about me."

Reggie's eyes darkened and filled with a look that I suddenly realized was hurt. Deeply wounded kind of hurt. Hurt that I had inflicted. I glanced away, no longer able to meet his gaze as I tried to find the words to apologize. When he spoke again, his voice was far less warm. He dropped the file on the floor next to my phone and cold half-cup of black coffee. "That paperwork is for you. I came to tell you that Charles named me as executor of his will, and you as the primary beneficiary. He left Hanford Legal, and all the business assets, including the office building and all of the contents therein... to you, as well as a substantial sum of money."

"Say... huh?" Normally, I'm pretty good at oratory and fairly decent at thinking on my feet, but right that instant, I ran out of words. Not just of the "I'm sorry" variety of vocabulary, either. The entire Oxford English Dictionary seemed to have abandoned me all at once. "He what?"

Fortunately, Reginald was no stranger to grief-hazed clientele. "Charles' will, Kami. He owned the building, free and clear. It's yours now. The contents of the office, the business assets, his clientele list, his art collections? Everything that was here is all yours." Reggie's glance trailed around the room, his gaze darkening. "Not that the contents matter now. Possession really is nine tenths and all. If we manage to get half of it back, that will be a miracle. I don't suppose you inventoried anything before Juliet stripped the place?"

Oh, Charles. Too worn and tired out for tears, I could feel myself standing there, mouth open, eyes burning, overwhelmed with gratitude for the generosity of the man I loved, and feeling stupidly like I'd betrayed him by opening the door to Juliet. I was suddenly shaking. "I...I... didn't know. I thought she was next of kin. Are you sure? I mean, I had no idea he left anything to me."

"I didn't either until I opened the paperwork this morning. He'd arranged it with Oslo, not a word to me. He left his house to …" Reggie's voice dropped off, dark memories of friendships lost behind his eyes.

"To be auctioned for the American Brain Tumor foundation." My mind was racing as it tried to add Reggie's declaration to the muddle of grief and loss I was processing, but failed to finish the equation. I was never good at math, especially of the emotional kind. "He set that up right after Arthur died. Did he leave anything at all to Juliet?"

"The family home in Leicester, England, with all contents, the portrait of their grandfather, and sixty thousand pounds, on the condition that she not contest the will." Reggie glanced around at the empty office. "But it looks like she wants to contest." He cleared his throat, eyes focused out the window on the mid-day street traffic. "I assume you'll want to sell this place? It's a good location, can fetch a pretty penny."

Sell it. Yes. That would be the sensible thing to do. Not a chance.

"Reggie? What about the business? I mean, he left me the assets but…" Egads, this was going to sound horribly petty. He left me a commercial building, and I needed rent money. "What about the business accounts? Payday should have been a week ago, and I don't even know… How does any of this even work?"

"All of the business and personal assets are yours, but that's really not my bailiwick. Call the accountant. He'll know about payroll. And come by my office later this week, we'll get things sorted, papers signed, etcetera. Probate will have to be filed, and you and I both know how long the courts can take with that."

Etcetera. I didn't want to think about all the etceteras. "Who was Charles' accountant? He never said." And I never asked.

"Jack Austin. I've his card right here."

"Austin? ..." Ugh! No wonder Charles never told me! That traitor!

Reggie mistook my groan for something else, confusion maybe. "He's excellent. We use him, too." I stuck out my hand. Reggie tucked the card into it and then gave it a warm squeeze.

"Don't worry," he encouraged. "We'll get this sorted out. Make a list of everything that was here before Juliet came."

I snorted, trying hard not to think about Jack Austin. "I don't think there was anything before Juliet. She's prehistoric. A dinosaur."

Reggie chuckled, gave a small bow, and scratched Hoover's pointed-alien ears on the way out the door.

It was only after he was sliding back into his Tesla that I remembered common courtesy and ran after him, diving around to pull the car door open and lean in. "Thanks, Reggie. I mean... really, thank you. For everything."

He smiled, a genuine smile for the first time since I'd dissed him earlier. "Anytime, kiddo."

"Reg?" I hesitated, feeling stupid for asking. "Did Juliet know she wasn't inheriting? I mean, did she take everything to steal it from me? Or did she honestly think she was getting everything?"

The lawyer shook his head sadly. "Peter told her this afternoon. He was actually on his way over here when I told him I would come instead. She knows now, but I don't think it's going to be a matter of asking pretty-please to get your inheritance back."

I caught his gaze and held it. "If she thought she was inheriting everything, you don't think she could have been involved somehow in Charles' drowning?"

"You think a sixty-year-old woman of Juliet's size and stature waded out into the ocean and took away his surfboard? Maybe sat on him until he drowned? What then? She got off the beach somehow without anyone seeing her? That's a pretty big stretch."

"Sounds pretty stupid, huh?"

Reggie shook his head. "She's greedy and something of entitled snob, but can you see her killing someone?"

I shook my head.

Reggie's voice was soft as he said, "He drowned, Kami. That's all. It's time to let go."

I thanked Reggie again, and stood on the sidewalk to watch him drive way. Could I see Juliet killing someone herself? No. But Juliet had money and means, and people with money and means were capable of a great many things.

Reggie's Tesla faded quietly down the street, and I was left alone to face the new problem he'd dropped in my lap. And it was a huge problem. A problem named Jack Austin. You see, I hate Jack Austin. I hate his shoes, his car and his word choices. I hate his little smiles and his tendency to hum when he knows something I don't. I hate the way he made me laugh when I wanted to cry, or cry when I wanted to laugh.

And then, when my back is against the wall and the deadlines were looming, he's not only there to help, but does it in the most amazing, gracious way possible. And that would make me want to start loving him all over again. But I couldn't, because I hated him entirely.

It's even more infuriating because he's my ex-husband. Well, not exactly husband. We never tied the knot, after all. Or rather, I didn't. I caught a bus and landed three states away in my stained, dusty wedding gown, calling him from an Idaho truck stop somewhere outside Boise. I blamed the bus station for being across the street from the church. Jack blamed me. And who could blame him?

Now, just when I wanted him least, I needed him most.

CHAPTER 6

———

Fremont & San Amoro: Tuesday

I ARRIVED AT JACK AUSTIN'S uptown office the next day, hopeful that he might not actually be there only to find his car sitting directly in front. He drives a boxy-looking silver BMW that's supposedly all cushy and expensive but merely succeeds in looking ugly and intrusive. Or at least, it should be ugly and intrusive. Not sexy. Leather seats are not sexy. Especially if they're heated.

"Kam! I'm glad you came by. Peter Oslo told me to expect you. He explained everything. I've just been going over Charles' accounts." Jack smiled, and I was reminded, as always, of Cary Elwes. I always hated that moment, when Jack looks like that, because I loved Cary Elwes, just as much as I hated Jack.

"I don't want to take too much of your time," I babbled quickly. "It's just… Charles left me the business… but I don't know about the money. Is there any? How am I supposed to keep the business running? Is my current pay still forthcoming? Are there death duties I have to pay? I'm broke! And the building? Are the taxes current? How much will I owe in estate tax? What's the …"

He lifted both hands from the desk. "Stop. Stop now and breathe a bit."

I tried to do as he said before remembering that I don't want to do anything he says. I took one deep breath and felt my heart-rate slow down. Damn him for being right. "Look, I just want to know what kind of mess I've gotten myself into. You don't need to rub it in or anything, or try to fix it. Just tell me where I stand."

"In front of my desk, obviously." And he had that damned twinkle in his eye. (For the record, I hate that, too.) "Come on, sit down. Relax. It's not as bad as it seems."

He said that all the time. It's not as bad as it seems. Even when it doesn't seem bad at all, he has to tell you it's not as bad. That only makes me worry more.

"The building at 542 Marin is current on federal taxes, permitting and repairs." He slid a folder over to me. "You might have a problem with the San Amoro city use tax."

"Use tax?"

"You're in a commercial zone. As long as you continue to rent out the offices and your renters are commercial users with commercial interests, the use tax will be a trifle of your income on the building."

"Oh, that doesn't sound bad," I said hopefully.

"No, not at all." He smiled, and it wasn't as smug as I expected it to be. "I told you it wasn't so bad. But all the offices need to be in use. You've got one sitting vacant right now."

"I can find a renter," I said confidently, even though I wasn't. It had been empty since the great chiro-scandal of Marin Street. I didn't think stashing Hoover up there counted as tenancy. "What about the business itself? I mean, I know we still have to go through probate, and it's the new month already and I haven't been paid for last month. Is there provision for business expenses like, oh, say… the electricity? Phone? Internet? My salary?"

Now Jack frowned, and I knew it was bad news. Not the "not so bad" kind of news, but the worse-than-you-expected kind of news. "The sister, Juliet Hanford, has already filed an injunction against all of the accounts. She's contesting the will and all its provisions. You'll get it all, but it's going to take some work. In the meantime, all outgoing payments will have to go through an escrow account. Charles and I worked to make this is as easy a transfer as possible but with his sister contesting the will? It'll take time to sort out."

"How much time?" I had about six-hundred in my checking account, about two-hundred in savings.

"I won't lie, Kam. These things can drag on for years. Don't worry, though. I'm working with Oslo and Burroughs. We'll get it sorted."

Years? I had a month. Maybe. If Reese was generous with the day-old bagels. I refused to cry in front of Jack Austin. "Right. I'll just go move into my car."

I hate Jack's laugh. It's so warm and happy, like he really means it every time he finds something amusing. It's disgusting. Really. Especially the way his eyes sparkle when he's amused. Such beautiful eyes shouldn't ever be so sparkly.

"Don't panic. Let me see what I can do."

"I don't want your charity, Jack," I snapped before I thought about it. Something that felt familiarly like guilt kicked me in the gut and I added meekly, "I only meant I can take care of myself."

"And I only meant let me see what I can do to expedite the escrow process and see about getting a stipend fund set up for you run the business with. God, Kam! You're so fired up all the time. Do you ever manage to cool off?"

"I do cool. I do cool all the time." I tried to smile, already backing toward the door. "Thanks, Jack. I appreciate all your help."

"Wait up a moment. I wanted to ask you about something..." Jack rifled through the paperwork for a moment. "Do you know what this is? Is it some kind of recurring business expense that he established an account for?"

I glanced it over. It was a bank account statement that showed quarterly withdrawals of five thousand dollars being transferred from over a quarter-million-dollar balance into some kind of fund. "Twenty K a year? And there's how much in here? Jack, I have no idea what this could be for. Is it part of the estate?"

Jack nodded. "Charles had me put it in his personal file, but I think the money was transferred from Arthur's estate when Arthur died. Either way, it should go to you. I'd just like to sort out what the payments are for."

I looked at the numbers again. "Maybe he was funding brain tumor research? Arthur's tumor was discovered too late to be viable for treatment, but only months after he died they found a new treatment that could have worked. Charles was furious that the research hadn't been done and available sooner. I know he wanted the house to be auctioned for research. If that's what it's for, it should all go there."

Jack frowned faintly. "I don't know, but I don't like the idea of your bequest just wandering out to heaven only knows where. I'll track down this account transfer number and find out what's behind it. Shouldn't take me long. Don't worry. We'll take care of it."

See what I mean about Jack. Why does he have to be so dang nice all the time? "So, you'll call me if anything comes up...I mean...for the finances?"

"Yeah." And as long as I waited for his smile, it never came. He waved a hand. "I'll call you. Be safe out there."

"You, too."

Ouch. Had I really just said that? I gave him a small wave and stepped backward out the door. So. What now?

MY MIND WAS REELING AFTER my conversations with the lawyer and the accountant. Charles had left me so much? Was he out of his mind? I had a near-fortune just out of my fingertips: Just selling one painting would mean I could go to any law school that would take me, and not have to worry about books or supplies while I did. That was, if anything at all ended up with me after a legal battle with Juliet. Would she really risk the family home back in England for a few paintings and old knick-knacks?

I BICYCLED TO MY APARTMENT. I hadn't been home in two days, not that I had much of a home to start with. I rented a single-bedroom efficiency that was roughly equivalent in size to Ivana Trump's closet. I kept planning to save enough money to move to something better, but never quite managed it. It's not like I did badly with my job or things are that hard-up normally, but there's always the car to get fixed, or tuition to pay, or a dental bill. Something always seemed to come up when I least expected it.

Now I stood in the doorway and gazed around with fresh eyes. The yellowing paint made the place seem smaller than it was, and the industrial cream and brown-flecked carpet did nothing for the dinginess. In my years there, it had been a place to sleep, a place to have a late-night snack in front of the TV. It suddenly struck me that I never really lived there. It was a crash-pad. A storage space. It wasn't somewhere to live. Life was too short to dump money into a place I didn't want to be and I didn't have next month's rent in hand, anyway. I was going to get out of there. And today.

I tracked down the landlord. He was playing pinochle with the senior residents in the recreation room and seemed pretty sanguine about my giving notice. He didn't have a big problem finding renters. The neighborhood was decent and the building was affordable, had a laundry and a rec-room, no cockroaches, and, amazingly enough, secure gated parking. But it was also smallish, had plumbing issues, and more often than not there was an ambulance service calling for one of the senior citizens that lives there. Nothing says home for the holidays like the twinkling of red and white emergency lights at three in the morning.

I was halfway through packing up when I remembered that I didn't have my car with me. Well, it wasn't like I could take it all to the office anyway, was it? I turned on my laptop and put an ad on Craigslist with just about everything I owned. If I could sell half of it, I would be able to eat and make the car insurance payment for another month or so at least, right? The rest I could call a donation truck for.

My few more precious things were boxed up and I called U-Store-It across town. They pick up and deliver for a minimal fee that would cost me less than renting a truck to move it myself. We used them at the office from time to time. If I mentioned their Yelp ad, fifty bucks would get me an eight-by-five space, and another twenty-five got me pick up. It really should have been thirty, but I didn't tell them that it was personal and not Hanford Legal business.

I went back down to my bicycle wearing two huge duffle-bags strapped across my chest bandolier-style. With a cheap blue ice-chest stuffed with perishables from the half-sized fridge strapped to my handlebars and a black garbage bag full of essentials tied to the back of the seat, I looked like a homeless person. Scratch that. I looked like a homeless toothpick in a purple bike-helmet riding a rust-bucket second (or maybe third or fourth) hand bicycle.

I DIDN'T THINK I COULD sleep, but I curled up again on Charles' sofa, the space where we'd shared so many laughs, cups of coffee, and late-night brief preparations. It was mine now, and no one could take it from me. I closed my eyes and pretended he was there across from me, but there was no sound, no movement. He was gone. I drifted off to the rhythm of Hoover's deep purr against my chest, soothing into the borders between waking and slumber. My world was the yielding softness of the sofa, the distant hum of the office fridge, and the peaceful darkness behind my own eyelids. Then came a faint brush of cold air along my cheek, gone as swiftly as I felt it. The back of my neck prickled and goose-bumps ran down my arms.

"Evrett?" I whispered into the silence. I wanted Charles to

be there with me, but I knew, deep down, that it was only our Crusader Knight. But why? I reached out a hand, touched only open air, and, not expecting an answer, asked, "Evrett, what is it?"

A sudden thud resounded through the room, followed by the all-too familiar slip-sliding of files and paperwork scattering across the File Room floor.

"Evrett!" I leaped straight up and flipped on the desk-lamp. Hoover flashed down from the sofa and ran full-tilt for the file room. Chevalier Evrett rarely wasted what energy he could glean on physically moving objects. He saved that for important things, serious things.

Heart pounding, brain still verge-of-sleep muddled, I crept off the sofa and went to the file room. Hoover was sitting princely upon a tall stack of files in the middle of the floor. And beside him, sprawled across the floor in a fairly-tidy landslide of paperwork, was another stack, the victim of whatever late-night bug had crawled up Evrett's chain-maille.

Hoover gave a faint "meep" and I gave him a glare and a warning. "You knock those over and you're going to the animal shelter."

He tipped his wrinkly bare nose in my direction, but remained where he was. He either didn't take my threat seriously, or didn't care to let me know that he was concerned. It's hard to tell with cats.

"Okay, Evrett. You've made a mess. Now what does it mean?" Maybe the knight just didn't like having all the files stacked on the floor? I turned on the electric tea-kettle and filled a tea-steeper with Mom's special Mind Over Matter blend. According to the label, which read "Jaxine's Herbal Tisanes & Teas" it was supposed to improve mental acumen and intensify "higher thinking." It smelled like licorice and wintergreen. My mother's tea recipes might not taste the best, but I'd had enough poured down my throat over the years to know they were fairly effective.

Hot mug of tea in hand, I settled cross-legged on the floor

in front of the scattered files. "You want to give me a clue what I'm looking for?"

There was no answer. I really hadn't expected one.

I gathered up the files that Evrett had knocked over and took them back out front where I settled on the floor in the acid-yellow glow from the streetlights outside. Slowly, I flipped through them, one by one. Old cases that Charles had handled before I started working for him began to spread out over the bare-wood floor.

The thickest file was one that had spilt the furthest, paperwork scattered out of order. It was, I noted with some surprise, Vanny's back-file, the one I'd set aside earlier. I scanned over all the paperwork in the file. Vanny's first divorce had been one of Charles' first cases after opening his practice in California. Jewel vs Osborne. Freeman Osborne was an entrepreneur in the early days of Silicon Valley, and at the time, Vanessa Jewel had been a shining newly risen star on the San Francisco music scene. By the time Vanessa was through with Freeman Osborne, he was paying obscene alimony, and Vanessa was a major stock-holder in his company. After Osborne, she moved on to Ryan Johnson, a former football player turned sports promoter, who, according to the divorce filing, was an alcoholic. After that, there was Anders Whisfeld, a North Sea oil tycoon. Vanny may have come from Central Valley sheep-farming stock, but she'd moved up fast in the world. There was little in the file that I didn't already know. I set it aside with a chuckle. Loyalty apparently extended to business where it didn't to husbands: She'd always come back to Hanford Legal.

Hanford Legal. That's what the window said. Sitting there in the shadows, staring out through the carefully stenciled letters, glowing gold in the streetlight, with the taste of my mother's licorice tea on my tongue, I didn't want to think about tomorrow. Or about the decisions I'd made that day. The lettering obscured the view of the empty street, and it no longer held any meaning. Hanford Legal. Hanford was gone.

I grabbed my silver letter opener from the box of things Julie didn't take and started scraping away the gold painted letters, careful not to scratch the glass. I didn't want to think about how much repairing that would cost. Slowly, bit by bit, the gold lettering came away, the view clearing. It took over an hour, and when I finished, I scrubbed the whole window down with Windex and paper towels until the streetlights twinkled as they faded into the coming dawn.

It was a cool greyish sunrise with only a few hints of pink brushed against the jet-streaked sky, and I watched it come. Watched until the first cars began to move down the street. Watched until Reese's Cafe opened its doors for breakfast. Until it felt like I was no longer all alone with a cat and a ghost.

CHAPTER 7

San Amoro: Wednesday Morning

I ESCAPED TO THE WARM comfort of Reese's, bought a latte and a cheese croissant, and sat looking out at my building. My building. 542 Marin, with its turreted corners and elegant curved windows that I loved. The window looked empty now, scraped clean. It seemed sad, too, missing "Hanford" the way I missed him. Maybe it was a little bit of owner's pride, but I could hardly bear to see it empty like that.

Reese wandered by my table and casually asked, "So, what do you plan to do now?"

Reese was in her forties, a tall willowy woman with black hair and dark brown eyes and usually dressed in brown, "so it won't show the coffee stains." She's born and raised in Oakland brand of tough. She ran the café with her husband until he ran off to the Caribbean with a club singer a few years back. With Charles' help, Reese took everything she could get in the divorce; house, car, boat and café. She sold the first three, and kept the last. She loved what she did, and like Charles, she'd given me a break when I most needed it. I'd walk through broken glass for Reese if she asked me to.

I considered her question, and finally shrugged. "I don't know."

She stood over me now with one eyebrow arched. "What do you mean, you don't know?"

"Maybe I could come back and work for you?" I asked hopefully. Because minimum wage was better than no wage at all, wasn't it?

"Hell no!" Reese snapped. Flagging her counter-helper to take her tray, she plunked down in the chair opposite me. "You got skills, girl! You got an education and a career. You aren't a coffee-girl anymore."

"I could be a coffee-cake girl. I'm sure of it. Maybe a bagel girl?"

Reese shook her head. "Charlie was a good man, Kami. He did a lot for you. For me, too. Do you think he'd forgive me if I let you give up your career? Don't be an idiot!"

She pointed across the street to the arched and empty window of 1A. "I want that window reading 'Kamera White, Attorney at Law' one day. And until then, it should read whatever you can do. You're a paralegal, right?"

"Well, yes," I agreed amiably, but quantified it with the reality of my situation. "But usually they work for lawyers. It's not easy to be on your own as a paralegal. I can't really give legal advice. Not, well, legally."

"No, but you can file stuff, right? Like injunctions and divorce papers and small claims? You help me with the business filings for the café, right?"

"I'm a licensed document preparer. But…"

"Weren't you doing investigations? If I suspected I had an employee stealing from me or something, you could investigate, right?"

"Not anymore. I can't complete my license requirements without Charles." I still had some classes to take and my internship period to complete. Which wasn't likely now. "Uh, do you? Have an employee stealing from you?"

Reese shook her head. "No, but when I do, I'll call you. Not to investigate, mind you, but because I'll need a new bagel girl. In the meantime, get over there, get your business going, and quit feeling sorry for yourself."

"I don't even have a desk," I grumbled, recognizing my self-defeatist demeanor for what it was; my own special brand of pathetic. I should trademark it and sell it on the Internet. You could sell anything on the Internet. How much was self-defeatism worth on eBay? "Juliet took everything."

Reese was undeterred, a smile splitting across her face. "I've got a folding computer desk in back I'm not using. Take it. Take a chair, too. Here…Max? Grab that desk I have in the storeroom and take it across for Kami! And hustle before we get busy."

I stood there kind of stunned while Max, a hyperactive (Maybe that was the free coffee?) college student, hauled the cheap folding desk and a wood and aluminum café chair across the street. Reese gave me a hug, topped off my latte with steamed milk—whole, not that non-fat stuff—and pushed me out the door. "Go on, girl. Pick yourself up."

So much for going back in time.

THE REST OF MY MORNING was spent trying to return my office space to official-looking normalcy. Juliet had taken the hand-painted oriental divider that shaved the main front room in half, giving me separate space for work and organization. Now I had just one huge empty open area. The built-in wall shelves looked barren, halved in their contents. She'd taken all but the more esoteric legal books. Whitish squares on the pale cream walls showed the gaps where Charles' collections of artwork and artifacts had hung.

I dragged Evrett to a new position, helping fill some of the empty space. I turned him slightly so that he had a view of the door and the front window and tucked his helmet back in place. As an afterthought, I turned back and opened the visor on his helmet. "There, better?"

There was no response. Was he still mad at me for the middle of the night scolding? Or had he worn himself out with his file-spilling trick? Poor old Evrett. Being nearly six-hundred years old had to be rough. Not to mention being dead on top of that. And I still didn't understand why he dumped the files, if he'd had a reason at all.

"Evrett always has a reason," I told Hoover, but whether to convince him or convince myself I didn't know.

As morning wore away into noon, some clients came by to pick up their files and a few more called to see who I would recommend they go to for legal help. (Oslo and Burroughs, of course.) Hoover kept leaping on the desk, stepping on my laptop, poking his paw in my face, stealing my pen, and all the other things that cats of any stripe do when something in their environment has changed and they don't understand why. I gave up pretending to work and got down on the floor on my knees and elbows to play paws under the door with him.

That was the undignified position I was in when Mallory Kent stopped by to check in on me. When I told him what Charles had done, leaving me the building, he was astounded.

"I guess you'll be selling it?" His pudgy face was crestfallen. "I'll miss this place."

Another surge of certainty flooded me. "No one is leaving. I'm keeping it."

"Really? Really? Well... Really?"

"Yeah, really. Don't suppose you know anyone who wants to rent out upstairs?" I asked hopefully.

"No, but can I offer some advice?"

"I can use all the advice I can get. I'm kind of floating here, I'm afraid."

Mallory shot me a greedy grin. "When you find someone, tell them they have to have renter's insurance as part of their lease..."

"And recommend you? Opportunistic bastard." I chuckled. "I'll do it. Anything else?"

"Yeah." He glanced around the barren office with pursed lips. "Get some furniture in here. It looks like a tomb."

"Yeah, well. Juliet took everything. I didn't have any sort

of inventory or anything, so I can't even prove what was here. Oslo & Burroughs is working on it, but, without any proof of what was here..." I looked around, struck again by the loss. Not just of the assorted decorations and collected artworks, but of everything that was Charles.

Mallory's expression turned thoughtful. "Kami, you inherited everything?"

"The building and all of its contents, as well as all of the business assets." I confirmed. "I just didn't know it before the harpy-hag of the Hanford family showed up. She's filed injunctions against the terms of the will, too. I filed a police report, but there's not a lot they can do."

"Who's managing your case? Give me their number."

Mallory's gaze didn't lose its intense concentration, even as I dug out Reggie's card and handed it to him with an inquisitive stare. "Come on, Mallory. Spill."

"Charles had everything in here, all the artifacts he collected and all of the business assets, insured through me. Technically, his insurance has to be dealt with by his next of kin, but if Oslo & Burroughs is executor and handling the estate, I can submit all the paperwork to them. Kam, there's an inventory, all right, and I have it in his file. Along with pictures of everything Charles had insured."

I had never felt more like hugging someone in my entire life. "Mallory! You're my knight in shining lilac tie today!"

"Yeah, well." He straightened said tie and shrugged, head ducked. "Just doing my job. I'll e-mail the files over to them right away. I hope it helps. This place looks like an abandoned mine-shaft."

"Feels like one, too." As my Hero Insurance Man left, I decided he was right. I needed to make the place look more lived in. Still elated from his revelations, I drove Charles' SUV to my apartment and loaded it up with my more presentable books and some of the framed calendar pictures that graced my apartment. Everything that didn't fit in the SUV, I packed up for delivery to my new storage unit.

By the time I returned to the office, there was no parking directly in front. The taxi cab drivers liked to hog the street in the afternoon so they could grab a quick lunch at Reese's between fares, and even the metered spots filled up fast at mealtimes. I pulled into the alley instead and walked around to the front of the building. It was good, I told myself, because it gave me a chance to study the building. My building. Was I ever going to get tired of saying that? It looked solid and sound, for what that was worth. Everything I know about building structures and engineering I learned watching This Old House with my grandfather. Give me a lease agreement for a structure, and I'll amend the heck out of it, but the structure itself? Not a clue.

As I came around the front of the building, I wished I'd ducked in the back door. Jude Booder, Doc, and Patrick were waiting in front of the Be Right Back sign I'd hung on the front door. "Hey, guys." I greeted, but I didn't even bother to give Jude the cat-nod as I unlocked the door and let them in.

"Sorry for the lack of chairs. What brings you over the hill?"

"The Paddle Out..." Jude started, but he was glancing curiously around the empty office. "Didn't you used to have, like, furniture or something in here?"

If I'd been speaking to him, I would have told him to shut up.

"Weather and tide are favorable for a sunset Paddle Out on Saturday." Doc pointed to the calendar on the wall. "If that works for you."

"I called Maverick's BBQ and they're available to do the catering," Patrick added, and I wondered how he managed to remember that Charles loved American style barbecue. "We just have to let them know by Wednesday."

"Whatever you guys want to do." I shook my head. I wasn't going. I wasn't going to forgive the ocean that easily. "I'm happy to spread the word, but ... I've said good-bye enough for now."

They exchanged glances, then Doc nodded. "Okay, if that's

what you want."

"Hey, though, while I'm thinking about it… Did you find out anything more about the green van?"

"What green van?" Was it my imagination or did Jude Booder's eyes just pop out of his head momentarily? With Jude it was hard to tell.

"Both Manny and I saw a green van at the beach the morning Charles died." Doc explained.

Patrick followed up with, "Kami's convinced it has something to do with Charles' drowning."

"I thought he just drowned? Came off the board and hit his head or something?"

I looked to Patrick, hoping he'd speak up so I didn't have to, but my cousin was silent, his eyes following Hoover as the cat restlessly circled the uninvited guests trying to decide if they were friend or foe. Or maybe just if they had tuna in their pockets.

"Not convinced. Just …curious." I amended as I shifted to watch Jude's face, though I still addressed my words to Doc. "It doesn't make sense to me that he just wiped out and drowned. We all know how well he surfed and how careful he was."

Doc kept talking. "Autopsy shows he drowned, but there weren't any extenuating circumstances, no head injury or heart-attack. Kami just wants to be thorough, Jude. Grief always seems easier if you can find a reason."

Now Jude was looking at me, but his eyes were dark. "I didn't see no green van at the beach. An' you know Manny. How much alcohol and other stuff he puts down it's a wonder he didn't see flying dolphins or something."

Patrick laughed at that. "It's true, cuz. Manny isn't exactly a star witness sort."

No one could deny that Manny had more than a few self-inflicted short-circuits in his brain. "Doc saw…" Darn it! I snapped my mouth shut, realizing that I'd almost spoken to Jude Booder. "You saw it, too, right Doc?"

"Yes, but that doesn't mean anything, Kam. Lots of people

drive green vans. Could have been a tourist, someone camping at the park, or even a parks employee."

"I know. I'm more concerned about his feet..."

"Feet?" Doc stopped and stared at me.

Careful, Kami. So careful! Fortunately, Patrick finally spoke up. Oh, he'd talk to Doc for me, but not to Jude Booder? "There were some marks that the coroner couldn't identify. Some kind of lesions. Non-specific lesions is what the autopsy report labeled them. We thought maybe they were jellyfish stings at first."

Doc closed his eyes for a second, and I wondered if he was doing his memory recall trick. "I don't remember seeing any lesions. We surfed together on Monday, too, and I didn't notice anything then, either. And I notice feet. I also notice jellies, and I didn't see any that day. Of course, that doesn't mean they weren't out there."

"After seeing your office, yeah, I can imagine you notice feet." I considered for a second. And if you were responsible for them, you wouldn't tell me now, would you? "So, whatever caused them happened after Monday, and before he drowned. He was here all day Tuesday and he was fine then."

"Maybe it really was nothing? Abrasions from being tossed in the surf. Stepped on a sharp shell on the beach. Kami, there may not be an explanation for what happened." Doc shook his head again, his pale green eyes scanning my face. "Have you even slept since the funeral?"

"Here and there." I admitted.

"Get some sleep. You can't go on like this. You're getting paranoid. If you need me to prescribe something to help you sleep, I'm happy to."

"No, thanks." I held up a canister of Mom's Lavender Chamomile Tisane blend, for a sweet night's sleep. "Mom's herbal tea should do the trick."

"Aunt Jaxine is a botanist," Patrick informed a skeptical looking Doc. "She runs a plant nursery that specializes in medicinal herbs. Her stuff tends to work."

"She made me and Kenny drink like eighty gallons of her gunk when we got chicken pox. Didn't do nothin' but made me pee a lot," Jude grumbled.

"That means you stayed hydrated through your fever, so it did work." Doc smirked as he checked the ingredients listed on the canister label and nodded in approval. "Your mom knows her stuff. Okay. Get some rest. And don't worry about the Paddle Out, we'll take care of everything. And you should come, whether you paddle or not. People want to see you."

Patrick gave me a quick hug. "We're going to pick up a few things for Saturday and then head back over the hill. Call us if you need anything."

I nodded, but Patrick yelled back over his shoulder as they climbed into his jeep, "And get some sleep! You look like a zombie!"

"I love you, too!" I yelled back.

I WATCHED THEM LEAVE, WAVING as they pulled away, but the earlier enthusiasm for my new independent career path had faded away, and I was feeling morbid and tired, which wasn't surprising considering the events of the past week. Had it really been a whole week? I glanced at the clock. Exactly one week and ten minutes since the office phone had rung and that official voice had asked if I was Kamera White. A week and ten minutes. The longest week and ten minutes in my entire life.

Hoover wandered up and nudged at my elbow, demanding attention, and I scratched his naked ears and rubbed his bare neck. "Poor baby. You don't understand what's going on at all, do you? You want Charles, too."

The cat rolled on his back, lolling bonelessly in my lap, and for the first time since Charles died, I just stopped. Stopped thinking, stopped worrying, stopped solving, stopped being afraid and stopped grieving. It wouldn't last, I knew it, this moment when autumn started to pass and winter loomed on the horizon, not quite ready to break into storms. It was a respite, nothing more, as I sat on the bare floor and closed my eyes and snuggled a lost lonely cat.

Only one thing was very clear to me. Something had happened to Charles on the beach that morning. And it felt like everyone I talked to about it was hiding something. What was that look on Jude's face when we mentioned the van? What did he know about it? And why when I mentioned feet did the "foot doctor" suddenly look concerned? Telling me I was being paranoid and that I needed to get some sleep didn't make me any less paranoid.

And I didn't want any stupid herbal tea. I tossed the canister at the wastebasket, missed, and left it on the floor where Hoover sniffed hopefully at it.

Settling at my desk, I phoned a few more clients, those who hadn't decided yet what to do with their files. Many demanded to know why they couldn't just keep using me as their legal counsel. They could, I told some of them (not the ones I couldn't stand, of course) but that if they needed something done that was out of my expertise and the limits of my knowledge and licensed abilities, I would have to refer them to someone else anyway. I was a paralegal and document preparer. I wasn't allowed to give them legal advice unless under advisement of a board-licensed lawyer.

The problem was that they all liked Charles. They trusted him. And if they couldn't have Charles then they wanted me. And if they couldn't have me, they were just going to wait until they could.

"Hurry up and pass your Bar, Kami!" the recently widowed Mrs. Judkins exclaimed. "I'm too old to find a new lawyer."

I was a long way off from my Bar exams, with at least two years of school, picked at through night school programs, left to go. That was, if I could even make enough of a go of things to support myself and pay tuition on top of it all. "I will, Mrs. Judkins. In the meantime, if anything comes up that I can't address, I'll send your information to Oslo and Burroughs."

I would miss Mrs. Judkins. I would miss all my clients.

And I would miss a steady paycheck. I didn't dare dream of the inheritance Charles was kind enough to leave me. What I could do with that money, if I ever saw it, that was. I had Oslo & Burroughs and Jack Austin on my side, but Juliet was a woman used to getting her way. Even if the courts found in my favor, by the time lawyers and court fees were paid, would I even see any of it? I Googled "how to win the lottery" and came up with over sixty-two million results. The second link was to a story about saving a dollar a week then investing the dollars in a high-interest savings account instead of buying a lottery ticket. Well, what kind of stupid advice was that?

I closed and locked the petty cash drawer, stuffed it in the back of the safe, and put the key behind Hoover's bag of kitty litter. Why tempt myself, after all?

CHAPTER 8

~~~

San Amoro: Wednesday Afternoon

PARANOID OR NOT, I was becoming more and more convinced that Charles didn't just paddle out beyond the break-water and drown himself swimming back in. I didn't care what Doc said. I didn't care what the coroner said. I didn't care, honestly, what anyone said. I tucked in at the little folding desk, pulled up my laptop, and I picked up my legal pad and wrote down all the questions to which I needed answers.

Why did Charles go in the water alone?

Who was driving the green van?

What were the lesions on Charles' feet and hand?

Why had Evrett knocked over the divorce case filings? What did Vanessa have to do with anything?

And why was I suddenly suspecting anyone and everyone I talked to?

Well, that last one, I was pretty sure was all about me, not them. Maybe Doc was on to something with the paranoia. Or maybe he was just trying to gaslight me. Because, you know, thinking you're being gaslighted isn't paranoid at all? I laughed as I ripped the page off my notepad, crumpled it into a ball, and threw it toward the recycling bin. It missed and joined the canister of tea, but was immediately attacked, pummeled and batted away down the hallway and into the file room. If the office ever comes under attack from balls of crumpled paper, Hoover will have us covered.

My cell phone sang out with the Reggae Carpet Cleaning jingle, and the caller identifier "Hate Him" came up on my screen. I answered it with a grimace, "Hi, Jack."

"Hey, Kam. How you holding up?"

"One more person asks me that and I'm gonna explode," I warned only half-heartedly. Jack didn't deserve me exploding all over him, but it was tempting nonetheless. "What's up?"

"I tracked down that account number. It's a private trust account in Canada."

"Canada?"

"Vancouver, to be exact. The name on the account is Willits."

"Willits…" I blinked. "Is there a first name?"

"Sara. S.A.R.A. Willets. The bank won't give out contact information to me, so I'm passing it over to Reggie. He can file an injunction."

"That's just weird. I've never heard the name. I'll check the office records and see what I can find out." I hesitated, then swallowed my pride. "Thank you, Jack. I appreciate all of your help."

"That's what I get paid for, darling."

Darling. I knew he meant it as a pet-endearment, the same as he'd call his dog, if he had one, or a neighbor-lady, but it shot a surge of something, something strangely sentimental, through me. "Well, thanks, anyway."

He was about to hang up when I stopped him, remembering what Patrick said about Andelle. There was only one other person I knew who had been in New Zealand. "Hey, Jack?"

"Yeah?"

"When you went to New Zealand, did you go surfing?"

I could almost hear his puzzlement over the phone. "You know I'm a lousy surfer. I went for the wine and the caving. We did go to Wailani beach, but I mostly watched the guys make asses out of themselves. Why?"

"What was the surf like?"

"You thinking about running away to New Zealand?"

"Well, you know me..." My big fat mouth blurted words before my brain caught up. "Running away is what I'm best at."

I hung up before he could respond and scribbled down on my new empty page, "Is Andelle who she says she is?"

Not that it mattered if she wasn't. Everyone who came to California seemed to want to reinvent themselves.

Sara Willits. I went to the file room and found the stack with the W's. Willits. Willits. Nada. Nothing. I checked the S's, just in case.

I called Reggie, but he was stumped, too. "Yes, Austin just called me about that. It's a substantial sum of money, and Juliet's injunction against the estate is going to stop those payments until it can get straightened out."

"Just like Charles dying and leaving the accounts to me in his will would have?" I groaned as a thought occurred to me. "Reggie? What if wherever that money is going is behind Charles' death? What if they thought it would all be paid out at once instead of coming in installments?"

There was a long silence at the other end of the phone, then finally he said in a very low voice, "When was the last time you slept?"

"I don't need sleep!" I hung up on Reggie. Quarter of a million in a high-interest account, even paying out twenty K a year, was a decent amount of money. And who knew how much had been in that account to start with. Well, Jack would know, or could find out, but I was full up on Jack-favors for the day. I turned to the second-best tool that I had: The Internet. Unfortunately, there were thousands of Sara Willits on the Internet, but none that I could find specifically in Vancouver. It was time to return to Evrett's lead, such as it was. Although what he would know about it, I couldn't fathom. I pulled up Vanessa's latest filing on my laptop, but it was all standard. "Evrett? Did Vanessa kill Charles?"

He didn't answer, at least not that I could see or hear.

Vanny Toreski and her eight husbands. Ex-husbands. All of whom she'd taken to the cleaners with Charles' help over the years. Eight husbands, eight suspects, well, except maybe Number Eight, Mr. Toreski. He didn't know about the avalanche barreling down on him yet. I scanned the folders, but none of the names looked familiar. On crime shows, the heroes always have pictures in the files, but divorces don't need picture ID. They just need signatures. "Who? Who?"

I flipped through them, mind racing, finally grabbing the phone. "Vanny? This is Kami from Hanford Legal. I'm sorry I put you off last week, but with..."

"Charles' death. Yes. I heard. I'm sorry."

I cleared my throat. "You don't have to worry about your case. I've completed your paperwork for you, but I'd like to meet with you. Do you have time today if I come by?"

"Well..." There was a long pause. "Yes, that would be fine. Robert is gone for the afternoon so the coast is clear."

I hung up. "Evrett, I owe you an apology. I think you were trying to tell me this all along."

The Crusader was reproachfully silent.

GRABBING THE FILES, I HEADED across town. I took my time and it was nearly 2 pm when I reached the gated community in Fremont where Vanny Toreski lived. I had to show my ID to a guard at the gate, then I was directed to Vanny's house, warned not to park blocking anyone's driveway, and the gates swung open. I rolled past a worn-looking grey pool-cleaning van, and a small black economy car where women in maid's uniforms were gathered, smoking before they returned to work. This was so not my neighborhood.

Vanny greeted me at the door. She was wearing jeans and a T-shirt along with diamond earrings and a gold necklace with a diamond garnished "V." Her feet were bare, showing off what was probably a two-hundred-dollar pedicure with tiny black and yellow butterflies painted on her big toenails. "Thanks for coming over. I just don't know how I could have found time to get downtown today."

She led the way to a flagstone patio in the back of the house, classy wrought iron chairs and a table laid with ice-tea and a plate of crackers, all overhung with a striped blue canopy. A sunken pool glittered like a palm-tree-surrounded oasis in an otherwise lush green lawn. So much for the California drought. I settled uncomfortably on a chair and let Vanny pour me a glass of ice tea.

"You have to stay hydrated. Dehydration is bad for the skin." She settled across from me, crossing her bare ankles neatly under her chair. A beam of sunlight glittered across her dyed blonde hair, revealing the faintest of grey roots. "Now, tell me what's going on with my divorce?"

"Can we speak freely?" I glanced around.

"Robert is on the yacht. Robert loves the yacht."

"And you don't?"

"Salt air is bad for the skin and hair." She eyed me carefully. "I don't even like to swim. And beaches? All that sand?" A delicate shudder shivered through her perfectly shaped shoulders.

I shrugged. I liked salt air. But that pretty much ruled out Vanny as a suspect, didn't it? I couldn't really see her traipsing down a sandy, salty, wind-blown beach to drown Charles. I changed the subject. "I brought you these to sign, and then I'll have someone from Oslo & Burroughs' review them before I file."

"Oh, very good." She scanned through the papers. "I've changed my mind about one thing... Let Robert have that stupid boat."

I blinked. She'd said she wanted the yacht. I'd rewritten the papers to include the yacht!

"You want to let Robert have the yacht?"

"Well, I don't need it." She fluttered a hand.

"Then sign these three, and I'll rewrite the distribution of property. I don't know if I can have it done before the end of the week, though. We might not be able to file until next week."

"That's all right. I'm in no rush. I've been with the schlub for two years. Another few weeks won't matter." She signed and initialed where I indicated.

"Vanny, I wanted to ask you… Your ex-husbands…" I hesitated, not sure how to ask if any of them were killers.

"If you're about to ask where they are today, I have no idea. Except for Ryan. He married my cousin Lydia. They live in Walnut Creek now. So silly. He should have married her all along. I think I was just a poor substitute."

I resisted raising my eyebrows. Okay, I could probably rule out Ryan. Six to go. "Were any of them really angry about your divorce? Angry at you, or at Charles, maybe, for how the divorce went?"

Vanny sat up straight, her tea glass tapping the table. "What's this about, Kami?"

"I'm not sure," I lied, not wanting another pile of disbelief stacked in front of me. "There's just something about Charles' death that bothers me. Vanny, were any of your ex's…"

"Violent? Lord no. I grew up with a violent father. I wouldn't marry a man like that."

"What about devious? Did underhanded things to undermine you after the divorce, maybe?"

Vanny flashed a handful of gold and gemstones in a dismissive wave. "Joseph was a stock broker—devious was in his blood. Alton? Anders? Anselm? What was his name? He was a… gosh…What was he again? I don't know. He was always on about drilling, and was always flying up to Alaska. I used neglect as the basis for the divorce suit. Let's see. My first husband…"

"Sherman?… the file says his name was Sherman Osborne?"

"Right. Ozzie, he went by. Like the rock star." She continued as if she hadn't heard me. "He had a business, some technology parts company. Profitable little thing, too. I sold it for half a fortune. Of course, he would never have sold it. Kept saying it was his life. He was angry, a bit, I think, when I left him. But he never loved me, not really. I was just some trophy to have on his arm at corporate events."

"Where is he today?"

"Oh, I have no idea. I haven't even thought about him in years."

"Were you ever afraid of any of them? Maybe something they said or did that frightened you?"

"Oh, sweetie. Aren't you adorable?" She laughed merrily. "I'm the scary one. Not them."

"Yes, but you wouldn't have a reason to hurt Charles."

Vanny blinked. "Never. Charles was the best man I've ever known. Terribly embarrassing for me when I realized that, well, I wasn't his type." Vanny started to laugh, but then stopped and stared at me. "My god, Kami. Are you suggesting someone killed him?"

I gathered up the files. "Can you think of anyone who might want to?"

"No man likes being bested by another, even if it's just in a court of law. But one of them?" She waved a perfectly manicured hand at the files in my arms. "Those losers just aren't capable."

I smiled but it felt thin. "Thanks, Vanny. I'll get the filing started and be in touch soon." But the little voice in the back of my mind was whispering over and over. If you lose enough, you're capable of anything.

MY MIND FULL OF MORE questions than answers, I was on my way to Reese's for a spot of dinner when a gleaming silver Rolls slid up in front of my door and Ms. Juliet Hanford got out. She was wearing peach today, including a peach colored hat that reminded me of the British sit-com "Keeping Up Appearances." She opened the office door without knocking, taking in the empty window as she passed.

"I see you didn't waste any time erasing my dear brother's

memory."

I stood my ground. "What do you want, Juliet?"

"I understand you're intending to fight my contestation of the will."

"I'm sorry." I smiled tightly. "Charles left me the business. He had faith in me."

She sniffed as though she smelled something unpleasant. "Misplaced, I'm sure. Oh…" Uh oh. Her eagle eyes had spotted Evrett. "Where were you hiding that?"

"Doesn't matter. It's mine." I planted myself between the knight and the witch. Not that I thought Evrett couldn't handle himself. For that matter, against Juliet he could probably handle himself better than me. At least he was genuine nobility. "I'm sorry, Juliet, but I intend to respect Charles' wishes."

"Charles was my brother, not yours." Juliet eyed me again. "What was his should come back to the family."

"He left you the house in England, and the family portraits and stuff, didn't he?" My heart was pounding and my tongue seemed to stick to the roof of my mouth. I was cowed, but there was no way I was going to let her see it. I clenched my teeth and kept my voice even. "Everything that belonged to the family went to you. He left me the business I've helped him build. I think that was more than fair."

"Fair? What do you know about fair? I came to the U.S. first, did you know? This was my fresh start! My new place. And he had to go ruin it, moving here, flaunting his shame all over, just like back in Leicester. How was I supposed to hold my head up in polite company with him in my way?"

"Shame?" I blinked as slow realization washed over me. "Oh. Oh my god. You mean because he was gay?"

"He ruined our family name back home. Ruined me. And then he had the gall to come here!"

I was stunned into silence. I had no idea how to even answer that. I moved to the door, opened it, and pointed.

"Throwing me out?"

I cleared my throat. "This is my building, after all."

She paused beside me. "Not for long, missy. Not for long."

She was almost back to the driver's side of her car when something occurred to me. "Wait? Juliet?"

"I won't stand for any more of your insults." She flung open the door of the Rolls so hard that the hinge creaked.

"No, that's not it. The name Sara Willits? Does that mean anything to you?"

She stopped, staring at me for a long moment. "Speaking of women that man ruined…"

And then she jumped into her car and squealed from the curb, narrowly missing a taxi angling for Reese's parking lot.

Women he ruined? Charles?

And how did ruined equate to twenty thousand dollars a year?

Now I had even more questions.

CHAPTER 9

San Amoro & Santa Cruz: Saturday Afternoon

PATRICK'S CHERRY RED Jeep Wrangler Unlimited, sporting its black hard top and luggage rack topped with surf boards and gear, rolled up in front of the office door, and I watched through the window as he walked up to the office and then strode in without knocking. "You ready to go?"

"Go where? What are you doing on this side of the hill?"

"The Paddle-Out. C'mon. Grab your stuff."

I held my ground, but at the same time was somewhat astounded. He'd driven all the way over from Santa Cruz to fetch me? "Not going. Sorry you drove all this way."

"You're going. Where's your jacket? Where are your shoes?" Patrick looked around and located my denim jacket on the coat hook behind the door and my sneakers under the folding desk. He waved them at me. "Put them on."

"I said, no."

He crossed his arms and stared at me. "People want to see you. And you need to see people."

"I do?" I did?

Patrick stared at me for a second, then apparently decided to change tacks. In fact, he put up the mainsail and pointed the rudder straight at me. "Think about it. If someone really did hurt Charles, don't you think the Paddle Out is the prime chance to see who had a grudge? It could say as much about the people who are there as who aren't."

Dang it all. I had too many questions and not enough answers, and I had a feeling that the only way to learn what I wanted to know was to attend. I would be there, but I wasn't going out. "Maybe you're right. But I don't feel like..."

"I'm dragging you whether you want to go or not, so put your shoes on."

I had a feeling that if I didn't give in, he was going to carry me. "Okay, but I'm not paddling. I'll go, but I'm not going out."

"Yeah. Sure." Trick looked smug.

I fed Hoover, patted Evrett's helmet, promised them I would be home before midnight, and then I climbed into the passenger seat of Trick's Jeep and let him drive me to Santa Cruz.

LATE SUMMER IN SURF COUNTRY is delicious. As we pulled into the lot above the beach, the full sun gleamed low on the horizon and a salt-brisk breeze swept in with the changing tide. The air was ocean-sweet with faint traces of sunbaked eucalyptus and old dried seaweed, combined with intermingled scents of apple-wood and charcoal. Patrick and Doc had rented out the picnic area at the head of the beach, and the caterer had arrived and had a barbecue trailer up and running. Down at the shoreline, a crowd was gathering with surf and paddle boards, and kayaks. It was a huge turn-out: over a hundred people by my rough estimate. "Wow. I didn't expect so many."

"Charles meant a lot to a lot of people, Kam." Patrick chided gently, reminding me that I'd been living inside of my own grief. I wasn't surprised to see Reggie and his life-partner, Skyler, among the crowd. I was a little surprised to see Jude Booder carrying what looked like a brand-new Krypto board under his arm. I was even more surprised to see Jack Austin heading down the stair, unmistakable with his red and white kayak balanced on his shoulder.

"Jack's here."

"Is that a problem?" Patrick was pulling on his wetsuit behind the door of the Wrangler and glanced over the top at me.

I wondered what would happen if I said yes? Would Patrick throw Jack off the beach? Or kick me off? Probably the latter. "No. I'm glad he came."

"I've got your spare board and your wetsuit from Grandma Jazzy's."

How had I missed that my old blue practice board was strapped to the roof rack of the Jeep? "I won't need them. But thanks anyway."

"Are you sure you won't paddle?"

I shook my head and watched Patrick unload his sleek hybrid board from among the several boards on top of the Jeep. Then he pulled down a yellow and white Walden Magic longboard. I felt a jolt of recognition followed by a wave of sadness and ducked my head to let it wash over me. "You brought Charles' board?"

"Of course. One last ride." Patrick hooked a board under each arm and jogged down the sea-stair to the beach. I followed more sedately, hanging near the BBQ area, grabbing a soda, and finding a seat on a picnic table where I could watch the Paddle Out kick-off. They moved out in a wave from the beach, a flow of brilliant colors that washed over the pale yellow sand, splashed down into the white surf, and then paddled out beyond the breakwater to the green-black Pacific waters. The mourners took turns dragging Charles' Walden Magic between them until they were out beyond the break, and there it floated alone, encircled and surrounded by those who had loved him.

The sun dropped to caress the ocean and the dark water lit up with orange and gold, the choppy swells glimmering like flames on the water. The caterers lit dozens of tiki torches, a bright light to guide the paddlers home, and I sat in the warm glow and wondered what words were being said, what songs were being sung. I trusted Doc and the others. And I didn't trust myself.

I sat alone on a picnic bench, my eyes focused out to sea, to the paddlers, and beyond.

"Quite a sight," a low voice murmured, and I realized that Manny was standing nearby, watching me.

"You didn't paddle?"

"Nah. More 'n enough folk on the water." He sat down next to me. "Hell of a sight, though. Don't reckon anyone will do that for me some day."

"Sure they will." But I wasn't sure. He was too migrant, too inconstant. Manny floated with the tides, bobbing along up and down the coast. Would anyone notice if he didn't return one day?

"You find out anything more 'bout that green van?"

I didn't want to talk about green vans, or secret suspicions. I shook my head. "Stopped looking. Coroner says it was an accident. Van was just a coincidence."

"Hmmm," was all Manny replied.

The ocean breeze turned cool, sand puffing along the rocks as the first stars started to twinkle overhead and the evening mist turned the horizon to shadowed haze. The turning tide caught the footprints the paddlers had left in the sand and carried them away out to sea, washing the sands clean. Good-bye, Charles. Good-bye. I miss you. Lord, how I miss you. You always knew what to do. And I never do.

Tears dragged themselves from my eyes, and I leaned my head on Manny's shoulder and let the grief wash over me as surely as the sea washed the shore. Focusing on the shadows of the paddlers out on the waters, I found myself holding my breath until they all turned back toward shore, paddling solemnly and safely to the sands. They came up the beach, and most moved to the showers and bathrooms to change into dry clothes before the feasting. It wasn't traditional luau fare, but I knew that Charles would have approved of the barbecued chicken, the corn on the cob, and the fat tubs of potato salad. No pretension, just good food and good friends. This was his kind of party.

"Let me take these back up to the rig," Patrick told me, a surfboard under each arm, his wet-suit half-stripped and hanging around his waist. I didn't miss the sideways glances Andelle was firing his way. I couldn't blame her. My cousin was an extremely well-built man. "I'll grab some dry clothes, and I'll be right back."

"You don't need to coddle me." I retorted, turning my back on him as he carried the boards away toward the stair.

"Believe me, no one would dare." Jack's voice came from my elbow and I gave him a grateful half-smile.

"Thanks for being here, Jack. I wasn't expecting to see you."

"Well, I figured that the funeral was for you to grieve. This was my chance to say good-bye."

Tears sprang to my eyes. "Oh, no. No… I didn't mean to keep you from…"

"No, don't worry about it. You were friends with him. I only knew him professionally." Jack was wearing a casual lightweight canvas jacket and khaki shorts. His pale hair was sprinkled with salt-water from the surf, and he looked comfortable and relaxed. And so incredibly handsome that had my heart not been broken, he might have taken my breath away.

"We don't have to segregate our friends, Jack. Or our grieving." I reached for his hand, stopped, and, not sure what to do with my own hand, rubbed my denim-clad thigh. Slick move, sister. You look like an idiot. "I'm glad you're here."

His beautiful blue eyes met mine and then looked away again. The sky had turned dusk grey and the golden light of the torches glinted off his sea-damp hair.

"So, who's this?" Andelle's accented voice interrupted. "Another cousin?"

Because he was blonde? But it was a sandy blond. And his boyishly handsome features were totally different from the chiseled lean look of Grandma Jazzy's lineage. And for some reason I didn't want him anywhere Andelle. "Not exactly. And I thought you were after Patrick?"

Andelle was sizing up Jack, and she leaned in with a smile. "A girl's gotta keep her options open."

Jack smiled back, his delicious sweet smile. "I'm Jack…" He held out his hand to Andelle, eyebrow raising in amusement. "…Kami's fiancé."

Andelle's hand had been halfway to his, and she froze, glancing to me before giving Jack's hand a cursory shake and letting go. "Oh! I didn't know you were engaged."

I didn't know whether to be mortified or amused. I hid my amusement by pressing my cold soda can to my blazing cheek. "Were is the operative word."

"Oh…so…you're not…?"

"She's far too amazing to remain with a boring old accountant, don't you think?" Jack gave me a gentle smile, and then turned his attention elsewhere. "Oh, Reginald and Skyler are here. I should say hello. Excuse me."

As he walked away, Andelle whistled. "Who woulda thought you'd be with that? He's fine."

Only she didn't say "fine." She said "faaayiiiyn," stretching it to five syllables. And really, I supposed he was. "Well, if you can catch him, you can have him." I told her with a shrug, "But if you're headed back to Auckland in the fall, I wouldn't do it. He's had enough heartbreak…" Because of me. "…already."

"Headed where?" She gave me a puzzled glance, then shrugged. "Yeah. Right. Well, nothing's set in stone, yah?"

"Not even wedding vows." I shrugged back. Not that I'd actually said them.

"Kam?" Patrick's voice came from my elbow. He'd changed into jeans and a T-shirt, but his hair was still wet, and sand clung to his bare feet. He had a bottle of water in his hand and was taking deep sips.

"Hey, Patrick." Andelle greeted him with a flirtatious wave. Jack was apparently already forgotten.

"Hi." Patrick practically ignored her and turned to me.

"Kam, I'm sorry. I'm not feeling so hot. If I'm going to drive you back to San Amoro, we should go soon."

"Lemme guess. You ate shrimp off that skanky lunch truck again? You'll never learn." I teased. "Let me just say good-bye to Doc and we can go."

Good-byes took a little longer than necessary, since everyone stopped me to say hi, but soon we climbed back up the sea-stair.

PATRICK TURNED ON THE RADIO as we drove out of Santa Cruz and merged onto Highway 17. We sang along with the first song, and then he fell silent. The evening was turning dark, the road delineated by reflected headlights, the trees turning to ominous grey shadows lining the road. I stared straight ahead, until I heard Patrick give a tired exhale. "You okay?"

"Yeah."

He didn't look okay. Beads of sweat were gathering on his forehead and his breath was coming faster.

"You need me to drive?"

"No." No one was allowed to drive his Wrangler. Except Grandma Jazzy. Grandma Jazzy got a pass on a lot of things. He shook his head like it was a snow globe. "I'm okay."

Traffic was surprisingly light, and we wended our way up to the top of the pass in good time. As we started down the twisting portion, the Jeep curved over the double yellow line and Patrick jerked the wheel, overcompensating before leveling back out.

"Sorry...."

"Cuz?" He was pale beneath his tan and his lips were practically white. "You should pull over. You really don't look good."

"Yeah..." He said it, but it was like the words didn't connect between his brain and his mouth. And then he slumped over the wheel, his foot mashing the accelerator, sending the Jeep rocketing off the road with a roar of the engine, tires screaming and metal shrieking.

CHAPTER 10

―――

Santa Cruz: Saturday Evening

I REMEMBER SCREAMING HIS name just before we crashed through the worn metal guardrail, and the airbag exploded into me, slamming me back and pinning me down as we plunged down the tree-filled embankment. Branches lashed at the Wrangler, shattering the windows, screeching across the metal and the plastic hard-top. I was screaming again as we slammed to a stop against the thick trunk of a California Redwood tree, my head snapping into the doorframe with a painful crack.

"Patrick!" I had to use both hands to punch down the slowly deflating airbag. Patrick was slumped against his airbag, seatbelt tight over his chest. He was alive. I could hear his breathing, short, rapid breaths. I was breathing, too, but my thoughts were a messy scramble. Ambulance. Need ambulance. Need help. My hands were as shaky as Patrick's pulse as I felt frantically at his neck. Everything in the Jeep had scattered, including my brain apparently, because it took me several frantic seconds of panic before I remembered that my cell phone was in the pocket of my denim jacket.

I somehow managed to navigate to the dial-pad and push 911 while trying to open my door, but it was jammed shut. I crawled over the seat and into the back to force open the back hatch. We'd come down a steep, rocky, fern and tree covered slope, and it was a good twenty or thirty yards to the top. Scrub brush pressed close on my side of the car, broken branches jutting around the flattened tires, scratching and clawing at me as I tried to get around the side of the Jeep to get to Patrick's door. The reek of leaking oil and ground redwood needles assaulted my senses.

The operator answered on the second ring. "911. What is the nature of your emergency?"

"Car accident. My name is Kami White." I told the operator. "Highway 17, we've gone through the rail."

"Can you see a mile marker?"

I could barely see the top of the cliff. "We went over the edge. I can't see anything. Please, my cousin is unconscious! We need an ambulance."

"Help is on the way," the operator responded. "Just stay on the line with me. Is your cousin breathing?"

Was he?

I struggled through the chaparral, manzanita, and, hopefully, not too much poison oak, adding to my scrapes and scratches, until I reached Patrick's door. It was caved in, and the window was smashed. I gingerly reached my hand through, feeling for the pulse at his neck, reassured when I still felt it. "He's breathing. I can feel his pulse, but he feels cold to me. I can't get the door open. It's stuck. There's trees, branches everywhere…" Something wet trickled down my face and I hoped it was tears and not blood. "Please, I need help."

"Help is on the way. Just stay with me. Are you hurt?"

Was I? I looked down at my body, then reached up. "Hit my head. Banged up a bit, but I don't think it's anything serious."

"Okay. Hold on. I have emergency services in route."

I put the phone on speaker and propped the hood to leave my hands free. "Patrick? Wake up, Patrick."

"Is he bleeding?" the 911 operator asked helpfully.

"It's pretty dark," I tried to explain, surprised when my

voice shook. "I can't see anything." I turned my attention back to Patrick, leaning into the car as far as I could, slowly pushing down the airbag and easing him back into his seat. He was like a rag doll. A six foot plus, all-dead-weight muscle rag doll. I used the flashlight feature on my phone, but the dim blue light didn't help much, and it was draining my battery fast.

"Patrick? Please wake up. Wake up."

There was no sign that he'd heard me, and I tilted my face up to the faint sounds of traffic above. "Help! Someone help me!"

"They're on their way, just stay on the line with me," the operator assured, but my phone was beeping.

"The phone's dying..." That was all I able to say before the screen went black. I was all alone. I slumped against the car, my fingers staying on Patrick's throat. Blood was trickling out of his mouth when he exhaled, and I realized that he had internal injuries. He was dying in my hands. "Hang on, 'Trick. Please just hang on."

The words became a mantra, darkness closing around me, the echoing roll of traffic above, the tiny crackles and crunches of the dried leaves and tired trees hanging over me, the faint gasping of air in and out of Patrick's lungs. Alone in the dark, years went by. Seconds, minutes, hours, months, eons of Patrick's labored breathing, my own shallow gasps, and my mantra. "Just hang on. Just hang on."

My hand went to my pocket, not even sure what I was looking for, and felt metal, cool and reassuring. Charles' Suunto Elementum Aqua watch. I fumbled for a moment with the buttons, and then the luminescent backlight gleamed pale blue, a lifeline in numbers. I counted the seconds with Patrick's pulse, erratic and faint under my fingertips. Time grounded, became solid, the eons falling to seconds which in turn counted their way into minutes, but I was no longer lost in them. They were a promise. There was help on the way. I just had to hold on.

The distant wail of sirens seemed like a dream when I first

heard them. Was I losing my mind, imagining rescue that was never coming? The sound grew louder and more strident until it was a scream that suddenly fell silent. Into the void it left, a sturdy deep voice yelled down to me, "Santa Cruz Fire Department! Is anyone down there?"

"I'm here! We're here! He's trapped in the wreckage! Please, help us!" I screamed at the top of my lungs, shock and relief rocketing a joyous hum through me. In moments, I was surrounded by men and women in uniform, their ropes unfurling around me and the broken Jeep as they rappelled down the cliff to my rescue.

My clothing was full of broken glass that left tiny scratches as it fell away as I was harnessed and guided back up the slope to the highway, where red and white flashing lights were being joined by blue and red, and I'd never been so happy to see an accident response crew in my life. There was a scream of a metal saw behind me as they cut Patrick free of the Jeep and strapped him into a buckboard to haul him up the cliff.

I managed to grab the EMT's arm. "Something was wrong before we crashed. He collapsed before we went over the embankment."

That was all they gave me the chance to say before the ambulance doors closed and it roared off with sirens wailing. A CHP officer started asking me questions, things like my name, Patrick's name, who owned the vehicle, how did the accident happen... I could barely form answers. My chest hurt from slamming into the seat-belt and I was aware of a slowly growing pain in my head and neck. A slow trembling started deep in my bones and rose through my entire body. The fire truck EMT came over, told the cop his questions could wait. The initial adrenalin was wearing off and I was shaking. Was this shock? The EMTs wrapped me up in an emergency blanket and I was toted off to the hospital.

PATRICK'S MOTHER WAS OUT OF the picture; our grandparents

had done most of his raising while Uncle Bill worked long-haul fishing rigs. Grandma Jazzy and Grandpa Dan had been Patrick's legal guardians for most of his childhood, and Grandma Jazzy wasn't about to let a little matter like adulthood stand in the way of that. I called them from the fire department ambulance but I don't remember what words I said. They arrived at the emergency room shortly after I did, and I could hear Granny Jazzy's strident voice echoing down the corridor. "My grandchildren are here, brought by ambulance. Kamera White and Patrick Tamsin... No, I will not wait over there. They need their grandmother! Where is my Patty?"

I'm sure it was the shock speaking, but I was willing to bet that Patrick would have died of embarrassment to hear the way she made it sound like my Coast Guard Captain cousin was a helpless six-year-old. For me, just the sound of her voice reduced to me to tears of gratitude and simultaneous laugher at calling Patrick "Patty." He despised the name Patty. The nurse cleaning my abrasions gave me a strange look as I laughed, probably wondering if she needed to recommend a psych admit.

The staff must have felt it was safer to let our grandparents through to us than to argue with Granny Jazzy. Grandpa Dan stayed with me while Granny was escorted away to find Patrick. Despite Grandpa Dan's repeated requests, no one in the busy ER could tell us what was happening with Patrick, but Grandpa never left my side. He even held my hand when they gave me a tetanus shot. I went through a thorough exam and X-rays to confirm that not only did I actually have a head, it was still attached to my neck and it had a perfectly fine brain in it. (Now wasn't that a miracle?) I was released with a diagnosis of concussion and bruised ribs, given a prescription for pain medicine, an ice pack, and orders to take it easy. They told me to come back if I experienced a range of symptoms that I hoped were written down on the release paper because I'd never remember them

We found Grandma Jazzy pacing back and forth in a

corridor. She wore a bright floral-print sundress and her long silver-blond hair was pulled up in a bun on her head. Her hands were splotched with paint—she must have been in her studio when I called. "The doctor says he'll come talk to us soon." Her smooth high-cheekboned face, so like my own, was wreathed with worry. "They said he's not doing well."

My legs were done holding me up, and I slumped into a chair and rested my head against the wall, gingerly pressing the ice pack to my bruised ribs. I could hear Granny Jazzy on the phone to Patrick's commanding officer. Grandpa Dan took my prescription and disappeared, presumably to the hospital pharmacy. Sometime later, he returned, pressing a pill and a paper cup of machine-made hot cocoa into my hand. "Take those. Keep your strength up."

"Should we call Uncle Bill?"

"He's up north."

North. That meant Alaskan waters. King crab or salmon. It also meant he was out of touch until he had a chance to call home. If the news was serious enough, Patrick's Coast Guard connections would get a message to his boat.

"What happened?" Grandpa Dan asked me at last. He'd said nothing, held all of his questions at bay until he knew that I was all right. But now, he wanted answers.

"I don't know. We were at the memorial, a Paddle-Out for Charles. Patrick said he wasn't feeling well, so we left. He was driving me back home. I thought…" I grimaced, thinking back. "No. I knew. I knew something was wrong. I asked if he wanted me to drive…"

"Not on your life." Grandpa Dan chuckled. No one drove Grandpa's classic '67 Chevy, either. Not even Grandma Jazzy.

I told them how the accident happened, but something was bothering me. Something besides the growing ache in my neck. "He was fine all day. He was fine for the Paddle-Out. They were on the water, oh, a half-hour maybe? Forty-five minutes?"

"You didn't go out?" Grandpa Dan had always encouraged me at water sports, but I shook my head.

"I'm mad at the ocean right now."

He patted my curls. Bits of broken glass from the windshield and door window fell away with his hand. I stood up and shook my head over the wastebasket in the corner, eyes closed tight against the cascading shards.

The doctor, a stressed looking emergency surgeon with thinning hair and thin face, came out and approached us just as Patrick's C/O from the Coast Guard arrived. We all stood together to hear the news. I held my breath.

"He's stable. He has a cracked vertebra in his neck, several broken ribs, a punctured lung, and a concussion. Healing is going to take time, but he's a strong young man. We'll need to keep him until his lung is clear and we're sending his x-rays to a spine specialist for review, but unless there are complications, he should be fine."

I'd never heard more beautiful words in my entire life. Grandpa Dan gave me a gentle one-armed hug, and I wasn't sure if it was for me, or if it was to steady him. I bore up straight and hugged him back.

"Our real concern is his heart-rate," the doctor continued. "He was tachycardic when he came in, though it seems to have stabilized on its own. Once he's recovered a bit, we'll run an EKG and a few other tests, but you can see him now if you'd like."

I let Grandma Jazzy go first, and she swept into the small hospital room with a theatrical flourish. "Oh, Patrick. What have you done to yourself this time?"

Grandpa Dan gave me a knowing grin, and I smiled back. Poor Patrick. Just thank heavens that my mother wasn't here because that was the last thing I...

"Kamera!"

Nuts.

Jaxine Tamsin White, eldest child of Jasmine "Jazzy" Tamsin, stepdaughter to Daniel Tamsin, swept down the corridor toward me. Her long blond hair, streaked with grey, was bound in a braid and her flowing floral broomstick skirt

swept around her Birkenstock sandals as she came toward us.
Behind her, to my everlasting surprise, was my brother Kenny
in worn jeans and Converse sneakers.

"You called Mom?" I gave Grandpa my best "how could
you betray me this way" glower, but he just shrugged.

"Well, I knew you wouldn't."

Jaxine's eyes, just a shade darker than my own, scanned
over me from head to toe, and, seemingly satisfied that I was
in one piece, she demanded, "Where's Patrick? Is he okay?"

"I'm great, Mom. Thanks for asking." I moved into her
arms to give her a hug, which she returned with a little more
force than necessary. Every muscle in my body was starting to
ache. My ribs were on fire, and the pain pill had yet to do start
its magic.

"Oh, baby, I can see that you're fine." She turned her head,
pretending that she wasn't tearing up. What the heck had
Grandpa told her on the phone? Was she expecting to find me
dying?

Kenny looked me up and down. "They have to put you
back together with Superglue?"

"Nah. It was an Elmer's Paste job." I wanted to smile at him,
but my face hurt.

I slipped in behind Grandma Jazzy to see Patrick. He was
hooked up to all kinds of monitors. There was a drain-tube
from his chest, a neck brace cradling his head, and he had a big
bruise across his forehead, but overall, he looked pretty good
for a guy who'd just driven over a cliff.

"I dunno what happened. I know I wasn't feeling very
good, but I thought I was okay... then I just blacked out," he
was explaining. He looked as confused as I felt.

"You hadn't been drinking, right?" His C/O obviously
wasn't one to pussy-foot around.

"Just bottled water," I answered. "I was with him the whole
time, except when they were paddling."

"It's just so weird. I don't get sick..."

It was true. Patrick's one of the healthiest people I know. He eats right, exercises regularly, and overall has the constitution of a rhino.

Suddenly, he blinked and stared wildly around at us. "What about my Jeep? Where's my Jeep?"

"At the bottom of a cliff, cuz." I answered abruptly. "That's where we ended up. The EMTs had to cut you out of it. I'm not sure it's still Jeep-shaped."

"Oooooh." His eyes slid shut again. "Guess I should have let you drive, huh?"

"Guess so." I reached down to squeeze his hand, the one that didn't have an IV line hanging out of it. And stopped. "Patrick? What's that? Did you have that before?"

There was a small lesion, almost like a mosquito bite, on the inside of Patrick's arm. There were two of them, in fact. Patrick lifted his arm and gingerly poked at it with his other hand.

"Looks like bug bites. Mosquitos are bad this year because of the late rain." Grandma Jazzy leaned over, lowering her glasses to take a good look. "You should put some calamine on that."

"Does it itch? I've got something right here..." Jaxine was rummaging in her purse. "It's a nice soothing aloe with calendula in a coconut oil base..."

"It doesn't itch. It's tender..." Patrick was poking at it. "Like, sensitive. It doesn't hurt, though."

"You have a morphine drip, cuz," I reminded him. "You probably aren't feeling much of anything right now."

"I feel pretty good, actually... like, you know, I drove over a cliff...but hey, good."

"I just bet you do," his CO joked. "See how you feel when that stuff starts to wear off."

"Probably a glass sliver." Grandpa Dan took Patrick's wrist and held it up to the light. "Kami's practically covered in broken glass."

"From my Jeep?" The pained look on Patrick's face had very little to do with any broken ribs.

"No, cuz. From the trees you ran over on the way down." I smiled to take the sarcastic sting from my words.

You know that look that most pre-teens figure out right about the age of eleven? The one that squints one eye and pops the other one wide, and half-smirks the mouth? The one that says, "You are such a moron, freak."? It's harder to do effectively when one has a black eye and a huge bruise on the forehead, but somehow Patrick managed it. If Grandma Jazzy hadn't been there, he probably would have followed it up by sticking out his tongue. Yup. Maturity runs in our family.

"It feels more like a sliver, but I can't see anything there..." Patrick turned his arm left and right, but couldn't turn his head for a closer look. The painkillers were keeping his eyes from focusing. "Maybe the nurse can look at it."

"Look, I hate to sound crazy or anything, but..." Crazy was my specialty, wasn't it? I took a deep breath. I didn't want Jaxine and my grandparents to worry about us. "Isn't that kind of like the marks they found on Charles during his autopsy? I assume you'd know if you were stung by a jellyfish, right?"

"There were no sea nettles in the water today." Patrick and I exchanged glances. This wasn't something to discuss in front of the parental units or commanding officers.

While my grandparents and mother fawned over Patrick, I tugged my brother out into the hallway. "Hey. What have you been up to?"

"My art, mostly. Trying to find a buyer for my book." He shrugged.

His "book" was a graphic novel project that he'd been working on since high school, some kind of sci-fi post-apocalyptic thing. I really didn't know that much about it. To tell the truth, a lot of the artwork just freaked me out; women with the bodies of cars, mechanical men, giant robots with human faces in their abdomens. It was just freaky. "Working?"

Kenny shrugged again. "Gotta real sweet gig right now. Free rent and base salary in exchange for looking after my landlord. He's in Vegas half the time anyway, so I just have to feed his cat and water the plants. Nice old guy. I have an apartment over the garage. Gives me lots of time to work on the book."

I sighed. I was unemployed and sleeping on a sofa in my office. For once, my brother's slacker lifestyle sounded more responsible than my own life. "Listen, have you talked to Jude Booder lately?"

Kenny looked surprised. "Yeah. Pretty much every week. Why?"

"Just wondered if he's working too, or if he's got some kind of side gig going. I mean, he just bought a new surf board, and he's acting like it's no big deal. But it's an expensive board. Just think it's weird."

Kenny tugged at his long blond braid. Yeah, that's right. I've got hellish wild curls but my brother has gorgeous blond hair that Christina Aguilera would kill for. "I kinda wondered myself. He's been buying art lately."

"Buying art?"

"Yeah. He just goes through my sketches and finds things he likes and has me dress them up. Just little stuff, mostly from my emo phase, like skulls and roses, wolves, anime faces; that kind of thing. Mostly stuff I'd even forgotten I'd done."

"And he's paying for it?" Okay, that was weird.

"Well, mostly we trade for it. You know, pot and stuff."

That I didn't want to know. "Where's he getting the money?"

Kenny shrugged again. "I'm not his babysitter, Kam. Why do you care, anyway? You thinking about givin' the Booder a second chance?"

I gagged. "He never had any chance. If I didn't feel like crap, I'd kill you for that."

Kenny just grinned. "You'd try, anyway."

My grandparents joined us in the corridor, as did my mother. "They're kicking us out. Said he needs to rest."

"So do I." I moaned. "Everything aches. Mom? Can you take me back to San Amoro? Hoover's been alone all day and I still have work to do."

And research to catch up on.

"Nonsense." Granny Jazzy planted herself firmly in front of me. "You need spoiling. You're staying with Grandma and Grandpa tonight. Give your key to Jaxine so she can fetch that little muskrat back to her place."

"He's a hairless Sphynx cat, not a muskrat." But Hoover did love my mother. She was a source of naughty forbidden foods, like creamed tuna and chicken salad. "No, I want to go home."

WHAT I WANTED APPARENTLY COUNTED for little because an hour later, I was tucked away in Grandma Jazzy's north-facing guest bedroom, the one with the wild horse motif and the carved wooden lamp shaped like a rearing mustang. When we were kids, there'd been two sets of bunk beds in here, but now that the grandkids were all grown, there was a comfortable queen-sized bed with a pull-out roller bed underneath. The old flannel camp sheets had been replaced with heavenly eight-hundred thread count cotton and my sore and grateful body eased down into a goose-down mattress cover. Grandma Jazzy had tried to get me to eat some clam chowder and garlic bread, but I felt nauseous and not very hungry. The second painkiller kicked in, erasing the sharper of the pains, and I drifted off to sleep to the comforting sounds of crickets drifting through the half-open window.

CHAPTER 11

Santa Cruz: Sunday Morning

I WOKE TO THE SOUNDS of Reba McEntire and the heavenly scent of Grandma Jazzy's blueberry pancakes drifting up the stairs from the kitchen. I discovered, much to my chagrin, that waking up and actually getting up were two very different things. The doctor had warned that I'd feel worse today, but every muscle in my body seemed to have locked up. My head hurt, my neck hurt; I had bruises on both my knees that I knew must have come from the accident but that I hadn't felt the day before. Every muscle in my back, shoulders and legs seemed to have gone on strike. Even breathing was torture.

With heroic effort, I rolled myself out of bed and onto the floor. Score one for me! I crawled into the guest bathroom and discovered that Granny Jazzy had laid out fresh towels, along with a clean T-shirt blazoned with a screen-printed floral design that read "Jazzy Art Studios, Santa Cruz" on it, and cotton Bermuda shorts in dark blue that I was betting were fresh from the gift shop right next to Granny's studio. The hot shower soaked enough of the ache out of my bones that I was able to limp down to breakfast in my fashionable tourist-wear.

MAKING COPIOUS USE OF THE wooden stair-rail, I trailed downstairs to find Granny Jazzy in the kitchen, bustling about over her electric grill, the same one she'd had when we were kids. The most amazing things come off that grill.

"Your mother called," Granny Jazzy informed as she slapped a plate on the table for me. Gran still served breakfast on the same melamine plates with the teal flower design that she'd served us on when we were kids, the cheap unbreakable ones. Like we were still as prone to breaking them at twenty-eight as we were at eight. "Your muskrat is happy as a clam at her house. They've been having adventures."

I hoped those adventures didn't include the kind that were going to mean stinky litterboxes for days. Hoover, for all that he'll eat anything, really does have a delicate constitution. And Jaxine loves to indulge him. "Oh good. He's been so lost without Charles." So had I, to tell the truth. Granny Jazzy poured me coffee from the French press, dosing it with milk just the way I liked it, heaped my plate with pancakes and added a bowl of strawberries and diced honeydew melon. I dutifully picked up my fork and dug in. Hey, if she was determined to coddle me, who was I to say no?

The mudroom door banged open and I was surprised to see Grandpa Dan holding the door open for Nicky. I glanced to Granny Jazzy, but she just shrugged, her crystal blue gaze inscrutable.

"Hey, Nicky. Thanks for dropping by." Grandpa Dan settled down across from me and reached for a coffee cup. "That alternator was a tough one to find."

Like I really thought he'd called my best friend over to bring him an alternator? I wasn't five anymore. He'd called a babysitter for me, not an auto mechanic for his Chevy.

"Sure, no problem." Nicky bobbed her head and I knew darn well it was to try to hide their little ruse from me. I was a poor liar, but Nicky had more tells than poker-playing mobsters. She scooted in a chair and within seconds was being served a huge pile of pancakes and bacon. Her hair was back in a pony-tail, and her expression was dark with concern as she eyed me head to toe. Her voice, however, was anything but concerned. "Hey, girl. You kinda look like crap."

That was Nicky for you. Straight to the point. But somehow, her tough-love attitude made me feel better. "Yeah, I kinda feel like it. Alternator, huh?" I would have raised an eyebrow but my whole face hurt.

Grandpa ignored me to exchange a conspiratorial glance with Nicky. "So, what's on your agenda today? Back to bed with you?"

I really wanted nothing more than to lie down somewhere dark and quiet until all the aches went away, but I didn't suppose that was an option. "I think I need to talk to some of the surfers who were at the Paddle Out. Something happened to Patrick yesterday, and someone has to have seen something."

Granny Jazzy eyed me seriously over her coffee cup, a black mug that read "Artists Do It With Flair" in hot pink letters. "Kami, do you really think someone tried to hurt Patrick?"

Did I? "I don't know, Gran. I hope not. But he was fine before we got to the Paddle-Out, and then by the time the barbecue was on, he wanted to go home. Patrick doesn't get sick, like, ever." I sipped my coffee and instantly felt comforting warmth shoot through my veins. Granny Jazzy didn't mess around with her bean.

Nicky gave me a long look. "Why would anyone want to hurt Patrick? Everyone likes him."

"Except Kelli-Ann." I mentioned his ex-wife and got a swift stare-down from Granny Jazzy. She was a big believer in the once-family-always-family way of thinking. Kelli-Ann didn't stop being family just because she stopped being married to Patrick. And I had to admit that I was being unfair. Kelli-Ann loved Patrick but couldn't stand watching on the shore as he sailed into the worst of storms on rescue missions. I think if he'd been willing to give up the sea, she might have stayed, but he wasn't a giving-up kind of guy. So, she gave up on him. We all had to make choices, and some of them resulted in cross-state bus rides.

"Is there still a spare bicycle in the shed?" Even as I said it, my swollen bruised knees protested. There was no way I was cycling anywhere today.

"There is, but you're in no shape to ride it." Grandpa said sternly. "Have you looked in the mirror this morning?"

I actually hadn't. I'd been afraid to. Granny Jazzy opened the utility closet door where a full-length mirror hung on the back. Oooh. Nicky's adjective didn't begin to cover it. I looked halfway to zombiefied. There was a purple swollen bruise all the way down my cheekbone, myriad glass scratches on my face and arms, and another ugly purple-blue mark from the seat-belt that spread down the side of my neck and into my T-shirt. Tugging the collar of my T-shirt aside I could see that it continued all the way across my chest. I looked like I'd rolled over a cliff, with or without a Jeep Wrangler wrapped around me. "Ouch."

"Ouch, indeed." Granny Jazzy laughed a little. "Nicky can drive you, can't you, sweetie? You can take my Fiat if you want. Just drop me at the studio first."

"No need. I've got the FrankenStang today." Nicky grinned over her last bite of pancake.

Grandpa dusted off his grey Carhartt jacket that he'd had as long I could remember. "I'll be at the hospital with Patrick, but I want you girls to call me if you need anything." He waved his cell phone, a gleaming white iPhone that sent a jolt of envy through me. Even Grandpa had a better phone than me. The envy was erased by his next words. "I think I've mostly figured out how this thing works"

Granny Jazzy handed the sheet of instructions from the hospital and my bottle of prescription pain medicine to Nicky. "She can have one every four hours if she needs it. If she starts getting confused, or nauseous again, take her straight back to the ER, and give me a ring at the studio. I'll be right there."

That was my grandparents. Free range parenting, but there when you needed them.

I was tempted to just lean the car seat back and let Nicky drive me around Santa Cruz all morning, but instead, I listened to the surf report and figured out where the gang would be. When most people think Santa Cruz and surfing, they think of Pleasure Point, or The Mavericks. Pleasure Point had the advantage of regular consistently good surf, but it was also a tourist magnet. If there's better surf running, the locals know the secret spots. The Mavericks only come in during winter, and are up past Half-Moon Bay. They were also only for crazy people who loved deadly big waves. In other words, not for me. "I'm guessing they'll be at Manresa."

"Manresa it is." Nicky flipped on her blinker and made the sharp turn onto Ocean.

We'd just arrived at the beach parking lot when my cell phone jingled its way through the Nino's Pizza song. The caller ID read "Hate Him." I stepped out of the car and answered. "Hi, Jack. What's up?"

Nicky heard Jack's name and sidled around the hood to put her head close to my ear. I pushed her away but she reached for the phone to take it from me. I tried to listen to Jack through the battle for my phone.

"I just dropped by your office, but you aren't here."

Was that an accusation? "No, sorry. I'm in Santa Cruz. Bit of an emergency." I evaded explaining about the accident, and to my relief, Jack didn't press the issue.

Nicky managed to get the phone for a half for a half-second. "Hey, Jack. Kami can't talk right now. She bonked her head last night, and..."

I wrested the phone back and reached to stamp on her foot, but my knee was too sore and swollen. Not only did I miss, but I sent a jarring stab of pain through my leg that left me gasping and leaning against the FrankenStang for support.

"Hi, Nicky..." Jack was saying in long suffering tones.

"I'm back. Nicky can't mind her own business."

"As I'm well aware." Was it just me, or was he genuinely

amused by that. "What was Nicky saying about you bonking your head?"

"Little accident, no big thing." I downplayed.

"Are you okay?"

"Yes, of course I am. Patrick's a little messed up, though."

There was a moment of silence, and I knew Jack was wondering how much he should press for details. Finally, he said in a low voice, "How's Patrick?"

"Like I said. Messed up bit. He's in the hospital with a punctured lung, broken ribs, that kind of thing. He'll take time to heal. But you know 'Trick. He's a rock." I glanced at the clock. Tide was going to be going out soon. "Really, Jack. There's nothing to worry about. I stayed with Granny Jazzy last night and apparently, she and Grandpa conspired to get Nicky to babysit me today. You know how Granny gets."

"Yes. Yes, I do. I also know how you are. Thank Nicky for me." Damn it, he really was amused! "Well, the reason I called is that I have some paperwork for you to sign. It establishes a stipend on the business accounts, so that you can keep the office open, pay your salary, etcetera. Juliet's injunction won't apply to it, like it will to the bulk of the inheritance."

It hadn't been a bad morning so far, but now it looked so much better. "Oh, Jack. That's awesome! Thank you!"

"That's my job." His voice was matter-of-fact.

Of course it was. Just doing his job.

"I also looked into that account you asked me about. It was transferred from Arthur's estate when he died. Kami, did you know Arthur was married before he met Charles?"

Arthur. Charles' life partner? I suddenly remembered what Juliet had said about ruining lives. Had Arthur left some poor woman for Charles? "I had no idea. Charles never mentioned it."

Nicky stopped fighting for the phone and leaned on the car hood, head tilted to try to catch Jack's words. I gave in and put the phone on speaker.

"Well, that money is paying into a trust fund. Sara Willets

is Arthur's ex-wife's name but the account is set up so that she couldn't touch it until last year. But she hasn't. Kam, there's almost four hundred thousand in there."

"Okay, you're the money guy. Why would someone do that?"

"Lots of reasons. It could be some kind of retirement fund for her, or some kind of long-term medical care. I don't know." I could visualize Jack's sexy little one-shouldered shrug over the phone. I mean, his weird deprecating shrug that was just annoying. Because, well, not sexy. "I just know that Arthur set it up and Charles has maintained the payments. Now that account funding the withdrawals goes to you. You can stop the payments into the trust if you want to."

I shook my head, then remembered he couldn't see me over the phone. "Not until I know what it's for. It was important to Arthur. And clearly it was important to Charles to keep it going after Arthur died. I won't go against their wishes."

"Okay, right. So, you're in Santa Cruz?"

"I'll probably come back tomorrow. Mom has the cat, so I don't have worry about him."

"Well, meet up with me Tuesday and I'll take you to lunch so you can sign these things."

Nicky shook her head at me. Lunch with the ex-fiancé was a no-no in her book.

I glanced in the mismatched side-mirror on the FrankenStang. I looked like a walking advert for first aid supplies. I didn't think anything as simple as lunch could get out of hand. "Okay, sounds good."

I rang off with a cheery "See you Tuesday!" but inside I was kicking myself. Lunch? With Jack? I'd had worse ideas but I wasn't entirely sure when. I guess I was feeling reckless since Jack told me he could get a stipend on the accounts. I wasn't going to be stuck with a building and no way to pay for it. Yeah, that's it. It was all about the money.

Andelle, Jude, Rick, and Manny were all on the water when Nicky and I made our way down the sandy beach. The surf was coming in tall even rollers, perfect for practicing stunt moves. Andelle was sweeping back and forth, her smooth switchback making it look easy. (It wasn't, and I'd worn more than my fair share of rock-scrapings and sand-burns from wipe-outs.) The guys were further out, watching as she rode the wave until it mushed out on the shore. I caught her eye and waved, and she bundled her board under arm to meet us.

She was wearing a waist-length body-tee over her wetsuit and still looked cold, but she was wearing that grin, that one that doesn't go away for hours after you've caught a good wave and had an awesome ride. "Hey, Kam. What happened? You get in a fight??"

Nicky laughed. "Only with me."

So, then I had to explain about the accident, and that led to talking about Patrick being in the hospital.

"Oh, that sucks." Andelle's face fell as she pulled a bottle of sports-drink out of her bag and chugged half of it. "He's a good guy, 'Trick is."

"You've only known him a couple days."

"Yeah, but some of these guys, you can just tell, ya know."

Yeah. Except that I didn't trust my own judgement. It was from long experience that I knew that Patrick was a good guy. "Hey, I wanted to ask you… the other day when we met on the street, Patrick said something to you? Some word? Sounded foreign? What was that?"

Andelle shrugged. "Don't remember."

My heart was beating faster, and to hide my expression, just in case the swelling and bruising wouldn't, I turned my face toward the water. Jude was paddling hard to bridge a fresh wave and I stalled to buy time to think. "Jude's new board looks good."

"Yeah. Wasted on him, though. He shoulda stuck with a longboard."

He made the pop-up and curved the board to the wave.

So far so goo...oops! He overcompensated on his back foot as the wave started to roll and down he went, white foam crashing over him. I winced. "He'll get the hang of it." Why was I defending Jude Booder? Because Andelle was lying to me. She was an outsider. A summer person. Jude was family. Well, as close to family as a brother's best friend that I didn't speak to could be. "It means 'be well,' it's a greeting. In Maori. Like 'hello.'"

"What?"

"Kia ora." I shifted away from watching Jude Booder struggle out of the surf and paddle out again. "It means 'hello' in Maori. And if you were really from New Zealand you would know that."

Andelle froze, her wide-set eyes staring me down, her wet black curls trailing drips of sea-water down her cheek like misplaced tears.

"Where are you really from?" I asked the question lightly, but followed it up with, "And why would you lie about it? Are you a fugitive or something?"

She clenched her drink bottle between her fingers, the plastic making crinkling noises under the pressure. Her eyes were focused out to the water where Manny was paddling adjacent to an incoming swell, but she finally said, "I really don't think that's any of your business."

Nicky stepped up behind me, ready to play Bad Cop. "I think when you lie to us, it starts being our business."

Andelle was bigger than either of us, and I was in no condition to take a pummeling. Nicky could handle her own, but I didn't want it to come to that. "I'm not asking for me, Andelle. Something happened to Charles the other morning, and something happened to Patrick last night. You said 'Trick's a good bloke. If you mean that, you'll help me find out what happened to him."

"I would never hurt Charlie." Watching, it seemed her expressions folded closed, a painful stillness, granite walled and thick, coming over her. "And I wouldn't hurt Trick."

"But someone did."

"And that someone needs to pay for it." Nicky took being Bad Cop very seriously.

"I just want to make sure it's the right someone," I reassured. "Why did you lie about where you're from? Are you Australian? English? Is your Visa expired? Something else?"

Andelle's gaze was on the ocean. "It was stupid. And now it's over. I'm going home next week, and I don't have anything to show for it."

"Where's home?"

Andelle glanced to me and then at Nicky, who was still playing the tough chick with crossed arms and splayed legs.

"Would you believe me if I just told you that I didn't have anything to do with what happened to either of them?"

"Not if you flee. If you leave, you'll never convince me that you're telling the truth."

"Flee? No!" Andelle's eyes flared in a horrified glance. "I just... Summer is almost over, and I have to go back to school in Vancouver. Canada, that's where I'm from."

Jude had given up wallowing in the surf and was extricating himself from the water, tucking his board under his arm.

"And where is school?"

Nicky, realizing Jude was coming, decided to pick up the pace. "Give it up, Kam. She's not sayin' nothin'. Let's just take what we have to the cops and let them deal with it."

"You don't have anything to take to the cops!" Andelle's tone was more hopeful than certain and I had to admit that Nicky's tough routine was working.

"Yeah, we do. You lied about who you are, and you were at the location of both incidents. That can easily make you an object of suspicion. And rumor has it you were spending a lot of time hanging around Charlie here at the beach. That's enough to go on." I tried to make it sound like I had more than I did, but what I had was bupkis.

Andelle grabbed my arm, and for a second I thought she was going to pummel me. Welp, walked into that one, didn't

I? Instead, she turned me back up the beach, away from Nicky and the rapidly approaching Jude. Her accent was suddenly faded, a pretense too heavy to keep up now that she'd been discovered. "Fine. But you won't like what I have to say."

"Try me," I deadpanned. "I almost died last night. Nothing you say could be worse than that."

She took a deep breath. "My name is Laura. Andelle is my middle name. My real last name is Ramone. I came here looking for my father."

"Arthur Ramone." I filled in, realizing the truth with a shock. Arthur's daughter. No wonder she'd pretended to be someone else. "Wow. Andelle, I'm so sorry."

"When I learned I was too late, that he was already dead, I just wanted... I wanted to get to know the man he left us for, you know, my mom and me. Mom didn't talk about him after he left us. I was just a little girl. Couldn't even remember his face. Mom burned all his pictures. I spent half my college money on a private detective, but by the time I could afford to come here, I was too late." She huffed, blowing a wisp of damp black hair from her face. "I didn't know what to do. I wanted to understand, but if I just showed up and said, 'Hey, your lover was my dad'... Would he slam the door in my face? Maybe he'd think I wanted something, money or something. The P.I. told me that he liked to surf, and I surf... So, I thought, maybe I could just meet him, you know. But I got to know him, and I wanted to tell him. I really did." Her words drifted off, then she turned to look carefully at me. "It just never seemed like the right time. Kam, you gotta believe me. I'd never have hurt Charlie. Never."

I nodded, my mind racing as it digested the revelation, "Andie, is your mom's name Sara?"

Andelle looked down at me with a tilted lost gaze, a little girl who didn't understand why her father had left her. Well, that was something I could relate to.

"Sara Willets. That's your mom, isn't it?"

Her eyes flickered wide again. "How'd you know that?"

"What I know is that your father set up a trust fund for you in your mother's name. Charles has been paying into it since Arthur died. No one could touch it until you turned twenty-one. Andelle, your father cared about you and wanted to make sure you were taken care of." I smiled as gently as I could with my bruised face. "And more importantly, Charles must have already known about you if he kept feeding into that trust fund. If you'd just been honest, he would have accepted you with open arms."

"Mom's proud. She would never have taken money from anyone, especially not Dad." A tear tipped over her cheek and she swiped it away with her wrist, leaving a sand-spot behind. "I just wish…" Andelle stopped herself and straightened, letting the brisk sea breeze flash dry her curly raven hair. "Too late for stupid wishes now. I take it you believe me?"

"Yeah, I do, though I might not have if I hadn't just talked to my accountant about that trust account. We should get that straightened out. It's your money after all." I dug around in my messenger bag and located Jack's card. "You met Jack at the Paddle-Out. He has all the details on the trust fund. The rest of the money earmarked for you is tied up in probate on Charles' estate right now, but it's yours. I'll make sure it gets to the trust."

Andelle dropped down on the sand, cradling her head in her hands and staring out to the ocean. "I don't give a damn about any money. It was my father I was looking for."

"Think about it." I'm not exactly touchy-feely, but I reached down and gave her wet-suited shoulder a squeeze. "It's kind of a lot of money. And your father wanted you to have it."

"I'll think about it." But her gaze was on the waves, and her mind, if I, as fellow daughter of an estranged father, had to guess, was elsewhere lingering on possible regrets and lost opportunities.

I started to walk away, back toward to Nicky and Jude, but suddenly Andelle called me back. "Kam? How well do you know Jude?"

"He was my brother's best friend when they were kids.

He's kind of always been around, like a second annoying little brother. Why?"

Andelle shrugged. "Maybe it's nothing, but Jude was at the Paddle-Out yesterday, and he was at the beach the day Charles' drowned. And… Well, this could be nothing."

I really didn't think Jude was capable of murder, but I also didn't trust him. That probably stems from the time he helped my brother raid my bra drawer and draped my intimates all over the neighbor's shrubbery. "What's nothing?"

"I don't think he's hanging out with good peeps." Andelle's gaze traveled up to the parking lot and back to me. "I hear him on the phone, talking about deals and meet-ups. Then, just when the swells are coming in good and the waves are perfect, he says he's gotta go and just takes off. I think he's into something. I don't know, you know him better than I do."

It all just added to my suspicions.

"Have you seen a green van hanging around at all?"

"Green van?" Her head tilted, her gaze shifting back to the water. "Can't say I've been paying attention. Why?"

"Something Manny said, is all. Doc saw it, too."

Andelle shook her head, and slumped back into the sand, her eyes watching the water. Our conversation was over, and I left her lost in reflection on the beach.

WHEN I REJOINED NICKY, SHE was listening to Jude yammer on about his new board. It was a beautiful board, sleek and smooth. And new. My good board was second-hand, at least eight years old. My practice board was ancient, if it still was a board. I needed to go track down Patrick's Jeep and find out what, if anything, of our gear had survived.

I waved at Jude's new board appreciatively. I hoped Jude wouldn't take it as some kind of innuendo.

Nicky caught my eye and spoke for me. In the years since I'd stopped talking to Jude, she'd become an awesome interpreter. "How much did that set you back?"

"It wasn't cheap." He gave me a grin that showed the chipped lower tooth where he'd gone over the handlebars of his bike when he was fifteen. We'd been racing down a hill. I won, purely by default since I didn't stop when he crashed and both Patrick and Kenny did.

"I didn't know you were working." Nicky was bad-cop-ing again, but I was pretty sure that wasn't the way to get to Jude Booder. "How'd you afford a board like that?"

"Did some odd jobs." Jude shifted to block our curious gazes from his board. "What were you and Delle powwowing about?"

"I could use a coffee," I told Nicky, giving Jude a "see ya later" kind of wave with one hand.

Nicky nodded and followed me. "I'm still jumping from Granny Jazzy's killer brew. I swear she puts meth in that stuff."

"She was a party-girl in the 60s," I reminded Nicky. "I try not to think too hard about her secret ingredients. But I'm pretty sure the coffee is unadulterated."

We headed back to the car. "So, what's Andelle's deal?"

"It's up to her if she wants to tell you," I knew I could trust Nicky not to pry. Too much, anyway. "But she's from Canada. She came here to find her father. I actually feel really bad for her."

"Did she find him?" Nicky gave me a sideways glance as we climbed back into the FrankenStang.

I shook my head. "She was too late."

We headed for Finn's and I told Nicky about the mysterious green van. "You don't remember seeing one, do you?"

"Green van? What year? What make? What model? Panel van? Camper van? Transport van? V8? V6?" Light green? Dark green?"

"I don't know. I haven't even seen it." I laughed despite that fact that my leads were all going cold. I should just leave detecting to the cops. Except that the cops thought Charles' death was a suicide. "I don't really want coffee, but I want to see if we can spot that van."

We spent the rest of the morning cruising around Santa Cruz in the FrankenStang, feeling a little like grown women trying to relive our high-school days, telling jokes and checking out the tourists, but there was no sign of a green van.

"Wanna hear a theory?" Nicky asked, as we drove through for burgers and milkshakes.

My face hurt and chewing was hard work. "There's no pickle on my burger. I'm sure it's a conspiracy. A pickle conspiracy theory. Who makes burgers without pickles?"

"No, it's not a pickle conspiracy theory. It's a van conspiracy theory. We should go cruise the campground near the beach and see if we can find it. If it's still in the area, it might be someone camping out." Nicky was picking apart her burger and eating it in bite-sized pieces with her fingers.

"Cruise the campground?" That was idea with merit.

Two hours later we had "wrong turned" into four campgrounds in search of a green van, but failed to find it. "That's enough." I sighed. "I'm exhausted. Let's go back to Granny's and put in a movie."

CHAPTER 12

Santa Cruz: Monday

I T TURNS OUT THAT a Patrick Dempsey-based movie marathon and Granny Jazzy's roast chicken does a lot to ease day-after-car-crash aches and pains. I was feeling almost human by the next morning when Nicky and I headed to the hospital to visit Patrick.

Grandpa Dan was sitting in a chair by Patrick's bed, a book on his knee, but my normally handsome, strong cousin was asleep, and he looked strange: frighteningly small and fragile, with an oxygen hose to his nose and IV tube in his arm.

"How is he?" It felt like a stupid question.

"He just had his pain meds. He'll sleep until they start to wear off. But he ate all of his breakfast this morning, so that's a good sign." Grandpa took my hand and gave it a gentle squeeze. "He'll be able to come home in a day or two." From Grandpa's tone, he intended fully that "home" meant his and Gran's house, not Patrick's bachelor apartment. "He's going to need a medical leave, physical therapy, all that."

"Did the doctor look at that rash on his arm?" It looked better today, just a small reddish spot. If I hadn't seen it the day before, I probably wouldn't have noticed it today.

"Said it looked like a splinter or something. Probably a

glass sliver. Didn't seem concerned." Grandpa shrugged his broad shoulders. "It's not life threatening, and it seems to be clearing up on its own. They're more worried about his lung draining properly."

"You'll call me if anything changes?"

Grandpa nodded as if I'd just asked him if the sun was going to set that day. "You headed home today?"

Home. Home was an office building in downtown San Amoro. "Yeah. I have a lot to do. But I'll be back over the hill soon."

"Do you have time to run an errand for me?"

He was wrangling to get me to stay another day. Why was I not surprised? "Do I have a choice?"

"They have Patrick's Jeep at the impound lot so the insurance company can appraise it. Not sure what's left, but I think he'd like to have his stuff when he wakes up."

"Oh, man. The surfboards are on it." I groaned. "Or at least, they were. I don't know how much will be left after the crash."

"Not much room in the FrankenStang for boards." Nicky's board was usually jutting three feet out the back end, with red flags taped to the fins.

Grandpa Dan handed me his keys. "Take my pick-up."

GRANDPA DAN'S PICK-UP WAS FIFTEEN years old, a burgundy red beast of a Ford full of scrapes and dents and marks. Driving it was like trying to drive a water buffalo, swaying and snorting, cornering with sturdy gracelessness. The consolation was that Grandpa had handed me the keys instead of handing them to Nicky. That must mean he thought I was feeling better.

The truth was that the more I did, the worse I felt. The aches and pains that had eased off in the morning were begging for a fresh painkiller and an ice pack. The rest of me wanted a nap. My head hurt, and my arms felt like lead as I turned the wheel of the big pickup. I found the lot, displayed my driver's license, explained that I'd been in the accident and needed to collect personal belongings and they let me through. Was it really that easy? Could just anyone come in here and say they'd been in accident and needed to look at a car? A glance in the rearview mirror reminded me that I looked like a walking first-aid station. Maybe they'd been a little biased by my appearance?

I found the remains of the Jeep towed to the side along with a couple other smash-ups deemed to be probable total losses. The Jeep qualified. The front axle was bent, the hood smashed in. The windows were all broken out, and dents and scrapes showed where more ambitious branches had taken on the metal flanks. Patrick's fine steed had been felled. I paused for a moment to put my hand on the remains of the hood, a last farewell.

To my surprise, the surf boards strapped to the luggage rack seemed to be in good condition. The Jeep's shape must have sheltered them from the worst of the tree branches. If we'd rolled or flipped, none of them would have survived. Nicky and I climbed into the back hatch of the Jeep, the same way I'd gotten out, and salvaged as much as Patrick's gear as we could. Everything was full of broken glass and we gingerly shook everything out, leaving piles of busted shards to join the other bits of glass and metal that littered the impound lot.

Finally, I hoisted myself gingerly up onto the runner-board to unhook the surfboard straps. Patrick's three boards, my own old blue practice board, and Charles' distinctive yellow striped Walden long board. I wrangled my own down first, then Patrick's three, passing each board to Nicky to put in the pickup. I pulled down Charles' longboard, unwieldy for someone as short as I am. It still had sticky pack from the last waxing on it, and a stab of sorrow flooded me. Charles cared for this board as he cared for everything in his life; with love and attention. He'd never let old wax layer up and dry out like that. This wax would have been freshly applied that morning, probably in the parking lot right before his fatal ride.

I clasped the board in both hands and slid it into the bed of the pick-up with the rest of the gear and then hoisted myself into the driver's seat of the pick-up. I'd barely put the truck in gear when a hot flush washed over me, and I vaguely became aware that my heart was racing. The pick-up skidded as I slammed on the brakes, Nicky's "Whoa!" echoing in my ear.

Her face was pale beneath her tan as she looked at me. "You okay?"

The uniformed guy from the booth sprinted over. "Ma'am? Maybe you should step out of the truck?"

"No, no, I'm okay." I shook my head, but my vision blurred out of focus, shards of light behind my eyes. I pulled up the emergency brake and turned the pickup off. I was not okay. I scrubbed my sweating palms on my shorts, closed my eyes and breathed against the wave of dizziness. "Do you guys have some water, maybe?"

Water. To help flush whatever this was out of my system? But I hadn't eaten anything since lunch. And Nicky ate the same thing I did. Someone handed me a bottle of warm water and I gulped it down gratefully. My heart was still pounding in my ears, but my vision had started to clear.

"Lady, maybe you should let us call someone for you…"

"No, it's okay. I'm okay. I think I was just dehydrated." Dehydrated? After Granny's jumbo-sized orange juice and a mango iced tea? Not a chance. I shook out my hands, blinked a few times, and felt better. "I'm all right."

But was I? I handed him back the empty water bottle. "Here. Recycle this." They didn't really look like the recycling type.

"You're going back to the ER. Right now." Nicky jumped out of the passenger seat and came around the pickup.

"Yeah, just… give me a second." I fumbled for the seatbelt. When I was sure that my heart wasn't going to race out of my chest, I grabbed the wheel and used it as leverage to start to scoot over, but seconds after my hands touched the wheel again, I felt woozy. Foot pressed solidly to the brake, I looked at my hands. Then at the wheel. Nothing there but a few flakes of surf wax from the aging layer on Charles' board.

Surf wax.

On Charles' board.

Son of a...

"Nicky! See if Grandpa has some Fast Orange in the truck box." I grabbed a rag out of the bundle of them that Grandpa Dan kept behind the seat and scrubbed the steering wheel. The guys with badges were still staring at me. "We're fine!" I hollered at them out of the open window.

"Kam? What's going on?" Nicky was staring at me as she handed over the plastic bottle of degreasing hand cleaner. I pumped a bunch onto a rag and cleaned the steering wheel, door handle and my own hands until I was sure there was no wax left. Then I scooted over and let Nicky behind the wheel.

She instantly started the truck and headed back to the hospital.

"Not the ER." I directed, pointing for her to turn. "We need the morgue."

"The morgue? Are you dead? I think you probably need a doctor."

"Chee is a doctor," I reassured, secretly glad I didn't need her for actual medicine on me.

DR. APRIL CHEE WAS SITTING at the front desk, eating a donut with one hand and reading something on the Internet that involved pictures of dead bugs. Lovely. She looked up when I came in, her eyes widened and then she leaped to her feet. For a second, I thought she was going to run away from me.

"You can't bring that in here!" She was pointing at the longboard that Nicky and I were carrying, gingerly wrapped in a towel I found in Patrick's bag of gear.

"You need this." I leaned it against her desk. "I need you to look at the wax."

Dr. Chee leaned across the desk, eyeing the flat surface of the board. "It... looks like wax." She reached out a hand to touch it.

I slapped it away without thinking. "Don't touch it! You don't want to touch it!"

"It's surf wax." Her almond brown eyes were wide, and I wondered if she was about to call the cops and have me arrested. I didn't have time for a 5150 psych admit, but had to confess, just quietly to myself, that a little time in a psychiatric ward might not be a bad thing for me. At least it would probably be safe there. Probably.

"Something is wrong with it." I sucked in a deep breath and evened out my tone. "This is Charles Hanford's surfboard."

"That file is closed." She informed me, crossing her arms. "Your tox screens came back negative for…"

"What can cause dizziness and rapid heart-rate?"

"Excuse me?"

"And be hidden in something like a surf wax?"

"Are you saying you touched this and it caused dizziness? Is that what happened to your face?"

And here I thought she hadn't noticed that I looked like an EMT training test dummy. I guess nothing gets past dead-people doctors. "No. I was in a car accident last night, and the person driving handled this surfboard just before the accident. He said he didn't feel well, and we crashed."

"You crashed…" Dr. Chee looked far less certain, staring unblinkingly at me. "And then you touched it?"

"Yes! Today, we went to the impound lot to get our stuff from the car. After I loaded the board, my heart started pounding, the world spun, my eyes got all jaggety…."

"Jaggety? You saw stars?"

"Stars, flares… whatever. My hands were sweating, but after I washed them off it stopped."

"And you think it was the surfboard?"

"I think something's wrong with the wax." If Charles' accident had been caused by defective surf wax… My concussed brain was racing and it was difficult to focus. I was winging it now. "If there's a contaminated batch of surf wax out there, how many other surfers are using it? Who else might drown? There could be hundreds of surfers out there with it in their gear, just waiting! Don't you understand? This is a matter of life and death!"

Dr. Chee held up a steady hand, slowing my words, her voice calm but finally convinced. "Okay. Okay. I'll test the board. I should have something for you tomorrow. If there's evidence the wax is contaminated, I'll have a public service announcement released."

I could have hugged her. "Thank you! Thank you! Thank you!"

"Is it possible to find out what brand wax he was using?" Chee looked the board up and down dubiously as Nicky and I leaned it against the wall.

His gear bag was still in the back of his SUV in the office parking lot. "It's in San Amoro. I'll have to go home and get it."

"Get it back to me as soon as you can." Dr. Chee was pulling on gloves, her expression determined.

"Thank you, Doctor." I half-smiled with relief. "I knew I could count on you."

She shook her head. "If this is some kind of joke, Miss White, I assure you it will come back to bite you."

"It's not. I swear."

Something in the deep brown of her eyes registered belief in me and I gave her a small smile as I slipped out of the office.

Nicky steered me out of the morgue and I left with my heart lighter than it had been in a full week's time.

"You think that's why Trick's team found the board in the surf," Nicky confirmed as she slid behind the wheel of the pickup. "That he realized there was something wrong with the wax and tried to swim in, but was too sick to swim?"

"My heart was pounding, I could barely see. If I'd been in the surf instead of dry land, I'm not sure I would have known which way was up." I glanced over at Nicky, finally certain. "Charles died of an accident, but not a bad wave. It was bad wax!"

CHAPTER 13

———— ~ ————

Santa Cruz: Monday Morning

W E PARKED GRANDPA'S TRUCK back in the hospital visitor's parking near the FrankenStang and the first thing Nicky did was open the trunk of her car, pull out three jars of surf wax, all different brands, and toss them directly into the parking-lot garbage can. "Not taking any chances," she told me as she grabbed a shop rag and wiped her hands thoroughly.

"You never wax your hybrid, you wear surf shoes. And I haven't seen you use your longboard in forever."

"Some of that is Rick's." She grabbed her phone and found him in the contacts. "I'm calling him now, telling him to throw away..."

"Nick." I grabbed her hand. "You can't. You tell Rick. He tells Jory, Jory tells Doc, Doc tells Jude, Jude tells Andelle, Andelle tells... well, who knows. If the wax was contaminated on purpose, intentionally, you'll tip off whoever did it." I saw doubt shoot into Nicky's eyes, and held her gaze, trying to slow my own fear. Was I still being paranoid? "And if it's an accidental bad batch from a manufacturer, you'll cause a panic. We need to wait until we know more."

She held her phone locked in her hand, but finally nodded. "Just, let me call Rick. I won't say anything, okay?"

I nodded and listened as she called Rick. True to her word, all she did was ask if he was planning on hitting the waves that evening. She rung off with a faint smile that told me he'd said something dirty. "He's working tonight and tomorrow. No time for surfing for a couple days."

I gave her a one-armed hug. "So, you two are back on again?"

"As much as we ever are. He doesn't like otters, so, you know, that could be a deal breaker."

"Yeah, who doesn't like otters?" I tried to laugh as we made our way into the hospital.

We took Grandpa back his keys, but we didn't say anything about Charles' surfboard and the contaminated wax. He had enough to worry about. Patrick was sound asleep and we whispered around him. "Tell Patrick his boards are okay. That should cheer him up."

Grandpa Dan gave me a gentle hug. "You go easy now, girl. Call us tomorrow. Nicky, you don't let her out of your sight now."

"Yes, sir," she chimed merrily.

"Seriously?"

She smiled at me. "Yup."

THE TRUTH WAS, I WAS relieved Nicky was behind the wheel. I'd been sore and tired all day, and the last hour had only served to amp up my mind while further exhausting my body. We swung by her parent's house to grab her stuff before heading back over the hill.

Nicky's dad met us as we pulled in, handing Nicky a few invoices to check off for clients while he appraised my bruises. "Oh, girl. What's the other guy look like?"

"Patrick's Jeep is totaled, but I'm not as bad as I look." Actually, I was feeling pretty bad right at that moment.

Mr. Gratz gave me a stern glance over his clipboard. "You have to come over for dinner one of these nights. Laurie will make her baked salmon."

Nicky's parents treasured my friendship with Nicky. They thought I was a good influence on her. Maybe I was. She was certainly a bad influence on me.

In Nicky's room, she quickly packed a backpack with a few essentials. "So back to your place?"

"Yeah." I answered before remembering that I didn't have a place. "No. The office. I'm crashing there currently. You'll wanna grab your airbed."

"You're sleeping at work?"

"It's my building now." I told her coolly. "I can sleep in it if I want to."

"Yeah, okay." She grinned as if to say, "no offense," but I felt a little bad anyway.

NICKY, FOR ALL HER LOVE affair with junk cars, was an excellent driver. Smooth starts, smooth stops, and ultra-smooth around even Highway 17's ugly curves. What the FrankenStang lacked in looks, it more than made up for in performance. All the same, as we started to climb the west side of Patchen Pass, I felt my heart rate speed up. What the heck? I hadn't touched the surfboard, or anything else that might have any surf wax on it since leaving Dr. Chee.

The road narrowed in my vision to just the solid white and yellow lines, the concrete dividers and steel guard rails, and the close pinch of trees on the right side of the car. I couldn't catch my breath. I checked my palms, but they were dry. Too dry. I scrubbed my face with them, the pain of the bruises and tiny scratches doing nothing to settle me down. What was wrong with me? I grabbed a bottle of Gatorade from the backseat and gulped at it.

Traffic was tight, and we were boxed in, creeping slowly along.

"We should have left sooner. Or waited another hour." Nicky groaned. "This sucks."

"Nick…" That was all I could say. I reached over and rolled down the window, trying to let fresh air in but the thick perfume of redwood trees in the heat of late summer mingled with exhaust fumes and old oil, and I instantly felt worse.

"You don't look good."

My chest was squeezing and I realized the Gatorade was a mistake. "Pull over…"

It was an agonizing few moments until she found a turn-out and I flung open the door, tumbling out into the gravel, staggering to the concrete guard rail and puking over it.

Nicky ran around the car and grabbed my arm. "Kam! You're shaking!"

"I don't know what's wrong…" I slumped down on the guard rail, but now that I was out of the car, I felt stronger, more in control.

"Let me guess. Heart's racing? Can't catch your breath? Felt like you were gonna puke?" Nicky opened her back-pack and handed me a piece of gum.

"Yeah, but it wasn't like before." Nothing at all like what happened in the impound lot.

"Before? The surfboard thing? No, it wouldn't be." She nudged my shoulder. "You're having a panic attack, nimwit."

"I don't panic."

"Yes, you do."

"Do not."

"Do, too. Remember gymnastics?"

"Lots of people are afraid of the balance beam."

"You are. Because you fell off it. Coach Jones finally excused you because you were shaking too bad to try again." Nicky recounted the memory that I'd pushed out of my mind with the kind of straight-forward matter-of-factness that only best friends can manage. Before I could come up with a reply, she helpfully pushed my head down between my knees. The tangy bite of peppermint gum filled my nostrils and replaced the scents of evergreen trees and road-grime.

"Breathe," she ordered.

Breathe. In and out. I felt better. Just plain better.

"See. Panic attack. I'm sorry, Kam." She met my gaze briefly, contritely. "I should have realized you might have a little PTSD after the accident. We can go back, go up the coast and come over 92 instead."

"That will take hours! No, we're not backtracking!" I stood up and shook myself off. Panic attack? PTSD? "That's ridiculous. It was just a little car accident and I'm having panic attacks?"

"A little car accident? You almost..." Nicky obviously thought better about completing the sentence and led the way back to the car. "Do you want to drive? You might feel more in control."

More in control? I was a wreck, literally, and I wasn't about to risk Nicky's life when driving. "No, you got this. It's all good."

We climbed back in the car, and this time I left my window all the way down. Nicky pulled up and waited for a gap in the wall-to-wall traffic. "We'll be through in a jiff. Here goes..."

She started to pull forward, and then gasped. "Did you see that?"

"See what?" I pulled my head back in the window and started to follow her pointed hand, but I'd seen it, too.

"The green van!" Nicky slammed the gas on the FrankenStang and it responded with a roar, rocketing through a gap in the traffic, forcing other drivers to hit their brakes. There were more than a few horn-honkings and impolite gestures behind us as she wrangled to get us close to the van.

"Did you see who was driving it?" It was too far for me to identify occupants, but I knew Nicky's distance vision was far better than mine.

She shook her head, focused on maneuvering traffic, changing lanes to get closer. The van was five cars in front of us, then four, then three, but that was close as we could get. "No, but I saw who the passenger was."

"Who?"

Her lips were pursed in a tight terra-cotta line.

"Nick! Who?"

"Jude Butthead Booder."

"Jude Booder!" I groaned, then waved to the car in front of us in a "we're not trying to run you off the road" gesture. In the Bay Area, that could be construed as friendly or it could come off as deserving of road-rage, but in this case, the driver just waved back.

"This is good." Nicky matched speed with the car in front of us. "Don't know if they saw us, so we'll just hang back and follow them."

I'd no sooner settled back into my seat when I recognized the road in front of us. There was a stretch of black streak on the asphalt where Patrick had twisted the wheel when he overcompensated, then broken branches and the twisted smashed edge of the old metal guard-rail. In daylight, it was easier to see how bad it could have been. On either side of the gap of metal, the new Cal-trans concrete barriers had been installed. A few feet left or right, and we would have slammed full speed into immovable walls. The broken branches and torn brush showed where we'd rocketed through the gap. I sucked in a breath as we inched closer. I felt sick all over again, my chest tightening until I was panting.

"Don't look!" Nicky reached over, grabbed the back of my head and shoved me down until my forehead touched the dashboard. "Don't look at it. Don't think about it! Just keep breathing."

How could I not think about it when Nicky's enthusiastic efforts to keep me from looking were pressing my seatbelt to my bruised chest, and just bending that far forward made every bone ache? I could hear the smash and crunch of metal and glass in my ears, feel the impact of the airbag against my torso.

"We're past it. Kam, it's gone."

I raised my head. The scene of the accident was behind us, and though the trees were still there, and the cliffs and the cars, I felt different. "This is crazy. I don't have PTSD."

"If you say so, sweetie." Nicky shook her head, her gaze focused on the road, and the green van, in front of us. "Things are speeding up. We'll be out of this soon."

As we drove, we speculated about the green van and Jude Booder. Nicky was unconvinced that it had anything to do with Charles' death. "Look, lots of people go to the beach. It's probably just some buddy of Jude's who was looking for him that morning."

"Looking for him in Santa Cruz when they're obviously headed back over the hill? And why did Jude pretend he didn't know anything about it?"

Nicky didn't answer that, but concentrated on keeping the van in sight. She was an excellent tail, hanging back, changing lanes to keep us just a few cars behind, out of the sight-line of the van's driver, off his radar. The FrankenStang didn't exactly blend in with traffic. We had to stay hidden. "Where'd you learn to tail cars?"

She grinned at me. "The less you know about that, the safer you are."

"The Transporter? Leverage?"

"Burn Notice." Nick's obsession with old television reruns was notorious, and second only to her bad car obsession.

WE FOLLOWED THE VAN NORTH onto 880. Sunlight was starting to fade, the light hazing orange out over the bayside. The afternoon marine front had started to blow in off the bay, turning the world to a glowy haze that would soon turn cold and dark. We passed Fremont, Union City, Hayward, and San Leandro. "San Amoro?" I asked Nicky with a raised eyebrow, but the van kept going.

"Let's hope they aren't rolling further than Oakland. We don't have enough gas to go much longer."

We exchanged relieved glances as the van pulled off in Alameda and wound through back streets, passing a line of restaurants, bars, and clubs before turning into a parking garage that climbed over a popular club in the central business district. Nicky followed them, sliding discreetly into a parking spot five spots down.

We waited, but no one got out of the van. Were they onto us? Breath held, I found myself glancing at Charles' watch, counting seconds. I was just starting to wonder if they'd somehow managed to get out of the van while we were parking when Nicky reached into her backpack and pulled out... an industrial sized aerosol can of engine cleaner? I raised an eyebrow.

"Better than mace and twice as nasty." She brandished the spray and jumped out of the car. I ran after her as best I could on my banged-up knees. Have I mentioned that Nicky scares me sometimes?

We sidled up to the van, but could see neither passenger nor driver. Nicky strode up to the back of the van, and we split up, each moving to cover the sides of the door, like cops in one of her TV shows.

"What do you want to do?" Nicky whispered.

I shrugged, reached out, and slid my finger around the back-catch of the door, preparing to hoist it open. Our eyes met silently, a thousand questions in our minds. What would we find? What was Jude Booder doing in this van? Drugs? Sex? Worse? And what did it have to do with the morning that Charles died?

Nicky mouthed, "Go!"

I flung the door open. Nicky leaped in front of it, engine degreaser held at arms-length. "FREEZE!"

Jude Booder and some guy I didn't recognize, wearing saggy jeans and a backward baseball cap, were sitting on stools, headphones on, an array of equipment mounted on the van wall between them. A wave of pot smoke rolled out around us. I held my breath. I didn't check to see if Nicky did.

"Whoa! Sis! What the hell!" Jude threw both hands up in the air.

"Sound's ruined! Totally bugged!" The other guy threw

down his headphones, staring at us, blinking in the light. "Who the hell are you two?"

"Unless you want a face-full of this," Nicky bounced the engine spray in her hand, "I suggest you start talking!"

"Talking about what?" Jude stared at us with wide bloodshot eyes.

"What you're doing in here, for starters. And what you were doing at the beach the day Charles died!" I temporarily forgot my moratorium on talking to Jude.

"What we're doin' ain't none of yer business," the other guy growled.

Nicky, just to keep him on task, aimed the degreaser at the equipment board and let out a tiny puff. Chemical stench wafted down and left greasy traces on the black knobs and slider switches. "Try again, smarty-pants."

Smarty pants? I raised an eyebrow at her, but the guy held out his hands.

"Okay, okay. Don't touch the mixer board, man. Leave it alone!"

"Then talk!" She let out another squeeze of poisonous aerosol.

"It's not what it looks like!" Jude Booder was staring at us with wide eyes.

"Look, you've been coming up all kinds of flush lately, and then this van was in the beach parking lot the day Charles died. It looks ugly." Nicky accused.

I followed up. "And you're standing here telling me it's not what it looks like? Did you kill Charles?"

Jude Booder is normally a kind of pale weaselly looking guy, but right that second, I thought he looked like a lump of stale sour cream; white, squishy, and defeated. "Seriously? No. No, never. How could you think that? Why'd I wanna hurt Charlie?" He was looking at me like he'd never seen me before. "Yer nuts!"

"Because he figured it out! This. Whatever you're doing?"

"What?" The other guy hadn't stopped staring at us, but

now he was inching slowly away from Nicky and her engine cleaner. "We're not doin' nothing!"

"Nothing? This doesn't look like nothing to me!" I waved a hand at the soundboard, the headphones, the … What the heck were they doing? That's when I saw the pile of uncut audio CDs on the floor, along with a stack of home-cut printer paper inserts. Inserts printed with familiar wolves, dragons, roses, and crosses. Undeniably it was Kenny's artwork. And that's when everything connected. The new surf gear, the van, Jude buying art from my brother. I said it as if I'd known it all along. "You're stealing music. You're stealing and pirating. Somehow, you're probably recording the early show at that nightclub downstairs right now!"

The way they gulped and stared told me I was right. "Let me guess. You secretly record the shows, sell the remixes through pirate music sites on the web? Probably sell the CDs out of the back of the van at festivals and street events? And Charles found out. So, you tampered with his board and waited for him to go into the surf."

They'd been nodding up until that point, but now Jude held up his hands, his lanky brown hair swaying around his face as he shook his head in denial. "No, no way! Charles didn't know. Nobody knows!"

I grabbed the can from Nicky and pointed it straight at Jude's oily pointed little face. "Shut up, Jude. I'm not speaking to you!"

The other guy glanced between us with wide eyes.

"Yes, you. I'm talking to you."

"I went to the beach to find Jude. I got some real hot stuff the night before, and I wanted to get it mixed and uploaded before anyone could beat us to it. He wasn't there. I saw the Coasties pull out a body and then I got the heck out of there. Cuz where there's bodies, there's cops, and I ain't 'zactly got good history with them. They'd wanna search the van, ya know."

Yeah, I did know. I lowered the can in defeat. "Did you see anyone—anything—on the beach while you were waiting for

Jude?"

"Huh uh. Just the Coasties. Looked like it was gonna be messy so I tailed it."

Nicky waved a discouraged hand. "These idiots don't know anything."

They didn't. The only thing they'd been hiding was a few ounces of pot and some music piracy. "You sure? You didn't see anyone? Anything?"

"No, man. Just, you know, surfer dudes watching from the lot."

Jude leaned forward. "You know I couldn't hurt a fly, right? I'm not …"

I slammed the door to the van in Jude Booder's face, feeling a satisfying click under my hand as it latched. Storming back to the car, I threw myself into the passenger seat, jerked the door shut, and leaned back. My head hurt.

Nicky climbed into the driver's seat and glanced across at me. "You okay?"

"Nope."

"Good answer. Want me to call the cops and tell them there's a couple losers smoking pot in a van?"

"This is Alameda. The cops won't care."

"We could tell them we think they have guns in there."

"Tempting, but I think I need all the good karma I can get right now." I closed my eyes. "I'm ready to go home. Oh, wait. Gotta get Hoover first."

WE DIDN'T SPEAK AGAIN AS she drove us back to San Amoro by way of the Seminary neighborhood of Oakland, and a small faux Eichler style house on a quiet tree-lined street filled with post-war two-bedroom, two-bath houses with single car garages, and post-card lawns that don't require a lot of maintenance. At least, most of them don't. My mother's yard is converted into raised gardening beds that stack in stair-step precision leading up to her front door. Normally, they were overflowing with herbs and sundry other plants, but with autumn coming, a number of the beds were mulched down, and only a few rows of cabbages, heavy sunflowers hanging from browning stems, and a stubborn bed of chives remained.

JAXINE ANSWERED THE DOOR AND dragged Nicky into a huge hug. "Nicklena! It's so good to see you! How have you been?"

"Hi, Mom. How are you?" I muttered under my breath as I stepped around her effusive greeting of my best friend. Of course, she hadn't seen Nicky in a week. Me, she'd seen at the hospital just Saturday night.

Hoover was lounging across the back of the old floral-print overstuffed sofa, his satellite-dish sized ears pricked toward the window. On seeing me, he rolled half-sideways, tilting his head at me as if to ask, "Where the heck have you been?" He was wearing a new knitted sweater, this one in autumnal pumpkin orange with burnt-auburn stripes.

"Nice threads, buddy." I settled on the sofa and pulled him down into my arms. His trademark vacuum-cleaner purr started instantly.

"He's been a perfect gentleman. We weeded the back garden together, and he slept on the bed with me," Jaxine doted fondly. "It's easy to see he's lonely. He misses Charles."

"I know. I miss him, too."

"You could have told me, you know." My mother busied herself with collected Hoover's harness and spare can of food. "I had to read about it in the paper! I didn't even know."

"What?"

"Charles. You didn't tell me. It was in the newspaper, otherwise I wouldn't even have known."

To my everlasting gratitude, Nicky waved to the window. "Looks like you've got the garden all ready for winter, Jaxine. It looks good."

And that was all it took to distract my mother.

"Oh, thanks! So much work, but it's worth it. I've ordered

seven varieties of heirloom basil to start over winter for next year. With luck and good propagation, we can have them in the nursery by next June. It's so exciting! The new trend for artisanal foods has really increased the demand for new varietals…"

I mouthed a silent "thank you" to Nicky. I never knew what to say to my mother, but Nicky somehow always did. While Mom yammered about her herbs and the gardening business in general, I got Hoover into his harness. Instead of the usual struggle and squirm, he lolled in my lap and rubbed his head on my arm. "Thanks for looking after Hoover, Mom."

"He's good company. It's lonely around here now that your brother has his own place. Maybe I should get a cat."

"You could grow catnip," I suggested jokingly.

"Oh, I already do!" Jaxine bustled into the kitchen and came back with a small Ziploc bag stuffed with dried herbs. "This is my new test blend for pets: catnip, catmint, and lemongrass. Hoover loves it! I'm considering adding a new line to my herbs and spices. Peace for Pets. What do you think?"

So that's why he was being so cooperative. He was stoned out of his gourd!

She also handed me a small jar. "And this is salve for your bumps and bruises. Put it anywhere you're sore. Comfrey, arnica, mint, and aloe in a coconut oil base."

I tentatively unscrewed the lid and was hit with a wave of powerful spearmint scent, strong enough to make my eyes water. "Thanks, Mom."

"You put that on your all your booboos and you'll feel better in no time!"

And it would keep my sinuses clear, too. But even at my age, it was nice to know my mom worried about my booboos.

Nicky steered me out the door. "We gotta run, Jaxine. Girl stuff to do."

"You kids have fun!" Mom stood on the porch and waved as we climbed back into the car, Hoover nestling happily in my arms.

"I love your mom." Nicky grinned at me.

I glanced in the rearview mirror. "Yeah. So do I."

CHAPTER 14

———— ✦ ————

San Amoro: Monday Evening

WE WANDERED INTO Reese's café just before closing, loaded up on day old bagels, remaindered fruit cups, and chocolate chip cookies, then slunk back across the street to the office. The Internet provided us with TV rerun heaven, and we coiled up on the sofa in Charles' old office and stuffed our faces to an NCIS marathon. In between munching, few words were needed.

"That guy totally did it."

"Gibbs knows it, too."

"Tony'd be hot if he wasn't such a nutcase."

"He kind of looks like Jack, a little, don't you think?"

Jack Austin was ten times better looking than Anthony DiNozzo. Not that I was going to admit that. I'd burned that bridge and pulled up the pylons behind me. "Shut up and eat another cookie, Nick."

Our impromptu slumber party eased toward sleep after the sugar wore off, but as we settled down into sleeping bags, Nicky on her air mattress on the floor and me on the sofa, a soft clank echoed through the office.

Nicky jerked upright, reaching into her bag for her engine cleaner, but I was familiar enough with it by now that I waved a hand. "It's just Evrett stirring around. He's been trying to tell me something, I think."

In the dim yellow streetlight that wafted through the blinds, Nicky's eyes were wide. "Has he been doing that a lot, like, since we last talked to him?"

I thought about it. "No more than usual. But you saw how helpful he was the last time. We just aren't on the same wavelength or something. Whatever he's trying to say, it's not getting through. He said follow the money, but that just led to Andelle, and she certainly didn't kill Charles."

Nicky squirmed out of her sleeping bag. "C'mon! We have to try again."

"What good is that going to do?" No sooner had I said the words than Evrett's visor slammed shut with a bang and I felt a shiver run down my spine. "Okay, maybe you have a point."

I didn't say another word as I opened the safe and collected the audio recorder and camera and handed them to her. Maybe she would have more luck than I did.

"Chevalier Evrett? It's Nicklena Gratz." Nicky started in with introductions as she set up the camera and recorder as we'd done before. Nothing to move this time, nothing to catch reflections. The room was completely empty except for Reese's folding desk, the café chair, and my laptop computer.

I was so tired that I only lasted about half an hour of Nicky's question and answer game, but this time, there were no responding knocks or clanks. Everything was silent. I finally gave her a small wave and headed for Charles' office. Hoover and Nicky remained up with Evrett. I curled up on the sofa and fell asleep listening to Nicky chatting to Evrett as though he was right beside her, asking him questions and leaving pauses for answers. Comforted, I drifted off to sleep.

WHEN SUNRISE CAME, NICKY WAS asleep sideways on the floor with my laptop inches from her face, the video program replaying the footage of the empty office from her investigation.

There wasn't much to see. The camera was designed for taking pictures of dents in cars, disputed material goods, and that kind of thing, not recording ghost-hunting videos in the dark. I watched the shadows replay for a few moments, and was just reaching to turn off the software when suddenly the camera picked up a shadow, a looming shape that leaned into the lens! What the heck...

I grabbed the laptop up and replayed the footage, maximizing the screen. A strange triangular shape, then a sharp curve, and then... a familiar yellow eye and set of fangs. Hoover's snout appeared in close-up, his pale pink tongue tentatively poking out to taste the camera lens. The shadow was just the cat; the bizarre triangle had been his oversized ear. I glanced over at the back of the sofa at the very real and very normal (despite the hairlessness) cat. "Really?"

He licked his paw and stared at me with wide blue eyes that seemed to say, 'What did you expect? I'm a cat.'

And cats needed to be fed. I gave him a half-can of his favorite food, then I showered and changed into clean jeans and my favorite blue button-up sweater. The damp cool of an East Bay late-summer morning was nothing to trifle with. While Nicky slept, I slipped across the street and fetched us mochas and scones for breakfast. My knee was less swollen today, but the bruises on my face, chest and arms had turned a sickly purplish-blue. I still felt like I'd been rolled over a waterfall in a barrel.

Reese greeted me with a hard stare. "What the hell happened to you?"

I explained about the wreck and watched her rich brown eyes nearly pop out of her head. "Concussion? Should you even be out of bed?"

"I'm fine. Well, maybe a little more dizzy than usual. I expect the cure is extra whipped cream on my mocha."

"Whipped cream doesn't cure concussions." But she sprayed an extra heap on anyway. "What about your cousin? Is he going to be okay?"

"It's going to take time to heal, but he'll live." I shuddered, realizing again just how close we'd come to not living. Thank Jeep for making indestructible vehicles.

"So, what are you going to do?" Reese pointed across the street. "Any decisions?"

Looking over at my building, I felt a surge of certainty. "You were right," I admitted, "Charles wouldn't want me to give up on the business. Just like he wouldn't want me to give up on finding his killer."

"You're so sure it was murder, then?" Reese's skeptical look was back, but it was so similar to her everyday expression that I wasn't sure that it was directed at me.

I briefly debated telling her about the surfboard and the contaminated wax, but remembered my warning to Nicky. We didn't want to cause a panic, at least not until we had some kind of proof. "I'm having the coroner run some more tests, but I don't think it was an accident. And I don't think the car wreck was one, either."

"17 is a dangerous road. Accidents happen."

That line was starting to feel like a lame excuse, and I collected the mochas and bagels with a shrug. "So do bad waves, but I'm over believing in coincidences this time."

I started to turn away from the counter, but a thought occurred to me and I shifted back. "Do you think Charles had any enemies?"

Reese almost smiled. "He made an enemy of my ex, I think. Not that I care. That loser was already in the Bahamas when the court orders came through. If it hadn't been for Charles, I'd be working the night shift at the Thrifty Mart to make ends meet. He made sure I got everything."

"And you deserved it." I flashed a half-wave, scooped up the tray and crossed back to the office. Nicky had moved from the floor to the air mattress and was curled up with just her long black pony-tail hanging out of the top of her sleeping bag. This was, apparently, the coolest thing that Hoover had ever seen and he was busily reaching out and digging his paw into

Nicky's hair, swatting it this way and that. Muffled mmmfff's of dismay were issuing from the depths of the sleeping bag.

As amusing as it was, I took pity on her. "There's coffee."

Instantly, her dark eyes emerged, framed by her dark blue sleeping bag, like some cave creature peering from the darkness. "Coffee?"

"Mochas. And scones."

Scones got her most of the way out of bed. "How late were you up last night?"

"Just long enough to know there's nothing on the audio recordings." She looked so disappointed. "He was so chatty, well, knocky, last time. I thought sure we'd get something good."

"You caught something cool on the video feed, though," I said mischievously.

"I did? What? Black shadows? Mystery shapes? Things moving on their own?" Nicky reached for the computer and fast-forwarded, stopping when the strange shape of Hoover's ear appeared. "Oh, wow! Oh wow! What is that? What is it!"

When she finally recognized Hoover's fangs as he licked the camera lens, she groaned. I started laughing, the first full real laugh I'd felt in days. "Sorry! I couldn't resist!"

"Well, you should have. Silly cat." She settled back into the sofa and cradled her mocha, and replayed the video just to amuse herself. "What's on the agenda for today? My orders are to stick with you like glue... Holy cannoli. Did you see that?"

"See what? All I saw was Hoover making a mockery of your investigative techniques."

Nicky backed up the video again, and then replayed it, pausing frequently. "Look. Look there, on your desk! Behind Hoover, right when his ear appears. Look!"

I put down my mocha and leaned over Nicky's shoulder. In the periphery of the camera-view, a file folder on my desk jerked, then slowly turned a quarter-turn. "No. No way. You bumped it!"

"How could I have?" Nicky grabbed my arm and dragged

me into the office. "Look! I was sitting in the chair right here. You'd gone to bed. Hoover was on the shelf. The file is there. I couldn't have bumped it."

"Earthquake? We get tremors all the time," I reminded her. "The Hayward fault pretty much runs right through town."

"I didn't feel anything. Did you?" Nicky touched her phone twice, and the USGS Earthquake application came up. She glanced at it and then pointed it at me. "Anything for 11:32 last night for the Bay Area? No. See."

She was right. The USGS wasn't showing anything.

"Could have been a micro-quake. That application doesn't show smaller than a 2.5 Richter."

Nicky's eyes rolled so hard I thought they'd fall out of her head. "Have you ever seen anything move like that from a micro-quake? Stuff bounces, rocks, maybe bounces a bit. But that file..." Nicky flung out her hand and pointed at it as though it was the thing that was haunted. "It turned, Kam. It turned a full quarter-turn."

I reached out and picked up the file. It was Vanny's master file, the one that Evrett had pointed me to before. I held it out to Nicky. "It's the divorce case I'm working on. Evrett knocked it over the other morning, and Hoover scattered it all over the floor once. I think he's just trying to tell me not to give up on the legal business, to keep working."

Nicky took the file and thumbed through it. "She's had this many husbands? What is she, like a black widow or something?"

I laughed. "All of her husbands are still alive. She just divorces them and takes them for all they're worth."

Nicky continued to flip through the file while we returned to Charles' office for our coffee and scones. "Maybe there's something here that we're just not seeing. We should look all these guys up."

"What were you asking Evrett when the file moved?"

Nicky uploaded the audio files to the laptop and synched the sound to the video.

"I was just chatting, asking him about himself, what kinds of things he liked, that kind of thing…" Nicky turned on the sound and we both listened along, our eyes on the video. We could hear Nicky's voice asking what Evrett's favorite food was, and then his favorite color.

"Seriously, Nick? Favorite color?"

She shrugged. The next question was about whether he wanted me to keep the office. And then she asked if he missed Charles.

God, didn't we all? But that's when the file slid.

"There you go. He misses Charles. There's a clue in there, Kam. We're just missing it!" Nicky waved the file in my face.

"Maybe. Or maybe it was in answer to me keeping the office. Telling me to get to work and finish the one paying job we have so we can keep the business going." I sighed tiredly. "I'm telling you, I've been over that thing a few times. I even went and talked to Vanny. I think she thinks I'm crazy. You know, she told me that if Charles was straight, she would have tried for him, too."

That made Nicky laugh. "Charles? Really? Now, Reginald Burroughs, that I could go for!"

"Couldn't we all? Why are all the good ones gay?"

"Not all the good ones." Nicky gave me the stink-eye. "You had the best one."

"Jack?" I snorted. "Speaking of Jack, you asked what was on the agenda for today. I'm meeting Jack for lunch."

"We are?" Nicky hopped up. "Let me grab a quick shower."

"I am! You aren't coming."

Have I mentioned Nicky has a hell of a pout? "I'm not?"

"Nope."

"Yes, I am."

"Nope."

"Yup."

"Nope."

Thankfully, our standoff was interrupted by the ringing of the office phone. I answered, "Hanford Legal" before I could stop myself, and instantly regretted it as Juliet Hanford's strident and proper British accent swamped my ears.

"You're suing me to return all these things on this list your lawyer sent me? Where did you even get this list?"

I took a deep breath and forced my trembling hand to loosen on the receiver before I shattered my borrowed phone. In court, you focus on the question being asked. Don't prevaricate, I tried to remind myself. Just answer her question. I was proud when my voice barely shook. I was done being helpless. And I was done being Juliet Hanford's whipping girl. It was time to do some whipping of my own. "The list is from the insurers. You didn't think that I would have had all those valuables here without having them insured and valuated, did you?"

"How could you?" Her voice radiated wounded pride.

"How can I? I can because legally, they're mine, not yours. Charles left them to me. He wanted me to have them. I'm sorry, but if you'd just asked instead of storming in and stealing it all, I might have been willing to be reasonable."

There was an arrogant sniff. At least, I assumed it was arrogant. It might have been real expression of grief. But I doubt it. "It's all I have of him. You're utterly heartless. A selfish evil creature."

Argh! Nicky was shaking her head at me, warning to me be calm, but I wanted to take the gloves off and lay into Juliet bare-fisted! Nasty wicked old hag! I grimaced, took a deep breath, and said, as genuinely as possible, "I'm terribly sorry you feel that way, Juliet. But just to clarify, when you say, 'It's all I have of him' are you referring to my thirty-thousand-dollar Civil War era oil painting? Or the twenty-two thousand-dollar framed antique map of the Ottoman Empire? Or maybe you're referring to my Oriental rug? I can't remember the appraisal number on that right away."

"Ah, now we see your greedy stripes!" Juliet crowed like a rooster at daybreak and I nearly laughed at her.

"Greed? No," I was admirably calm despite my eager desire

to crawl through the phone and dice her into tiny pieces with Evrett's sword. Damn shame the sword wouldn't fit through the phone. If it had, I would have stabbed her through the ear with it. But far better than any sword, I had words. And somehow, I found them and wielded them with righteous anger. "I don't care about the numbers, Juliet. I care about the pride in Charles' voice when he called to tell me he'd bargained a wonderful price on that rug, and could I arrange shipping home. I care about the light that used to glow in his eyes when he traced his fingers across that antique map and told how his Turkish ancestors, your ancestors, would have made the trek across it with little more than ponies and camels."

I care about those beautiful artifacts because your brother cared about them. And I loved him, and he was my best friend. And you…" My breath was coming faster now as I lost the will to quell my fury. Something warm and wet poured a waterfall in miniature down my cheeks. "…You never heard or saw those things. You never visited, except to hound him. Never spoke to him except to say you weren't listening. Charles left those things to me because he knew I would take care of them, love them and cherish them as though they were my own. You took them because it was one more way to hurt Charles, even though he's gone, and he's never coming back, and I hope… Oh, Juliet, how I hope! …that he's where your words and actions can never hurt him again."

There was a long silence when I stopped speaking, and for a moment I thought she'd hung up. Hell, I would have hung up on me, too. I was just about to drop the phone back into the cradle when she spoke again.

"My brother is in hell, where he deserves to be. And that's where you're going, too."

"Maybe so." And even to my own ears my voice was a cold and violently angry thing, a foreign distant monster growling in my throat. "Maybe that's where I'm going, Mizz Hanford. But first? I'm going to court. And I'm getting back everything you stole from me. If I'm going to hell, I'm taking my oriental rug with me."

Now she did hang up, the click resounding in my ear.

Good riddance, Juliet. I was shaking with fury when I stood up, full of aggression and action and nowhere to go with it. I slammed my fist on the little folding desk and it shuddered ominously as I screamed, "Argh! I hate her!"

Nicky started applauding and singing, "Atta girl! Way to go!" at the top of her lungs.

Hoover, apparently unfazed by my tantrum and Nicky's outburst, flopped over on his side on the bare floor and glowered up at me as if to say, "Yah! She took my rug!"

"You should have peed on it," I told him, but I didn't really mean it. I'd hate for anything bad to happen to that rug. Thankfully, Hoover was too fastidious to even consider such a thing and he gave me a squinty-eyed glare of rebuke for daring to suggest he would be involved in such a defiling act.

Nicky laughed and quipped, "Better pissed off than peed on. So, about meeting Jack…"

"You aren't going."

Two hours later, we were both in the car on the way to the local pub hangout, Magillies on Main.

CHAPTER 15

San Amoro: Tuesday, Noon

MAGILLIES ON MAIN had probably been a genuine Irish pub at some point, but attempts to keep up with the fast-moving Bay Area had led to mounted flat-screen TVs and a menu that offered grilled salmon, fresh ahi sushi, and braised apple blue-cheese salad along with the usual Guinness and corned beef sandwiches. The décor was dark wood and brown vinyl that wouldn't show beer stains, with yellow stained-glass lighting that, even during broad daylight, lent a cozy atmosphere to the place. Jack had arrived ahead of us and scoped out a table almost out of sight-line of the televisions. A bottle of the house-brewed root-beer was on the table for me, as well as Jack's usual micro-brew, and a glass of ice tea with extra lemon, Nicky's favorite. Wasn't that just like Jack?

When he saw me, he leapt to his feet, eyes wide and jaw tense with horror, which was swiftly followed by fury. "Who the hell did that to you…"

Nicky put her palm on his chest and pushed him lightly back toward the chair. "Chill! It was a what, Jack. Not a who."

He slumped back into his chair. "This was your 'little accident'? You told me you were fine."

And then we had to explain about the crash all over again.

"Jeez, Jack. When you saw me, I thought..." I shrugged. "You looked fit to kill."

"Yeah, well," His blazing blue eyes suddenly became very focused on the label on my root-beer. "I know you can handle yourself."

"Damn straight."

"Damn straight," Nicky echoed.

We both glanced at my unexpected third wheel. But that was Nicky. Always had my back. Apparently, so did Jack, but that was something I tended to forget.

Now that we'd all caught our breath, I explained to Jack about Arthur's daughter and the fund that Arthur had set up and Charles had continued paying into. "She had no idea the money was there. Her mother never told her."

"There's enough money in that account now that she can do whatever she wants, go to school, buy a house, or whatever." Jack said, handing me a slim file. "It's just been sitting, collecting interest all this time."

"It's so sad, really." I considered. "Andelle spent years hating a man she barely even knew, but he loved her, despite leaving her mother. If she'd just given him a chance, she might have had a father."

Both Nicky and Jack were giving me strange looks that I couldn't interpret, but before I could ask, the waitress came by to take our order. I ordered the salmon sandwich, but both Nicky and Jack went with traditional beef burgers stacked with bacon, mushrooms, and cheese. While we waited for food, Jack pulled out the business account paperwork for me to sign.

"It will still take a few weeks to get the banks notified and everything lined up, but the stipend should be enough to keep the lights on at the office," Jack encouraged. "Until Oslo & Burroughs can get the injunctions cleared, there's not much else I can do."

"Injunctions," I groaned in frustration. "Juliet won't stop, and she's got the money and the power to back herself up. I can live without the money. I mean, I've never had money before, so it's not like that matters. What matters is the stuff… all of Charles' antiques, his art, his collections. Why does she even want them? I should never have let her through the door of the office!"

"You think she'll try to sell them before the courts can process the injuncta-thingamabobs?" Nicky asked around a mouthful of bacon-burger.

"Injunctions. She can try, but Oslo & Burroughs has the full inventory now thanks to Charles' insurance. No auction house is going to take them without clear provenance." I considered the problem and had a terrifying thought. "But she can get them out of the country, ship them to England or something. Once that happens, they're gone. I'll never see them again!"

Jack held up his hand slowly. "You're getting worked up over something that hasn't even happened yet. Does that make sense to you?"

"Nothing makes sense," I resisted the urge to stick my tongue out at him. We were in public, after all. "Charles' death doesn't make sense; not the how, the why, or the what. Patrick wrecking the Jeep doesn't make sense. Juliet Hanford stealing stuff willed to me doesn't make sense." I could feel tears welling up and swiped them violently away with the back of my hand, my bruised cheek singing a sweet agony at the contact. "I feel like I'm watching the swells go by but I can't catch a wave."

Both of them, my former lover and my best friend, remained silent, staring at me over their burgers. Finally, when I'd broken eye contact and realized that my salmon burger was getting cold, dill sauce congealing unappetizingly on the edges, Jack spoke up.

"Just tell us what you need."

Just tell us what you need. If only it was that easy. "I need to eat my lunch, and after that, we need to take Charles' surf gear to the coroner, but as far as what else…" I paused to think, sandwich halfway to my mouth, but the thing that had been tugging at my subconscious all morning finally clicked into place, Reese's words coming back to me with the inexorable force of a rip tide. "He made an enemy of my ex…"

"What? Who did?" Jack frowned, his eyes flicking between me and Nicky. "I'm not an enemy. Am I?"

"No! Not you. The next ex! I gotta go." I crammed the last of my sandwich in my mouth and gulped my root beer. "I gotta run. Nicky, keys?"

"Not a chance."

"What? What next ex?" Jack asked, confusion riding across his handsome features. "Are you seeing someone?"

I snatched the keys off the table right out from under Nicky's elbow and was out the door before either of them could stop me, Jack's worried voice fading behind me.

I DASHED INTO THE OFFICE, nearly tripping over Hoover on the way in. The files that Evrett had shifted around were still on my desk, the piles of divorce filings.

Vanny Toreski and her eight husbands. All of whom she'd taken to the cleaners with Charles' help over the years. Seven ex-husbands. But what about Mr. Toreski? He didn't know about the avalanche barreling down on him yet, at least, as far as I knew. As far as Vanny knew. But I was pretty sure he hadn't gotten where he was today by being a fool. What if he knew? He spent all his time on the yacht. The yacht more than capable of sailing into Santa Cruz and out again.

My god. What about Vanny? If he'd killed Charles and learned the divorce was still going through, was he capable of killing her? Of killing me?

I flipped through them, mind racing, finally grabbing the phone. "Vanny? This is Kami from Hanford Legal. I need to see you. Right now. Today."

"Oh, Kami!" Vanessa's voice rolled through the phone, practically joyous. "I do need to see you, but I'm packing for a week in Sonoma right now. I need spa time. But if you don't mind talking while I pack, you can come to the house."

"Yes, I can do that."

I hung up. "Evrett, I owe you an apology. I think you were trying to tell me this all along."

The Crusader was reproachfully silent.

Grabbing the files, I headed across town. I felt sluggish and slow, after-effects of the concussion, and I realized that I probably shouldn't be driving. But the entire drive, I was fighting a nausea that had nothing to do with the concussion. What if I was too late? What if Robert was home, what if he was poisoning Vanny right now? I reached the gated community in Fremont, showed my ID and was buzzed through. No maid's car today, but the grey pool cleaning van was on the corner again. How often did these people have to get their pools cleaned?

There was a black Cadillac ELR in the driveway, so I parked on the curb. Robert's car, I recognized. She was suing for it in the divorce. Was Robert home? My heart sank a little further.

Vanny opened the door before I even knocked. "Kami, thank you for ... Oh, you look..."

"Terrible, I know. It's not as bad as it looks. I was in a little car accident."

"Well, I hope you got the other driver's information. You should take them to court! I don't need to tell you that accident injury suits can be very profitable."

I didn't bother to mention the driver in case was my cousin. "They can, but I'm healing fine. Vanny? Is your husband..."

My words fell off as I spotted Robert standing behind her. I watched helplessly as he came around the corner of the kitchen-bar, an enormous chef's knife in his hand. Stainless steel glittered in the brilliant midday sunlight that poured through the ceiling skylight. "Who's this, darling?"

"Vanny! Run!" I gasped, reaching for her arm. We needed to get out of the house, out into the street, into public. He wouldn't dare hurt us in broad daylight in a gated community, would he?

"What?" Vanny looked at me, and then back at Robert. Her smile never wavered. "Why?"

"Because he's the killer! He killed Charles!"

Vanny started to laugh. "Oh dear, sweetie, you really did hit your head, didn't you?"

I gaped wide-eyed at Vanny. In the periphery of my vision, I saw Robert put the knife down on the counter, staring back and forth between us. He was fairly handsome in an older-gentleman sort of way. Tall, strong, athletic looking—must be all the time on that yacht. His voice was soft, faintly amused, not even intimidating at all. "Do I even want to know what this is all about?"

Vanny's laughter gentled. "Darling, this is Kami White. She's the paralegal I told you about."

Robert came forward with long strides, his hand outstretched, and for some reason, I reached out mine, which he shook with genteel elegance. "Nice to meet you. Peachie has been telling me all about you."

Peachie? No wonder she wanted a divorce. But Vanny was tucking herself under Robert's arm with comfortable familiarity and smiling up at him with infatuation.

"Umm… Vanessa? Am I missing something here?"

"Oh, come in! Come here! You look ready to fall off your feet." She took my arm and guided me into the small informal dining area that overlooked the backyard. In back, a slump-shouldered figure in a baseball cap and a grey union suit that read Harry's Pool Service was slowly pushing a pool vacuum back and forth through the pristine-looking blue water.

That wasn't right. Robert wouldn't kill us in front of witnesses, would he?

"Darling? Go ahead and fetch some of that cake, will you?"

"And iced tea, I think." Robert disappeared back around the corner of the kitchens dining bar, and returned a half-moment later with the enormous chef's knife in one hand and a ganache covered chocolate cake garnished with fresh raspberries in the other. He settled them both gently on the tabletop before disappearing again. When he returned the second time, he was carrying a tray laden with a pitcher of iced tea, glasses, plates and forks.

Cake? Did murderers often serve cake and iced tea to people they wanted to kill? I didn't think so. They did if it was poisoned, though, right? But Robert made efficient use of the chef's knife to serve each of us a hearty slice of cake, pausing several times to swipe crumbs from the knife onto his fork and eat them. So the cake wasn't poisoned. Then he poured the tea and drank half of his before refilling his glass. The tea wasn't poisoned, either? I didn't know whether to be relieved or disappointed.

"So, umm... Vanny? You wanted to see me?" I took the tiniest bite of the cake and nearly melted in the heavenly flavors of sensuous dark chocolate and bittersweet raspberry ganache. If by chance it was poisoned, it was well worth dying for.

"You first, sweetie. What was so urgent that you rushed all the way over here? You didn't really think that Robert was going to kill me, did you? Well, no, of course you didn't. You're a smart girl. If you thought he was going to kill me, you'd call the police, wouldn't you?"

Calling the police really hadn't crossed my mind. But I didn't want to tell Vanny that. What had I been thinking, dashing over here to confront a killer? "I didn't think you would have said it was okay for me to come over if he was home," I admitted faintly. "I didn't really know what to think."

Robert smiled, a little sadly. "It seems nuts, but I can see where you'd get the idea. Vanny told me about your boss being killed."

"She did?" I glanced at Vanny. This was starting to make less and less sense.

"I told him everything, Kami." Vanny's hand slid across the table and cupped around Robert's fingers. "I told him how unhappy I've been, how I missed the excitement we had early on, how I felt like we'd settled down, gotten boring. I told him all of it. I told him I was filing for divorce."

"You did?" Flabbergasted is an awesome word. It's a shame there's not more use for it in everyday conversation. I sighed.

"I'm flabbergasted."

"I can imagine." Robert smiled broadly. "But she's right. We've been settling, going our own ways." He lifted her hand to his lips and kissed it. "I never wanted that. I love her. I just want her to be happy."

"And I want you to be happy, too, darling." Vanny gazed adoringly at Robert for a moment before turning her eyes back to me. "So, we're starting over. Right now. Today. Kami, do you have the divorce paperwork with you?"

Tentatively, I handed Vanny the file. "So, the yacht? The property in Mexico?"

"We're selling them both!" Robert declared. "We're going to Sonoma for a week, no distractions, no fuss, and then..."

"A cruise! Around the world! Every port we can find," Vanny effused. "I can't believe that I was about to make the worst mistake in my life. Thank you, Kami, for everything! If you hadn't come here, asking about my ex-husbands...Well, it just got me thinking that true love, real love. It's so hard to find. You can't just throw it away because you're a little unhappy. It takes work. Real work."

Or it takes a bus. It hadn't even been that great of a bus. I blinked, coming back to the problem at hand. How many hours had I logged on this divorce? I felt my bank account drain by double digits. But one look at them together, and I knew that filing those stupid papers was the worst thing either of them could have done.

Vanny took the file over to the kitchen sink and there was a grinding noise and the roar of running water as she put the papers one by one down the garbage disposal, and then brushed her hands off and returned to stand beside Robert and toast him with her tea-glass. "To starting over!"

"To starting over." I chanted along with them.

Robert walked me to the door. "Just send me the bill for whatever hours you put into that mess that just went down the drain."

"Oh, no. I don't charge for jobs that weren't completed." I

smiled but Robert shook his head.

"Just by working on my divorce, you saved my marriage." His dark eyes glittered with emotion. "That's worth whatever you charge."

I waved to the gatekeeper on my way out of the complex and turned right, rolling too slowly along the tree-lined one-way avenue, relief over getting paid for the unfinished job fading in the other questions I was carrying. If it wasn't Robert and it wasn't Vanny, then who? I needed to look at other divorce cases Charles had worked on. Anyone else who might have had a grudge against him. I dug my blue-tooth unit out of the glovebox and told my phone to call Reginald Burroughs. After misdials to Reggae Pizza and Right Way Carpet Cleaners, I finally got Reggie's office, and after that, it only took three threats to get Rayanne to put me through. I braked for a stoplight as Reggie answered.

"Kami. What's up?"

"Divorce cases that Charles worked on that might have turned hostile? Any he might have mentioned to you?"

"You think an angry ex killed him?" I could almost see his eyebrow arching in disbelief.

"Reggie, you keep safe-houses for your clients who are being threatened. You know better than me what kind of crazy exes are out there."

"And you have no idea. Your ex is an angel."

"An angel? Jack?"

"Like I said, you have no idea." Reggie laughed. "Let me think about it and I'll call you back."

I'd barely hung up with Reggie when my phone sang out. I answered it with a clipped, "Hullo?"

"Kamera White?"

The official tone was crisp, but familiar. "Doctor Chee?"

"Can you come to my office?"

I glanced at the dashboard clock and mentally adjusted an hour to compensate for my inability to change the time on my Kia. I figured it was correct during Daylight Savings Time, so that was half the year, right? "I'm in San Amoro. I couldn't get there before five o'clock."

"I'll stay late. I have plenty of work to do. I really need you to bring me whatever surf wax was used on that board."

"Did you find something? Can you give me a hint?"

"It's crazy, but you were right. The surf-wax was contaminated. I had to run it three times before I believed it."

Who knew relief and fear could happen simultaneously? I slowed and pulled over. "You're sure?"

"Positive."

"What was it? Am I poisoned? I touched it!" My gut lurched.

"No, you're fine. It's fast-acting, fast-dissipating, absorbed through the skin. Once you wiped the surf-wax off your hands, you were safe." Doctor Chee might not have a charming bedside manner, but sometimes just the facts were enough to make you feel better. Relief was like a cool wave splashing over me.

"What is it? The poison?"

"Nitroglycerin. It's technically not a poison at all."

"Nitro... Dynamite? There's dynamite in the surf-wax?" I blinked, suddenly relieved that I'd pulled over to the side of the road to have this conversation.

"Not dynamite. Medically, nitroglycerin compounds can be used for a number of treatments, including regulating blood pressure and heart rate. If I'm right, your friend Charles Hanford probably didn't feel the effects at first because the water would have kept the wax cool. When he paddled out, his body heat would have warmed it, but his wet suit would have protected him. It's my finding that it absorbed through his feet when he stood on the board to surf. Then it would have affected his blood pressure, and he would have felt dizzy, sick, possibly even have fallen unconscious."

"And fallen and drowned..."

His board was outside the break. That's what Patrick said. My mind was racing. "His board was outside the break. The Coast Guard told me that. He'd known something was wrong and tried to swim in to shore without the board!" I finally felt the dots connecting in my mind. "And then when Patrick handled the board after the Paddle Out, it was cold. It wasn't until the flaked wax on his arm warmed up in the car that he felt sick!" My god, the same board had nearly killed all three of us.

"When you handled the board," Dr. Chee's voice was calm and matter of fact. How could she be so calm? "the wax was already warm from the sun in the impound lot, so it absorbed through your hands right away. You were right to bring it to me immediately." She sighed, and I could almost hear a smile in her voice. "I admit, I thought you were probably suffering grief-related psychosis."

This time I laughed, more relieved over being right than being called crazy. "Wouldn't be the first time I've been accused of being crazy."

"There were also fiberglass slivers in the wax, just microscopic pieces, probably some contaminant. The slivers were probably what caused the lesions—they would have carried the nitro through the skin faster," Dr. Chee continued. "Did you check to see what brand of wax he was using? If you bring it to me, I can test it. We'll have to notify the county and we need to file a recall. We have to warn surfers."

I groaned. "I haven't had a chance." Charles' gear was still in the back of his SUV, which was still at the office, hidden under the tarp in the back lot. "I'll get it now."

The whole drive back to the office, my head was spinning and not just from the aftereffects of the concussion. Was it really that simple? No killer, just contaminated surf-wax? Every comment about my overactive imagination and suspicious mind was completely justified! I'd even accused Vanny's husband to his face! I glanced at the files on the seat beside me and laughed in sheer relief. Between Charles dying and the car accident, I was probably losing my mind. I pulled into the back lot of the office, but didn't bother to park, just pulling up alongside Charles' SUV long enough to unlock the door and fetch his duffle bag out of the rear door. I waved to Mallory Kent through his window as I pulled out again. My office was dark, which meant that Nicky hadn't returned. Was she still with Jack?

I drove to the end of Marin Avenue, cautiously made the no-light left onto 2nd Street, and started to turn toward the freeway. CRUNCH! I was thrown forward into my seatbelt, my already bruised ribs screaming in agony, my earpiece going dead as my phone flew out of the dashboard holder with a clatter and bounced across the passenger seat. What the hell?

A glance at the rearview mirror showed a big grey metal grill planted against my back bumper. A grey van? The pool van? Dang...

My rear door slung open with a groan and a clack, and in the rearview I saw only blue eyes through a black mask and the flash of a gun barrel. Gun. My brain registered that slowly. It was a revolver, silver and wood.

"Drive."

The voice was low, gravel, unrecognizable and familiar at the same time. Like he was trying to mask his tone.

I was panting and my hands sweated as I reached for the steering wheel. "Where to..."

"Drive. Now."

"If you want the car, it's yours. It's a piece of crap anyway. I don't have any money." I was stalling. We were on the edge of the business district in the middle of the afternoon. Someone had to have seen something, heard the accident, right? Someone would come, or call the cops. Wouldn't they? I looked around but if anyone had seen anything they weren't rushing to my rescue.

"Drive."

I put the car in gear and drove forward, feeling my crumpled bumper grind as it pulled free of the other machine.

"Where am I going?"

"Shut up. Drive."

"Okay. I'm driving." Surely somewhere a cop is going to

notice that I'm driving a car with a bashed in bumper. Was my license plate gone? Damaged? They'd have to stop me, wouldn't they? My abductor directed me onto 880 South. The freeway was quickly clogging with the early commuters, but he directed me to the carpool lane and told me to keep driving. In Bay Area rush hour, no one pays attention to other drivers. They barely pay attention to other cars. I tried to make eye contact, tried to signal with my fingers, but no one was watching.

A distant siren grew closer and I glanced in the rearview to see lights approaching. Oh, thank heavens! "You should give up now." I told my abductor, but his only answer was to poke the barrel of his gun into the back of my seat.

"Look! The cops are coming. What do you think happens next?"

The cop car was racing toward us now and I started to slow, panic making my stomach churn, hope singing so loudly in my ears they were practically ringing. The cop car flashed its headlights and pulled around us, the cop glaring at me as he whipped by on his way to wherever his real emergency was. I mouthed, "Help!" but from the way he sped away, I guess that a woman alone in the front seat of a sedan with a masked man in the backseat wasn't a huge priority.

I was on my own.

CHAPTER 16

San Amoro & Santa Cruz: Late Tuesday

"WHERE ARE YOU taking me?" Hope faded as I watched those red and blue lights fading into the stretch of traffic ahead of me. What now? Did I crash the car and hope I lived? Slam on the brakes and jump out of the car, hoping he dropped the gun instead of pulling the trigger? Roll down the window and scream "help me" at passing cars? My phone was still on the passenger seat and I eyed it, taking a moment to gather my thoughts. How to keep my captor from figuring out what I was doing?

"You know, someone saw you take me. I bet they've already..." I glanced down at my phone and tapped my Bluetooth unit. "Call nine-one-one!"

"With what? Where's your..."

"Calling Nino's Pizza..." My phone intoned helpfully.

"NO! Nine-one-one! Call Nine-one-one!"

In my blue-tooth unit, a distant phone started ringing.

My captor reached over the seat and snatched my phone just as a voice on the other end said, "Nino's Pizza. Will this be delivery or takeout?"

"CALL nine-one-one!" I yelled desperately, hoping Nino, at least, would know what I meant.

My captor rolled the window down and threw my free smartphone into traffic where the last I saw of it was in my rearview mirror colliding with the front bumper of a silver Toyota minivan. The bearded, tattooed driver glared at us for throwing litter and changed lanes as I mouthed, "Help me!" in my mirror to him. He kept driving. I really needed to get an iPhone.

"Knock it off. Drive. Or die right here."

The threat caused my heart to start racing again, despite the tears of frustration that sprang to my eyes. My captor was starting to sound irritated. But there was something about that voice. Something familiar.

"So," I gulped down the bile in the back of my throat and focused on not getting us smashed in traffic. "Where are we going? I probably know a short cut. Not that I'm eager to get there, wherever it is, but most of the cab drivers hang out at the café where I used to work, so I know…"

"I said, shut up."

"Okay, I'll shut up. But you know, if you're going to kill me anyway, you might as well tell me your name."

"Drive. Or die."

Since shooting me while I was driving seventy miles an hour in the commute lane would result in a crash that would probably prove fatal to both of us (assuming I survived the whole getting shot part of that plan), I'm afraid I didn't take it very seriously. I would be in far more danger if he ever got me where he wanted me to go. Ahead of me, traffic was slowing into a steady stream of brake-lights, and further ahead in the far right lane was an accumulation of emergency lights—the emergency situation that the cop must have been racing toward. I braked, too, downshifting as we slowed. "There's nowhere to drive to until the road clears."

There was a snarl from the backseat and I glanced into the rearview mirror, once and then again, studying the face of my captor as he looked at the traffic around us. His mask was a neoprene dive hood, designed to be worn with a diving mask and tank, exposing only his mouth, nose and eyes. The shape of the face, detail features, even hair, were entirely covered. "Pull over and take the next exit."

"We're in the commute lane! What do you want me to do, play leapfrog?"

"Get off the freeway."

I put on my signal and started wedging my way between cars. If he was trying to stay anonymous, this wasn't the way to do it. A black SUV honked as I forced my way in front of it, and the driver of a yellow sports car flipped me the bird. I flipped back, only to have my captor reach across the seat and slap my hand down. Couldn't anyone see that there was a man in a black mask in the backseat of my car? Did they think people wore those for fun? Then again, this was the Bay Area; stranger things were pretty normal here.

The exit lane opened in front of me, and just beyond it was the accident zone. Too far. My gut sank just a little further. I had no choice but to slide up the exit ramp, and follow his directions along surface streets until we merged back onto to the freeway. We were far south here, nearly to Mineta San Jose airport and the traffic was thick and deep. And then we were through San Jose and merging into Highway 17. Back to Santa Cruz? "Santa Cruz. Why didn't you say so? This is perfect. I've got an appointment on Ocean Street that I can't really miss. Hey, it's a little late to catch the surf today, so how about we get burgers after?"

The barrel of the gun tapped the back of my head.

I glanced in the rearview. "What? You aren't going to shoot me here and you know it. You shoot me, we crash, and we both die. I've already crashed once on this road already this week. And Dr. Chee is waiting for me. That's the coroner by the way. I'm not the only one who knows what's going on, so, you know, getting rid of me won't get you very far. She knows everything."

My captor seemed determined not to speak. His eyes were on me, through me, almost unfocused.

"She's not really patient, you know. If I'm late, she'll

probably call the cops. Besides…"

Finally, he waved. "Take the 101 merge."

The 101 to 1. Wild winds, sharp curves, high cliffs, short sandy beaches with some of the most dangerous undercurrents in the world. And some of the best surf.

"But my appointment is on Ocean." I said it as casually as I could, tipping the turn signal the opposite direction.

"101. Now!" The gun barrel shifted toward my head, but I ducked forward so that it missed jabbing me.

"You hit me with that thing one more time and I'm gonna turn this car around!" Wow. I sounded just like my mother.

"Shut the hell up or you won't get the chance," he growled. "Take the merge!"

I squeezed between a green Mazda and a metallic red H2, the latter dwarfing my little Kia like an elephant over a baby, and then I was merging onto 101, away from Ocean, away from help. The remaining distance of town, I tried casually to catch attention, lane drifting, slowing down and speeding up. I needed to get out of this car. I needed to get away from that gun. I needed to be where other people could protect me. But we were out of town in minutes, and the coastline opened up, the distant ocean grey-gold as the westering sun lowered slowly toward its boiling surface. Brown grasses on windblown cliffs leading to the water's edge swept away from the road on the left, while on the right, cattle grazed and small farm buildings dotted fertile fields. Hand-painted signs for fresh strawberries, homegrown pumpkins, and organic eggs spotted the sides of the highway.

"Here. Stop here."

We were in a spot where the road narrows, and on weekends and warm summer days cars park in the sandy edges to let people use the cliff-side hiking trails or slip down to the state park beaches without paying parking fees. This time of day, this time of year, there was no one parked. The traffic was mostly commuters travelling between Santa Cruz and Half Moon Bay further up the coast. I flicked on my signal and slid to the side, feeling my Kia's tires swamp slightly in the soft sand. This was it. If I left the car, left the roadway, my chances of surviving… Well, I didn't want to think too hard about that.

"Get out."

My captor opened the door the same time I did and stepped out, but kept his gun at my back, low enough that the car door hid it from oncoming traffic. He reached back into the car and picked up Charles' gear bag, tossing it over his shoulder, then slid his arm around me, gun in my side, hidden under his arm. How was the passing traffic not noticing that he was wearing a dive mask?

Because this was Santa Cruz. Just another water sports enthusiast on their way to the ocean. Nothing strange about that.

The moment there was a break in traffic, he pushed me across the road and up a small trail. This was my last chance. I had to stay in sight of the road.

"I know who you are," I said with a certainty I didn't feel. Courtroom manners, courtroom bluff. "I know who you are and what you did. Do you think I didn't tell anyone?"

"Doesn't matter. No one can prove anything."

"Don't be an idiot. If you kill me, they'll know you did it."

"You're the idiot. And you're grieving. You have a head injury." He shrugged, pushing me up the sandy path and through the windbreak, out of sight of the road. The harsh Pacific winds instantly whipped across my body, shaking my small frame, and I tried to duck back as much for cover as to return to the nominal safety of the road.

He grabbed my arm and yanked me back. Only a hundred yards ahead, the ocean sprawled far below the deadly cliffs. "You're all sad over Charlie. You'll kill yourself and no one will question it."

Kill myself? I jerked back, facing him. "My mother is Catholic and my father is a Buddhist. Do you really think anyone would believe I'd kill myself? If that's the best plan you've got…" I took a deep breath and said what I was becoming more sure of by the mile, "then, Manny, you've got some rethinking to do."

Manny. I was absolutely positive now. Manny with his custom-made surf waxes and his heart condition which required medication. His insistence that the green van was somehow involved deliberately planting a red herring. How blind could I have been? Crying my eyes out on his shoulder? Stupid, stupid girl. He'd gone very still and I half-smiled at those glittering blue eyes that wouldn't meet mine. "But you weren't always called Manny, were you, Sherman. Sherman Osbourne."

Now those eyes snapped to me and his hand ripped off the hood he was wearing. He stared, his sun-wrinkled eyes firing wide with fury before he grabbed my arm and dragged me toward the cliff. I dug in my heels, leaning all my weight away from him, like a recalcitrant toddler.

The sun was setting, the ocean ablaze with light. The buffeting wind was thick with salt and sand that it had ripped from the ancient cliffs and tasted like grit in my mouth, scouring my bare skin raw. "Manny! You don't have to do this. Just stop!"

He tugged me harder, pointing the gun at my face with the other hand.

My brain started playing one of those stupid "Which would be better" games. That kind where you're given two bad options and have to choose one. Better to be stranded on a deserted island with only a copy of the San Francisco Chronicle, or to be shot in the head? Shot in the head. Better to have nothing to eat but lunch truck shrimp for the rest of your life, or shot in the head? That one was a toss-up. Falling over that cliff and smashing on the barnacle-crusted rocks below? I was still leaning toward the shot in the head option. "You're going to have to shoot me there, because I'd rather die than go over that cliff, Sherman."

"Stop calling me that!" Rage flared over him like the orange-gold sun that was dropping over the blackening water.

"You don't know anything!"

His fingers were digging so hard into my arm that I was bruising. How much pressure could my wrist bones take? My brain was tumbling, just like my body would if I went over that rocky ledge. Terror almost stuck my tongue, but I sucked in a deep breath, digging the heels of my soft flats deeper into the sand. "I know you still love Vanessa!"

It worked. His fingers loosened, I screamed. And then I screamed again. only a bit, but enough. I jerked as hard as I could, yanking my whole body backward. And then I was free, rolling up and into a sprint, losing a shoe, sharp rocks, thorns and sand slashing at my bare foot. I made it four steps before he barreled into me, his body landing heavily on top of me, a tackle that knocked me breathless. My already bruised and battered chest flared with new agony.

A sharp short inhale and I screamed, screamed long and loud until that tight breath was gone. I was fighting for my life. Why didn't he shoot me? He was trying to grab my hands, trying to pin me down face first on the sandy trail. Dust clung to my face, clogged my nose, but somehow, I screamed again, twisting in his grasp, wriggling out from under him. He was an old man, a stiff old man with a heart problem! How could he be so strong? Wait. He was using both hands to grab my wrist. He'd let go of the gun! Where was it? The gun!

Sand grated my belly, thistles tearing through my lightweight blue sweater, rocks bruising my knees and hips as Manny struggled to capture me. My fingers closed around something, a piece of wood, windblown and smooth, and with a wild howl, I rolled and swung, managing to hit him in the shoulder. He responded with a swing of his fist that connected with my unbruised cheekbone. Stunned and jarred, my body stopped responding, and I was yanked to my feet and pushed toward the cliff, my hands locked behind my back.

At my feet, the gun was lying on the path, but he couldn't let go of my hands to pick it up. I hooked my bare foot under the trigger-guard and kicked high, sending it flying into the thistle scrub. Gun off the table, I resumed my fight, but my body was done, reeling from the punch, aching from abuse, and shaking all over. If the wind had been pushing me toward the cliff instead of away, I might have not have needed Manny to make me fall.

"Get the hell off me! I'm not going in that water." I growled. "Manny, think about this. Everyone is going to know it's you."

"How?" He laughed faintly, as though the whole situation was some poorly done sitcom in need of a real laugh track. "You're the only one who knows. You and this bag..." He tugged at the strap of Charles' gear bag. "Are the only things that will stop me."

Charles' gear bag. I twisted my head around to look over my shoulder. Manny's blue eyes were wide and sparkling with determination, his wrinkled tan face set with a bitter frown, his silver hair wind-whipped and wild. How could I ever have thought of him as good old Manny. "It doesn't matter," I lied, bluffing literally for my life. "I told Doctor Chee what was in Charles' surf bag, what kind of wax he was using. I told her he had your custom wax in there."

"Without the bag, where's the proof?" Manny shrugged, shoving me again, back toward the cliff. "Everyone's been usin' my wax. Everyone has a jar. They won't find nothin' in any of the other jars. If I'd just thought to take his bag that morning... Hell, shoulda taken the wax with me after I waxed his board for him that day."

"You killed Charles..." My voice stuck in my throat, sand clogging my words. I gulped and kept going. "You almost killed Patrick."

"Patrick?" Manny held up, looking confused.

"He carried Charles' board for the Paddle-Out..." I kept talking, kept stalling. Was it my imagination or could I hear sirens in the distance? "You know he crashed his Jeep? That's why! You almost killed us both. But why kill Charles at all? Why not just kill Vanny? She's the one who wronged you." My voice clutched in my throat and burning tears stung my wind-dried eyes as I asked the question I'd been screaming to myself for a week. "Why kill Charles? Why?"

"They ruined me," Manny muttered, but he'd resumed pushing me toward the cliff. "They took everything I had."

"I saw you." I said it with a certainty I didn't feel. "I saw you at her house. That was you cleaning the pool, with that van... that was your in. You knew where she was. You were watching her. You knew. You could easily have killed her but you didn't... Because you still love her. Don't you? You saw her today, how happy she was, and you realized that you still love her. You want her to be happy."

He shoved me again. My feet were near the edge of the cliff, but I refused to look, my still-shoed foot digging for purchase in the sandy ledge. Below, the ocean was roaring against the cliffs. I kept talking, desperation running my mouth and my mind, willing my body to find strength to fight. Salt and sea-rot filled my nostrils. Seabirds screamed from the rocks, their calls filling the air. A glance down to where the terns swept on wide wings up the cliffside left me dizzy with vertigo. "Look! Those are protected species down there, Manny! You don't want to mess with protected species, do you? Do you know what the fines are for that?"

He was standing still, his hands locked so hard around my wrists the bones were grating. My knees buckled from the pain, and my foot lost its leverage. I was falling!

"Let her go!" A new voice yelled from the trail, and Manny whipped around, dragging me with him.

A cop. A uniformed cop. Two cops. Running toward us over the uneven ground, guns drawn.

Relief and tears came at the same time.

Manny yanked me back up, dragging me away from the cliff, and I was so relieved to be away from the edge that it took a moment to realize there were thistles underfoot. We were off the trail. The gun. He was retrieving the gun.

And then it was a stand-off. Two cops with guns drawn and pointed at me. And me, locked in Manny's grip with his gun aimed over my shoulder. I'd become what Kenny's video game playing friends called a "meat shield." It was as unglamorous as it sounded. I raised my voice tentatively, "Umm, officers? This rescue? It's not really working for me."

"Shut up," Manny growled in my ear.

"For crying out loud, Manny, they're going to shoot you! Do you really want to go out this way?"

"Ma'am? Don't worry! We're here to help..." I suddenly recognized the officers as the Ortez and Bryant. The suicide theorists. Oh great. Tweedledee and Tweedledum. Best. Rescue. Ever. Not! Had April called them about the surf wax? How had they found me?

It didn't matter how they found me, they were going to get me killed. I felt a hysterical laugh bubbling up through the tears. "How the heck is pointing a gun at me helping?"

"I'll kill her!" Manny gave me a hard shake. "Back off!"

"Yeah, let's all back off." I agreed. "Maybe we can all put down the guns? Oh, right. I don't have a gun. So why don't you three all put down your guns, and we can...Oww!"

Manny twisted my arm back and up, efficiently jerking my shoulder to the limits of its socket. "Everyone shut up!"

"Manny? Manny." I whispered agonizingly, low enough that only he could hear. "What are you going to do? If you surrender, you get your day in court. You can tell them everything. Everyone will know what Charles and Vanessa did to you. If you try to fight this out, you know what happens. We both end up shot, right? Maybe we survive, probably we don't, but no one will ever know why. And you want them to know why."

I could feel him shaking against my back. When I looked at the hand holding his gun, it was trembling. He was gasping. In the golden light that poured across the ocean and turned the stubbled field around us to the color of ripe peaches, I could see the hand clasped around the butt of the gun, the tip of Manny's finger across the trigger. Turning blue.

My god.

"Manny!" I shoved his gun arm away as he suddenly released my arm and fell to his knees.

The cops started running, guns aimed at us. Manny was down, his hand, the one that had only just recently smashed into my face, clutching his chest, his weather-beaten face wreathed with pain.

The cops tore up beside us and tried to pull me away. "He's having a heart attack!" I tried to explain as I was pulled up. "He needs help! He needs medicine."

Manny was rolling to his side, agony on his face, fist clenched to his chest. The cop standing over him, gun pointed at his head, called for an ambulance. In a heart attack, every second matters. I remembered reading that somewhere. That's why you administer aspirin at the first symptom and go straight to the emergency room.

"It's okay, ma'am. You're safe now. You're safe." The other cop was trying to drag me away from Manny. It was a chaos of seconds, my own breath catching as the wind whistled past my ears, and in between Manny's ragged gasps and Officer Bryant's cries of remand, everything suddenly stood still.

And I saw him.

Charles.

He stood over Manny, staring down, his gentle face tight with concern, and then he looked at me and his hand raised, pointing to the duffle bag. The surfing bag that that hand, in life, had lifted so many times, that had so often been casually slung over that sturdy shoulder. That bag that held the poison that had killed him. Charles pointed, and then he looked at me. Could he be, looking at me? I wondered even as he smiled, smiled as if to say, "You know what to do." The way he had so many times when he was alive.

"You're okay," Officer Bryant was screaming in my ear.

"But he's not!" I jerked out of Bryant's gloved hand, grabbing Charles' duffle bag and digging through it. The plastic jar of homemade surf-wax was in the webbed pocket along with the other waxes Charles favored. I snatched it up, grabbing a small towel and dove back to Manny's side. The cop over him tried to push me away. I don't know why he couldn't. He was bigger, stronger, and I really didn't have any fight left.

"Ma'am! He's a killer," Ortez warned.

"He's dying!" Warm. It had to be warm! I smushed some of the wax into the towel, squishing it with my palm to heat it, careful not to let it touch my skin, then pressed it to Manny's throat where I could see his carotid artery fluttering frantically. For a dashed second of time, I felt a hand over mine, pressing lightly. Had the cop started to help?

"I forgive him."

Charles' voice. Quiet and stolid. Warm and alive.

"Charles?" I whispered his name, hardly daring to hope for an answer.

"Good job."

And then the hand was gone, and when I looked up, so was Charles. Had he ever really been there? Did it matter? I looked down at the aged surfer, the murderer saved by his own victim, his grey drawn skin, his tightly closed eyes like slits of darkness in his sunken face. "Breathe, Manny! You have to breathe!"

Like a snapping band, the tension in Manny's body released and he sucked in a deep breath, his eyelids fluttering. I pulled the towel away, gathering as much wax as I could from his skin. That was as far as I got before the cop pulled me away, keeping his gun trained on Manny's inert body. "Lady," he said with a tired frown, "you are one special kind of crazy."

I shrugged, sinking down on the sandy path to pick the stickers out of my foot. "So I've been told."

CHAPTER 17

⁓

Santa Cruz/San Amoro: Two Weeks Later

FAIRY LIGHTS TWINKLED from every corner of Granny
Jazzy's garden, where thick Japonica overlapped with late
summer roses in velvety whites and reds. The heady fragrance
of the roses was barely masked by the tantalizing barbecue
aromas that filled the evening sea-air. Around me, the sounds
of soft laughter and jazz music trickled, accompanied by
splashes from the hot tub and the ever-present burbling of the
small angel fountain at the back of the yard. It was my belated
birthday party and Patrick's welcome-home party, combined
into one long afternoon of barbecue, hot tubs, horse shoes, and
crazy charades.

On my left, Patrick was seated gingerly in a well-padded
lawn chair, and on my right, Kenny was cutting apart our
emptied soda and beer cans, folding them into twisted swans
and wallowing aluminum turtles.

"So, cuz, when you going back to work?" Kenny asked it of
Patrick with a half-smile. It had only been two weeks since the
accident, not even fourteen days since I'd almost been marched
off a cliff. Patrick was healing, but as promised, it was going to
take time. Still, I wasn't prepared for his next words.

"Well, I'm not. Not for the Coast Guard, anyway."

My heart stopped for a brief moment. "What? The Coast Guard's your life!"

Patrick shook his head. "I'm getting a Medical Discharge. It's either that, or spend the rest of my career behind a desk. My neck…" His pained expression said it all. I hadn't seen the MRI images, but Granny Jazzy had, and so had his commanding officer. "There's too much risk on active ship duty in a cutter like mine."

"Oh, Patrick, I'm so sorry." I felt another flare of anger at Manny rising up. Would that ever stop? He'd confessed to everything, and he was going to prison, but with his health problems, they were sending him to a prison hospital, and he might not ever be considered well enough for general populace. It was too good for him. Charles would want me to forgive, and I was trying, but apparently, I hold on to grudges. "I know you love that boat."

"So, you're. what? Gonna go into law like Granny Jazzy always wanted?" Kenny stacked a smaller aluminum turtle on top of a larger one. One was diet Coca-Cola silver and red, the other Heineken silver and green. Granny Jazzy's artist genes had somehow skipped over me and poured straight into Kenny.

Granny Jazzy's voice echoed from the barbecue, "Gonna have a lawyer for a granddaughter. Don't need one for a grandson. Pick your own path, pumpkin!"

Because calling a medically retired Coast Guard Captain "pumpkin" was always appropriate when you were his grandmother.

Patrick half-laughed, but his broken ribs protested and he winced. "Actually, I thought I might go up to eastern Oregon, see my cousins—you know, on my mom's side—I haven't been up there for a long time. My great aunt's ranch always needs some work."

"Isn't that like, miles from anywhere? In the desert?" Kenny's idea of geography was hazy. "Won't you miss the ocean?"

"High desert. And that's kinda the point…" Patrick's words faded but fortunately were cut off by Nicky bounding down the back steps.

"Look who I found out front?" She stacked bowls of salsa and guacamole on the patio table before waving to the back door and the next person coming out.

Jack Austin? Who invites someone's ex-fiancé to your birthday party? Oh, wait. That would be my family.

"Jack!" Patrick leaned forward to shake his hand. "How's it going?"

Kenny jumped up and gave him a back-slapping man-hug. "Hey, man! How you been?"

"Hi, Kam…" Jack hesitated, looking at me, and I hesitated right back.

"Hi, Jack. There's, umm… soda and beer in the cooler over there. Help yourself."

"Thanks!" He headed for the cooler, and I headed for the barbecue.

"No, YOU HAVE TO PUT a layer of glaze on the ribs right when you put them on…" Granny Jazzy was arguing good-naturedly with Grandpa Dan.

"If you put it on first, it chars! You have to brown the meat a little, then glaze them."

"You have to let the flavor soak in!" They were tussling mildly over the bowl of Grandpa's famously delicious rib sauce.

"Man's place is at the grill," Grandpa quipped, "And woman's place is…"

"Daniel, if you dare say 'kitchen'…"

"Entertaining her guests. You're hosting this shindig," Grandpa Dan finished, waving toward where Jaxine and Diane, her partner in the greenhouse business, were joking and laughing with some of the surfer crowd around the hot tub. "Quit neglecting your guests."

"Speaking of guests…" I glared at Granny. "Why on earth

did you invite Jack?"

Her eyes twinkled faintly as she relinquished the bowl of sauce to Grandpa Dan. "Oh, of course I didn't. I just told Nicky that she could invite whomever she thought you might like to see."

So, they'd conspired against me, had they? Why wasn't I surprised? "Traitors in my midst," I grumbled to Grandpa Dan, who merely shrugged and smiled as if to say, "What Jazzy wants, Jazzy gets."

I glanced around looking for somewhere to hide. My childhood bedroom perhaps? But I was stymied by Morri and his wife (with an enormous platter of treats from Happy Cookie), and with them, Father Joe. Behind them arrived Doc and Rodney, and then Andelle and a few more of the surfer crowd; it was a party in full swing.

LATE THAT EVENING, I FOUND myself ensconced near the fire pit, surrounded by friends and family, filled with good food, and with love. Granny Jazzy presented an enormous chocolate cake and I had to do the obligatory blowing out of candles while everyone sang, but despite the joy, I was tired. Nicky settled beside me with a slice of cake nearly as big as my head and two forks, one of which she handed to me. "Eat," she ordered.

I've mentioned that Nicky is nearly twice my size. I complied.

"So, you can tell me what really happened out there."

"Out where?" I knew exactly what she meant.

"Don't play games with me. The story is that you saved Manny's life out on the cliffs."

I took a deep breath. I could tell Nicky anything, had always told Nicky everything. "What would you say if I told you it wasn't me?"

I don't know if it was something in my tone of voice, or something in my expression that held her up. She tilted her head, dark ponytail falling to one side as she studied me.

"Someone else was there?"

I glanced up as Morri and Father Joe came up, slowly, respecting our space. If anyone would get it, it would be Morri. And if I needed to confess, Father Joe was the safest bet. I gestured to them to join us. "Sit. You might as well know, too." I crammed another bite of chocolate cake in my mouth for courage while they gathered around. "I'm not sure yet if there's going to be a trial. Manny confessed, but who knows what his public defender will try for. But there's no way I can say this in a court of law. I'm going to need all the help I can get to get around this under oath."

Nicky shoved a huge bite of cake into her mouth, and sat back, watching me. Now that I had a full audience, it seemed even more impossible. I swallowed down the lump in my throat, wondering why the smear of chocolate frosting on the side of the plate was suddenly the most interesting thing I'd ever seen. I couldn't take my eyes off it.

"Poppet? Whatever it is, you know we'll believe you." Morri didn't say more than that, but it was all I needed to hear.

"It was Charles." I finally confessed, heat rushing to my cheeks. My fingers trembled and I dropped the fork back on the plate.

They were all looking at me, not skeptically, as I'd feared, but curiously. The whole story tumbled out. Charles on the cliff, pointing to the bag, reminding me that the heart medicine was in the surf wax, his hand on mine. "I know it sounds crazy, but I wouldn't have thought to use the poisoned wax to save Manny. I'm not sure I would have tried to save him at all." And how easy would that have been? To let Officer Bryant drag me away, and let Manny die there on the windswept ground with guns pointed at him? "I heard his voice. He said he forgave Manny. I'm not making this up."

"You actually saw a ghost? It touched you?" Nicky was staring at me goggle-eyed behind her thick glasses.

"Not just any ghost. It was Charles. Just… Charles."

Father Joe was nodding, his dark hair falling over his

forehead. "You know it was. Sometimes those who have passed have to bring us messages. And that sounds just like Charlie, doesn't it?"

None of us could deny that it did. "What if this goes to court? I can't tell that story under oath. My law career would be over if I testified that a ghost made me save a murderer's life."

"If it comes to that, tell yourself that what you saw was a manifestation of your subconscious mind, seeing what you needed to see to do what was right." Morri's eyes were twinkling and he glanced at Father Joe. "Only you, and of course, the three of us now, have to know what really happened. But that brings me to something Joe and I were discussing earlier today. We have a little business proposal for you."

A business proposal from Morri and Joe? I glanced at Nicky and she grinned and nodded.

"Does it involve free Happy Cookies? Cuz, for that, I'm in." I agreed.

"It may test your faith," Father Joe cautioned. "What we're going to suggest is, well, unconventional."

I wasn't raised particularly religious. It was true that my mother came from a Catholic family, but Granny Jazzy wasn't strict in her faith, and my father had become Buddhist sometime after the move to India. Unconventional was pretty much what I did when it came to things that tested my faith. "So, what's this about? Do I need an exorcism?"

Father Joe laughed. "I hope not. No one does those anymore. But I do cleansings, blessings, and the like."

Morri was rocking back and forth in the oversized Adirondack chair, a gleeful joy on his face. He looked a little like a wizened merry Muppet. "You ladies did superlative searching with your investigation of Evrett."

"We did? He didn't even talk to us. Just knocked about a bit." I glanced at Nicky. "And I think he knew Manny killed Charles the entire time, but he didn't even bother to tell me. For that matter, was Charles around that whole time? Did Evrett know he was there?"

"There will always be unanswered questions," Morri answered seriously. "In investigating Evrett, you took a scientific approach but remained open to things outside of scientific understanding. That's what it takes."

"What it takes to do what, exactly?" Why did I not like the sound of that?

"Investigate hauntings." Father Joe tilted his head, his dark eyes twinkling seriously at me.

"Investigate hauntings?" I wrestled the remains of the cake away from Nicky. This conversation required more chocolate. And maybe a glass of wine or six.

Morri bobbed his head. "You see, we used to be part of a group that did that, but after those reality television shows became popular, everyone wanted to be a part of the media sensation. They splintered off and started groups associated with the shows. They stopped being pure researchers, stopped having the hearts, health, and minds of their clients in their best interests. You two... you two have what it takes."

"To investigate hauntings." I said it slowly, annunciating each word carefully. "I'm trying to become a lawyer. I'm a legal representative of the courts. I can't..."

"And I'm a priest, a vested representative of the Church." Father Joe interjected. "We can be more than one thing in this life, Kami. Look at Morri here."

I looked at Morri, who was gazing at me through sharply twinkling blue eyes, and I mentally tallied up everything he had been in his long life. War correspondent. Journalist. Chess champion. Loving husband. Cat rescuer. Cruciverbalist. Ghost hunter?

"What do we have to do?" Nicky asked, tilting back in her chair, black pony-tail swaying, combat boots scuffing in the sand around the fire pit. "Do we have to go find ghosts to hunt, or do they come to us?"

I laughed, but realized when she fired a glare at me that she was serious.

"People come to me from time to time," Father Joe

explained. "I can't always help them directly, but I can refer them to you. If you find evidence of actual haunting, then we all get together and do a full investigation, maybe even a cleansing or blessing. What do you say?"

"I say it's nuts. I have to focus on my career. Especially now." I knew I was fighting a losing battle when Morri and Joe turned to Nicky, Morri's eyebrows waggling in dangerous encouragement.

"I say I'm in." She leaned over and pushed my shoulder non-too-gently. "You're in, too, Kam."

"I am?"

"You are."

Morri raised his cup of coffee in a toast. "To the new investigators in town."

"To the investigators!" Nicky joined in enthusiastically.

"Amen." Father Joe agreed.

I toasted, too, but I kept my voice silent. I knew my life was a disaster but I wasn't sure about haunting investigations. "Look, I work with a ghost, but that's as far as this goes. I'll help out with this investigation stuff if Nicky wants to do it, but I can't risk my career on it."

Morri looked a little crestfallen but Nicky wagged her finger at him. "Don't go all frowny-puss. I'll talk her around."

There was a pretty slim chance of that, but I finished my cake, listening to the others plan out how things would work. Morri and Father Joe seemed to have a pretty solid grounding in what they were doing, and I knew that Morri had been the one to do all the research on Evrett when he first turned up. But I wasn't sure this was for me.

I was actually a little relieved when Jack appeared at my shoulder. "What are you four up to? You look thick as thieves over here?"

"Just telling ghost stories," I said hastily, standing up to shift Jack away from the others.

"I didn't think you believed in any of that stuff," Jack half-laughed. The firelight was glinting off his golden hair, and his

eyes were twinkling as brightly as the fairy lights that framed
him. I totally blame the chocolate overdose for the fact that he
suddenly seemed to be the most beautiful man I'd ever seen in
my life.

I closed my eyes for a second, but when I opened them,
he was still there. "There's a lot you don't know about me, Jack
Austin."

He nodded, but his expression was pensive. What was that?
Fear? Was there anything in this world that Jack was afraid
of? "Wanna get out of here? I'll give you a ride back to San
Amoro?"

Since my Kia was still impounded as evidence, I'd ridden
over with Jaxine and Diane, who were, at that moment, in the
hot tub and showing no evidence of wanting to leave any time
soon. I glanced around the party, surfers and Coast Guard
sailors, artists, lawyers, musicians, and family all crowded
around the backyard and throughout the house. I was suddenly
exhausted. "Let's slip out the side-gate," I whispered to Jack.

AUTUMN HAD BEGUN TO SET in for real, the sky thick with
coastal fog and the night air chill. I nestled into Jack's BMW
with its heated seats and watched him ease behind the wheel
and start the car. I was used to race-car starts and stops from
Jack, but he drove gently, slipping quietly up to stop lights and
pressing off from them as though he had all the time in the
world to chauffer me around.

We had merged onto Highway 17 before either of us spoke.
Somehow, we managed to try it at the same time. I laughed, fell
silent, and gestured for him to continue.

"I'm sorry I doubted you."

I looked out the window, but the fog was closing in,
cocooning the BMW in its own little bubble. "You had every
reason to doubt me, Jack. I mean, it all sounds crazy. I get that."

"Still…" He paused, his fingers clasping and unclasping
the wheel. I shifted to look at his face, his features soft in the

dashboard glow, his smile faint as he sighed. "I want to trust you. I still…"

Oh god. If he said he still loved me… my heart jolted.

"…think you're crazy." His smile turned to a wide grin. "But I think it's a good crazy."

I laughed in relief. Or was it? "Thanks. I'm glad you're not. Crazy I mean. I can only take so much crazy."

"Is that what the problem was? I'm too sane for you?"

The words were naked, raw, leaving us both vulnerable.

"I don't know what the problem was," I admitted, the vertigo of the cliffs-edge reopening at my feet. "And I think that's the problem. I've got issues, Jack."

He nodded. "You ever think, you know, maybe you'll figure it out?"

Ahead of us, outlined by the headlights, I could see the twisted old guardrail where the Jeep had plummeted through, but for the first time since the accident, there was no fear. "I want to. I don't know if we can try again, but… I want to."

Jack didn't say anything else. His gentle smile said it all for him.

Jack let me out at the curb, dashing around to open my door, even though I was perfectly capable of opening it myself. He leaned in for what I'm sure was intended to be a swift and somewhat shy kiss on the cheek. But some devil took me and turned my head into it, his lips landing against mine. Just briefly, before he drew back and smiled again.

"See you again soon," he whispered. Then he drove away, leaving me alone finally, except for the cat and the knight, I sat down at the desk and looked out the barren window. A sharp knock interrupted my one quiet moment. I glanced at the clock, realizing how late it had gotten, then flipped the dead bolt and, hoping it wasn't a burglar, opened the door. Reggie was standing on the doorstep, and I smiled in relief.

"You snuck out of your party without saying good-bye," he accused good-naturedly. "Exciting day."

"Exciting couple of weeks. I need a nap. Or three." I waved

him to my one folding chair and leaned on my flimsy desk. "What brings you by?"

"I tried to talk to you at the party, but didn't get the chance. I heard from a colleague of mine. Apparently, you made a bit of an impression when you stood up to that cop to save Manny's life."

"You heard about that?"

"The cop was wearing a body camera." Reggie gave me a sideways glance. "Manny's lawyer consulted with our firm, and we've all seen it. He's trying to get it released publicly, to sway opinion toward Manny in case there's a trial."

I buried my face in my hands. "Oh god, I almost wish Manny had shot me!"

"Rumor has it that his gun wasn't even loaded." Reggie laughed slightly. "Anyway, have you heard of Drury and Kane?"

"The liability lawyer guys? Sure. Their ads are all over the place. What? You think I should sue Manny? Dude barely has a penny to his name, and he's about to lose that."

"No, kiddo." Reggie steepled his fingers and leaned them against his chin. "Dennis Drury is a friend of mine. He knew Charles, too. Anyway, he says there's a paralegal position open for you if you want it. Full time with benefits and profit sharing. Competitive rates, too."

"Full time?"

Reggie nodded. "What do you say? One door closes and another opens."

"When one door closes and another opens, it just means that you probably have a ghost." I smiled faintly in Evrett's direction.

"It's a good deal, Kam. And Drury is a good guy." Reggie glanced around the empty office, his gaze lingering on my folding computer table. "You'd have a real desk."

I looked around the office, at Hoover reclining on the empty bookshelf, as close to the furnace vent as he could get. At Evrett, standing silent sentry by the corridor doorway. At my office. My building. My home.

I held out a hand to Reggie, shaking his with businesslike

crispness. "Thanks, Reggie. For everything. But you know... I think I'm going to give this a go. Independent paralegal. What do you think?"

He squeezed my hand and didn't let go. His eyes followed the same path mine had, from the scraps on the cheap plastic desk, to Hoover, to Evrett, and then around the empty walls where lighter patches of paint showed where pictures and artifacts had once hung. When he looked back at me, he smiled and a tear lingered in the corner of his left eye. "I think Charles would be proud of you."

I felt my own tears threatening to start again and let go of his hand. "I hope so. And, you know, if it doesn't work out, I may come crawling back."

Reggie's smile was warm. "Miss White, you've never crawled a day in your life."

After he left, I went to the back corridor and retrieved the paint cans that were stored there. The "auburn gold" looked like it was still good. I used my computer and printer to print up some plain Garamond font stencils. With Hoover sniffing around the paint jar, I lined up the stencils, one letter at a time, and dabbed in the paint. It's not as easy as it looks. I'm never going to be able to make money in a side-career as a window painter. There was a lot of scraping, cleaning and trying again, but finally it was done. I scooped up Hoover and ran out to the sidewalk to look at my handy-work. It didn't look half-bad. At least it was correctly spelled.

Kami White: Licensed

Paralegal / Research / LDP

There it was. I was in business. And I didn't know what would come next. All I knew was that the tide of my life had changed. The surf was washing in to shore, and for once, I was in the right spot. I closed my eyes and listened for the ocean, and somewhere inside I felt my feet find the board, felt the swell catch up underneath me. Maybe after all the bad waves, maybe I'd finally caught a good one.

THE END

E.L. Oakes lives in the San Francisco East Bay with her two cats and one of those Silicon Valley programmer types that she writes so freely about. Freelance web content editor by day, author by night, she loves nothing more than curling up on a rainy day with a good cup of coffee and a mystery novel. She's worked with various paranormal research groups throughout the northwest, though she now values a full night's sleep over drafty old buildings in the middle of the night.

For more information, go to www.eloakes.com